The Society of Friends

Also by Kelly Cherry

The Society of Friends

STORIES

by Kelly Cherry

University of Missouri Press

COLUMBIA AND LONDON

Copyright © 1999 by Kelly Cherry
University of Missouri Press, Columbia, Missouri 65201
Printed and bound in the United States of America
All rights reserved
5 4 3 2 1   03 02 01 00 99

Library of Congress Cataloging-in-Publication Data

Cherry, Kelly.
  The society of friends : stories / by Kelly Cherry.
    p.   cm.
  ISBN 0-8262-1243-3 (alk. paper)
  I. Title.
PS3553.H357S63   1999
813'.54—dc21   99-15516
                                                       CIP

Cover design: Mindy Shouse

Text design: Elizabeth K. Young

Typesetter: Crane Composition, Inc.

Printer and binder: Edwards Brothers, Inc.

Typefaces: Stuyvesant, Helvetica Light and Times

for some in town

Alix and Laird, Gail, George and Maline, Jan
and Don, Raphy and Tommy, Ron and Peg

and of course,

all the kids, always,
wherever life may find them

In all the houses and streets there is peace and quiet. Out of fifty thousand townsfolk there's not one ready to scream or protest aloud. We see people shopping for food in the market, eating by day, sleeping by night, talking their nonsense, marrying their wives, growing old, complacently dragging off their dead to the cemetery. But we have no eyes or ears for those who suffer. Life's real tragedies are enacted off stage. All is peace and quiet, the only protest comes from mute statistics: so many people driven mad, so many gallons of vodka drunk, so many children starved to death.

Oh yes, the need for such a system is obvious. Quite obviously, too, the happy man only feels happy because the *unhappy* man bears his burden in silence. And without that silence happiness would be impossible. It's collective hypnosis, this is. At the door of every contented, happy man there should be someone standing with a little hammer, someone to keep dinning into his head that unhappy people do exist— and that, happy though he may be, life will round on him sooner or later. Disaster will strike in the shape of sickness, poverty or bereavement. And no one will see *him* or hear *him*—just as he now has neither eyes nor ears for others. But there *is* no one with a hammer, and so the happy man lives happily away, while life's petty tribulations stir him gently, as the breeze stirs an aspen. And everything in the garden is lovely.

—CHEKHOV, "GOOSEBERRIES"

In his grief Tom Willard's face looked like the face of a little dog that has been out a long time in bitter weather.

—SHERWOOD ANDERSON, "DEATH," *WINESBURG, OHIO*

I get by with a little help from my friends.

—THE BEATLES

Contents

Acknowledgments

Some of the stories in this book previously appeared, sometimes in different versions or under different titles, in the following magazines and anthologies, to whose editors and publishers the author is pleasantly indebted:

"The Prowler": *Fiction* (New York)
"Tell Her": *The North American Review*
"The Society of Friends": *McCall's; Kobieta i Zycie* (Warsaw);
    Karogs (Riga)
"The Wedding Cake in the Middle of the Road": *The Wedding Cake in
    the Middle of the Road,* ed. Stamberg and Garrett (Norton, 1992);
    Karogs (Riga); *Tampa Review*
"Not the Phil Donahue Show": *The Virginia Quarterly Review; Prize
    Stories 1994: The O. Henry Awards; The Seasons of Women,* ed.
    Norris (Book-of-the-Month Club and Norton, 1996; Penguin UK,
    1997)
"Chores": *The Southern California Anthology; Světová Literatura*
    (Prague); *Karogs* (Riga)
"As It Is in Heaven": *Commentary*
"Lunachick": *The Virginia Quarterly Review*
"How It Goes": *Fiction* (New York)
"Love in the Middle Ages": *The Georgia Review; Voices from Home,*
    ed. Krawiec (Avisson, 1997)

"On Being in Jeopardy" (from "Chapters from *A Dog's Life*"):
  Jeopardy
"Where Love Is" (from "Chapters from *A Dog's Life*"): *Tampa Review; cold-drill*
"A Friend Came to the House" (from "Chapters from *A Dog's Life*"):
  Mangrove
"The Dog and the Water-Lily" (from "Chapters from *A Dog's Life*"):
  Mangrove
"Block Party": *The Greensboro Review*

For information about the place and period, I am indebted to the superb study *Northumbria in the Days of Bede* by Peter Hunter Blair (St. Martin's Press, 1976).

The Society of Friends

The Prowler

Someone is out there, in the dark, waiting. Maybe waiting to break in. Maybe waiting to— But no one quite dares to think what. They talk about the possibilities without naming them. They whisper. Meeting on the sidewalk by day, they huddle, shoulders drawn up like drawbridges. Home again, they check their drop bolts, the catch-locks on their windows. They worry. Nina most of all, or at least first of all, because it was she who first became aware of whoever or whatever it is they are aware of. She has a dog, a small dog, and one night her dog growled in a way he had never done before, a big-dog growl, while backing away from the back door, his tail tight between his legs. And because he is salt-and-pepper, with an overall charcoal look, he looked a little like an umbrella that had folded itself up and was putting itself away in the umbrella stand.

Nina's daughter was sleeping upstairs. Nina had come down, soundless in socks, holding onto the banister so she wouldn't slip on the bare oak stairs, to let her dog out for a minute. Silently she prayed that the fear she was feeling, the fear her dog was feeling, was not finding its own way upstairs into her daughter's dreams. She had wanted her daughter to know no fear. Fear got into a dream and it changed everything, it never really left even after you woke up. Nina knew this.

She picked up a knife. It was a carving knife, not a very sharp one because she wasn't much of a cook and didn't like the idea of having sharp knives around, but it could carve a roast, or a man.

Nina realized she was assuming it was a man.

Then, trying to visualize a woman because she did not want to be sexist about this, she saw herself standing in the yard—which was hedge-hidden from the street—ankle-deep in the blue scilla that year by year was taking over the grass, but when she thought of herself like this, she was out there in her white nightgown, not wearing a ski or stocking mask, the damp night heavy as wash, purple hyacinths inking the air with colorful scribbles of scent.

As a rapist, Nina thought, she lacked credibility.

The phone rang in the next room. It was Sarah. "Thank God it's you. Call the police, Sarah," Nina said in a low voice, striking what seemed to her the right note between urgency and calm, and she told Sarah about how her dog was growling.

Sarah listened to Nina and then said she couldn't call the police on the basis of Nina's dog growling. "Do you want me to call Sam?"

Sam Clementi, who lived across the street from Nina, was a private detective.

"No," said Nina. That would be like cornering a doctor at a party to ask about your symptoms.

In fact, by now the dog had stopped growling, and the lights on all over the downstairs made it seem like day, and Nina felt pretty silly clutching a carving knife while talking on the telephone with her friend Sarah. "I called to ask if you wanted to go to the Farmers' Market in the morning," Sarah said.

Sarah was frequently on the road, and she lived—a couple of blocks away on James R. Vineyard Street—in a condo instead of a house. The condo had a cathedral ceiling in the living room and a skylight in the bathroom, and over the fireplace hung a memento from one of her trips, a Cantonese folk-art painting depicting a busy village scene.

The only art Nina could afford was a poster of Renoir's *The Luncheon of the Boating Party,* which she loved because the little dog in the painting looked exactly like her own little dog. The young woman in the painting looked a little like an older version of her daughter. Nina fell in love easily like that, with art and life and—grateful for its steadfastness—even with furniture. The Green Bay Packers chair that had, so long ago, been on sale, the pale beige rug that was really a carpet remnant, the teak table inadvertently bleached where a friend had set a plant that Nina had agreed to house-sit, the poor old dependable-though-sometimes-shouted-at telephone, chipped and cracked, the exhausted couch, all seemed to be poised, like poor relations who live in the same house, for a word from her: Faithful servants, they would do whatever she wanted them to do, though their hearts were sprung upholstery and their souls tattered and fraying fabric.

Perhaps the downstairs furniture was a loyal patrol—chair, carpet, couch, table, and telephone taking turns on guard duty.

All the same, Nina left the lights on all night, like someone with Seasonal Affective Disorder, and didn't fall asleep until sometime around three, long after her dog had curled up next to her daughter in the other bedroom, his tiny rump against Tavy's outflung arm. He liked to sleep touching someone.

It had been a very long time since Nina had slept touching someone.

When people slept, they took a deep-dream voyage, sailing through miles of inner space to a planet hidden from view by layers of self, that obscuring, cloudy atmosphere. They went to the place where they were the bare essences of themselves, B.P.—Before Personality, before mannerism, trait, display and disguise. It was better, if you could, to sleep next to someone.

In the morning, the sky as blue as the scilla, she and her daughter and Sarah waved to Sophie as they got into Sarah's car. Sophie, a widow in her early seventies, shouted as they pulled out into the street, "Did you hear that noise last night?"

So Sophie had heard it too.

But Nina didn't try to reply, only kept waving, because Sarah, just back from Bucharest, was talking at the same time, telling them about a sign she had seen in the hotel lobby. *The lift is being fixed for the next day. During that time we regret that you will be unbearable.*

As Sarah talked about her trip to Bucharest, Nina watched Sophie, receding in the sideview mirror, watch the receding car.

Even after the car turned the corner Sophie stayed where she was, looking after nothing, thinking. Or not thinking, because, ever since he had died, inch by inch, his bones knocked down like dominoes by the cancer that rippled out from his lungs, Sophie had tried hard not to think about how, if Leland were alive, she wouldn't have to look after everything by herself. She might still have arthritis, if he were alive— well, not *might,* she *would* still have arthritis—but surely she wouldn't feel it the way she did, nasty twinges at erratic intervals, that kept her from ever really being able to think. As it was, she would sit by herself in her living room and simply try to think—about something positive, about how people in the world were basically good, most of them, for what would be the use of thinking something negative, such as that they were not, such as that they were too involved in their own lives to be aware of anybody else's?—and the next thing she knew an hour would have gone by, escaped like a thief or Houdini, and if she'd had a single thought in all that time, she couldn't remember it now. Not that she spent *much* time sitting around her living room. Her mother counted on her to visit, bringing pie and knitting yarn and mystery novels to the nursing home, and the church altar needed decorating, and she had lived in this neighborhood for so many years, and the neighbors had all been wonderful to her, knowing how she had felt when Leland died. *As if her heart had been cut out, she had felt as if her heart had been cut out with a carving knife.* And they had known it and had all been wonderful to her, the ones who had known Leland. Oh, people came and went, they moved in or moved away, but somehow the neighborhood stayed the same old neighborhood. She was always impressed with how good-hearted people were, whether they came or went. Her trifocals had misted up. She wiped them on her slacks and then resettled them on her face. As for the arthritis—there wasn't much a person could do about that except keep moving. That was why she did rather a bit of the yardwork, pruning, planting. Her brother came over if there was something she couldn't handle. She had thought about calling him last night about that noise that had been so . . . almost as if it were inside the house, but she didn't like to be after him all the time, pestering him to do this and that. He had a family of his own. She never for a moment thought of calling her mother. It was strange to think that that once attractive, quick-tongued woman was over there in the nursing home, shriveled as if all the feeling, the meat and moisture of a person, had evaporated out of her and silent, silent as a dream, because she never said anything, never answered questions, never asked any, never said thank you for the yarn or the paperback books or the pie. Silent silent silent, so what was the point, Sophie sometimes wondered, of going there and carrying on a one-way conversation. She missed having someone to talk with! Doing the shopping, fooling around in the yard, she had taken to talking to everyone she ran into. "Isn't it a beautiful day!" she said to the Wallaces when she went out to weed the flower bed, and they both beamed at her—they always beamed at her and that made her beam back and then she felt it truly *was* a wonderful day, or almost; no, *was,* even if there was a huge hole like an autopsy in the middle of it—and they inquired if she'd like them to pick up anything for her at the Farmers' Market.

No, but had they heard anything last night, something that, oh, she didn't know, a sound that just didn't seem to *belong* in the neighborhood?

And they said no, they hadn't, but they would certainly be on the alert.

In the Land Rover, while they looked for a parking place close to the Square, Shelley Wallace remarked to her husband how Madison had changed. It had grown—sprawled, wandered, crammed too many people in—traffic was congested—there was not one place left in the city where traffic noise was not a problem!

"Maybe we should have walked," Ian said.

"I just meant that's probably what Sophie heard last night. A traffic noise."

"Or a calliope," Ian offered, for, as it happened, the Six-State Calliope Convention was being held that weekend.

It was not so strange, really, to stumble into a calliope convention on the Square. During the summer, there was a public event almost every other weekend. In June, during Dairy Month, you could see cows on the Square, and even *milk* one. Later in the summer, during Paddle and Portage Weekend, you had to dodge crazed canoeists bearing boats on their heads—a sort of shared millinery, team hats—all of them scrambling across the Square from Lake Monona to Lake Mendota.

The calliopes were large or small, some like wagons and some more like overgrown accordions, some austerely beautiful and some kitschily embossed and beaded, some sounding like steam whistles and some like Steinways, some playing "The Art of the Fugue" and some playing "Alexander's Ragtime Band." "A cacophony of calliopes," said Ian, a tall man who could look out over most of the purchasing pedestrians.

In the middle of the Square stood the state capitol, serenely deaf. (The state legislature was also often serenely deaf.)

Ian had brought his large straw shopping basket, which he'd had since his days in the Peace Corps in Nigeria, and he slipped the handle over his left arm, the better to hold on to the cup of Mexican coffee Shelley had dispensed from a Thermos. Already numbers of people were walking—counterclockwise; no one knew why, but it had become an inviolate rule to circle the Square counterclockwise—and the vegetables were still jeweled with dew, the sky was the color of a chlorinated blue that might lead a bird to think itself a fish, or a fish to think it could fly, and the air had a racy, polo edge to it.

Shelley spotted Nina talking with the acclaimed novelist who also owned an apiary—two writers discussing literature, or, perhaps, bees.

Nina, Tavy, and Sarah were standing hand in hand in front of the calliope that was playing Bach. The child had on a knitted cap that fit close to her small head and covered her ears and made her look like an ambulatory raspberry. "I prefer oompah music, myself," Sarah was saying to Nina as Shelley and Ian came up to them, "but I never argue with a child." She spoke to Shelley. "How's life at the hospital?"

Shelley was a nurse, often working with the terminally ill.

Shelley smiled. "I'm happy to report there *is* life at the hospital," she said.

"And Isabel?"

"Who knows! College students live in another world, even when they're right here in Madison. The last time I asked her to come to dinner she said she couldn't because she had a date. And then she wouldn't tell me a single thing about him. I think she may be in love. You know how when you're in love you want to keep it private and special at the beginning?"

"Oh, God," said Sarah, feeling herself become edgy at the mention of love, feeling herself become all angles and sharp points, like a porcupine in heels, this was what modern life could do to a woman: make her feel like a porcupine in heels, "don't ask me anything about love. I don't know anything about love! Good-bye!" she called, as Shelley and Ian moved on to cucumbers and challah.

Shelley and Ian tried to go to the Farmers' Market every Saturday morning. Sometimes on Saturday night they made stirfry and invited a neighbor. Jasmine Evangeline Pierson, one of the brave few who circuited the Square clockwise, always appreciated an invitation. "Saved from another night at the singles bar," she would say, accepting, though, as Ian commented to Shelley later, he didn't know which bar she could have meant, because pretty much every bar in Madison was a singles bar. "I think even the State Bar Association is a singles bar," he said.

"Not entirely," Shelley said. "There's Lisa Adcock. She's married."

"And how long do we think that's going to last?"

Jasmine Evangeline Pierson had come to Madison from New York, and her black skin still had a cosmopolitan sheen to it, a Bloomingdale's burnish, a sexy Saksesque polish. "Like shoe polish," she mumbled to herself, facing the bathroom mirror in the house she had so daringly—would she get tenure? would she ever find funding out here in the hinterland for her performance art?—bought. She fluffed her hair as if it were a pillow, the purple streak in it like something sliding by. She changed the kitty litter and turned off the overhead light and left the room. *Hey, living in a house by yourself is bound to be strange at first,* she told herself when she heard the garbage can turned over and clanging out into the street, a one-can parade. A sudden noise like that didn't have to mean that someone was out there, keeping an eye on her, peering at her through the windows, noticing when she turned out the light in one room and flicked on the lamp in another. It could be the wind. There was almost always a big clean wind out here in the Midwest, nothing like the scissory little breezes of upstate New York that snipped at your skirt and hair, or the totally immobile thermal inversions that were New York City's summer norm. A big wind could probably knock over a garbage can, even one that had been chained to a tree. A big wind could probably snap the chain in two, send the garbage can barreling down the street. Couldn't it?

"I don't think so, Jazz," said Mary Clementi. "I'm going to talk to Sam about it."

Mary brought it up to Sam while they were cleaning the garage, tagging the items they thought they could sell. Jazz had come over to be company while they worked.

Jazz stretched her bare legs out on the picnic bench, but then she suddenly became self-conscious and sat up and swiveled her legs under the table: Larry Adcock, hard-working and handsome and with a Wall Street swing to his stride, was crossing the street in their direction.

Underneath that handsomeness, Jazz thought, there was something ready to give up. She suspected he was a man who'd been trading in futures for too long. He had the practiced *GQ* slouch-and-smile of a man who sensed himself slightly outlaw, or on loan and about to be called in. Or maybe it was just the look of someone who had cold-called more times than was good for a person.

He was moody, Jazz thought. She never trusted anyone with moods. Her mother had moods, and all you could do was steer clear of them.

"I saw you out here in your garage," he said—unnecessarily, but then, he was a man who felt he had to account for things. "Someone got into *our* garage last night. Into our *car.*"

"How? Why?" they clamored. "What makes you think— But *who?*"

"There were cigarette butts in the ashtray. There was a—" He glanced quickly at Jazz, Mary.

"Condom?" Mary said.

He nodded.

"Oh, it must just be teenagers." West High was a block away. The teenagers were omnipresent. They stood on the street at noon, smoking, leaning against their cars and playing the stereos loud. They disappeared again when the class bell rang. But they'd never done anything like this before—used a person's *garage,* for god's sake. This was too much!

Though Shelley said later, when she heard about it, that she was glad they were using protection.

Larry explained that he had gone back to the kitchen for a paper towel to use as a kind of mitten. An anonymous rubber on the floor in the back of his car in his own garage was not something he would have wanted to handle even in the old days, and it was definitely not something he wanted to handle these days. He had tried to tear the paper towel from the roll over the sink without letting Lisa see him, but she saw him. She wanted to know what he was doing. As she asked him this, she was pouring milk on granola. Her suit jacket hung over the chairback. "Nothing," he said, but she followed him to the garage. To Larry, Lisa's scent of milk and perfume was like a memory of being a child again, the only son. He remembered what it had been like to walk on the earth lightly, a boy, touching down only now and then, to eat or sleep, and he realized how deeply he had sunk into his own bones, how his bones pulled on him like gravity, how they would haul him down and bury him. Once he had not been able to walk beneath a lintel or arch without leaping up to touch it, so great had been the exhilaration of knowing that he was growing, was becoming a man, though to express that in words would have been beyond him, which was why he jumped instead for, yes, joy. Now he felt as if he were walking atop his own interred skeleton. His wife was silent as he deposited the rubber and paper towel in the outside garbage can. He felt as if he were discarding something that had been cut out of a body, as if by a knife—a heart, or a fetus. *Love or trash,* he thought, his breathing shallow and forced—as if he were dying, he felt as if he were dying—*it was hard, sometimes, to know the difference.*

"Lisa's going to call the school and ask the principal to make an announcement," Larry told them. "Lisa's legal mumbo-jumbo should get the principal moving."

"Maybe I better look at your garage," Sam said, and the two men went back across the street.

Sunshine poured down over the roofs and treetops like a golden rain, like a god in love. Furry little buds burst open, pointillistically stippling the canvas of sky. The green tongues of new leaves chattered in front of the houses, which looked on, silent and bemused, with red-brick or painted-wood or aluminum-siding forbearance.

"I don't think it's teenagers," said Jazz.

"Why not?" Mary asked.

Mary lifted her arms, clasping her own hands high over her head, twisting first to the right, then to the left, a morning stretch after bending over boxes, and the sun made her white arms and white cotton sleeves blaze in a detergent dazzle that seemed to Jazz—who had thought about things like how racial discrimination was like laundry, was a sort of sorting—whiter than white.

"I just don't think it is." In her mind Jazz heard the garbage can, saw the snapped chain.

Perhaps the chain had been not snapped so much as hacked.

Perhaps the chain had been hacked in half with a carving knife.

But she didn't want to press the matter. She certainly didn't wish to be an alarmist. She was still new to the neighborhood. She didn't even know everybody yet!

She didn't know the couple with the three boys. She'd see them hanging out in the yard in the late afternoon, playing ball or tag, but they seemed so contained, a unit, that she never did more than nod. In the late afternoon they called to one another, the parents to the boys, the boys to their parents, the boys among themselves, and their voices were a suburban choir, a cookout a capella. As the sun dropped lower it seemed to be slipping from a grasp, falling from the sky, as if accidentally let go; it rolled down the long, straight streets to the precipice of horizon and went right over the edge, a kind of Chappaquiddick—the way all can change in a moment, the fatal mistake—and the night, instead of cooling off, grew warmer. It was going to be a steambath summer, neighbors rising at six to mow the lawn before the day was too hot to think of any task more arduous than drinking iced tea. Sun-brewed-and-herbal iced tea, because that was the kind of city this was. This was the kind of city that, when you got off the plane coming back from anywhere, St. Louis or Atlanta or Seattle, and you flagged a cab because the limo was never there, the cab driver had a Kundera novel and a plastic bottle of spring water in the front seat beside him, and when you asked him if he liked the novel he said he wasn't far along enough to compare it with Kundera's previous books. All in all, it was that kind of a city.

But there were rumors of another existence here, too—handguns on the South Side, the mentally ill who roamed the University's deserted buildings after hours, the hookers on the Square at midnight. Landfills with toxic earth-fingers that reached out toward people, radon entering your pores when you weren't looking or when you were, blind deer-hunters who, the state legislature said, *may hunt only when accompanied by a seeing person.*

And there were rich folk, whose houses fronted on one of the lakes, and there were way too many overpaid double-income professional couples, the parents of the privileged West High kids, three cars to a family (Mama Bear, Papa Bear, Just-got-his-learner's-permit Bear), orthodontry and tai-chi lessons, and mountain bikes though there were no mountains, laser printers and plug-in woks and consciences made pure by recycling. *Soon they would just recycle their consciences. Then they wouldn't have to recycle the other stuff.* One night Nina heard a fierce pounding on her front door. She couldn't think of a single one of her friends who wouldn't have called before coming over so late. Upstairs, she held her breath and waited, a shushing finger over her lips as a signal to Tavy not to make a sound. The pounding went on for a good ten minutes. *All right, a bad ten minutes!* Finally it stopped.

One day there was an envelope in the mail with no return address. Inside was a copy of an article about her. A photograph of her had been published with the article, which appeared in the newspaper. Whoever sent the article had kept the photograph.

Shelley held the envelope up to the floor lamp next to the Green Bay Packers chair. She had come over to borrow a book. "There are these weirdos called stalkers," she said. "Maybe you'd better inform the police."

"Sam says there's nothing to go to the police *with.*"

"Well, if you get another one of these, I'd go anyway."

But Nina didn't get another letter like that. After that letter, there was no more pounding at the door, there were no more envelopes minus return addresses.

But Larry discovered that the latch on their backyard fence had been jimmied. And Sophie said someone had dialed her number and hung on, not saying anything, not even breathing heavily, but still there.

It was a puzzle, a mighty puzzle.

They wondered whose latchgate would turn up broken next. And whose answering machine would next fill up uselessly with unidentified staticky radio signals, a DJ spinning patter onto the incoming-message tape. And who, or god forbid what, was snaking through the dark from house to house, and why?

Sometimes, when it had not rung for a while, Sophie would pick up the telephone anyway, in spite of the arthritis that was starting to make her hands look, she thought, like tap roots, to make sure the line had not been cut. It never was; it always buzzed reassuringly, and she replaced the receiver.

She had had the thought—she couldn't help herself—that maybe it was Leland trying to call her. Maybe he missed talking to her as much as she missed talking to him. This might be a slightly insane thought, she knew, but she didn't think it could harm anyone if she kept it to herself, which she did, a secret treasure.

And then after a little longer while, they began to realize that nobody had had anything to report for several weeks. And then still more time passed, and there was still nothing to report. And they began to forget that there had ever been this particular puzzle.

They didn't even want to talk about how concerned they'd once been, because it seemed to make no sense to fret about something that wasn't happening. Even to talk about how they'd worried for no reason was to admit to a kind of temporary communal craziness, and no one wanted to be crazy even temporarily. You could find yourself living in luridly lit hallways, eating chalkdust. You could find yourself shooting, blindly, at anything that moved. It was true that sometimes this one or that one would hear a noise in the night, as before, but in the morning a logical explanation would always be revealed—there really had been a big wind, or Ian Wallace had actually found two teenagers asleep in each other's arms in a rusted-out secondhand Subaru parked right out in front on the street. Or somebody's *cat* was in heat. Trucks tore up and down Highland, a street never meant to support the traffic it was made to support. Sirens sounded, mufflers fell off, kids opened the sun-roofs on their parents' Preludes and turned the four-way speaker system up full blast.

There was always a logical explanation, and besides, they were always inside their houses after dark fell and so never saw the shadow thrown against the fence when the headlights passed. They never saw the figure tampering with the basement window. They were preoccupied, rushing silently through the deep space of their solitary dreams. They never heard the knife prying the wood frame from the sill.

Tell Her

Guy knows he has to tell her—this news that he has to tell her—but not yet. Not while she's practicing sex on the living room floor.

"By George I think she's got it," he says, Higginsishly.

His wife is wearing floppy black shorts and a white Jockey undershirt beneath which her braless breasts, as she lies on the floor, are as flat as a horizon, a bad EKG.

Dooley told her that women lack an understanding of the music of sex. They don't know how to lose themselves in the beat, he said.

"We've got three kids," Guy says now, using his normal voice, which is average for a man, nowhere near as deep as he had wanted it to be when he had hit puberty and thought he might grow up to become an infielder with the Chicago Cubs. But he's never even traveled to Wrigley Field to see a game.

At work he worries about telling her, because he knows he has to tell her sometime.

Meanwhile, there is inventory to take, there are orders to write up, books to shelve or send out. There are posters to print. *I believe in the viability of our downtown area,* he had told the loan officer. *I want to do my part to make the city of Madison attractive and useful to its residents.* The changes he was proposing, he told the loan officer, would increase his business by distinguishing it from the other bookstores. He did not point out that the other bookstores practically had a monopoly and that he was desperate to find a way to survive, but anyone in Madison could have guessed as much. The loan officer took the request to committee, and the bank handed him a home equity loan to expand his bookstore. Which he has done by adding a coffee shop and small stage. Now novelists, poets, and performance artists come to town to read their works and sign copies of their books—which he often can't sell and isn't allowed to return for credit. He suspects that some writers do this on purpose. He wouldn't be surprised if their publishers sent them out on tour with explicit directions. *Sign every book in sight,* they said. *If you don't want to use your own name, make one up. Play tic-tac-toe on the flyleaf. Do you want to publish your next book with us? Do you dream of a bigger advance? No returns!* He doesn't blame the writers. Everybody has to make a living.

Including himself! And why *shouldn't* it work, this idea of his! It *was* viable! It *was* downtown! On summer Sunday mornings a local string quartet played Mozart while customers munched on bagels, brioches, and croissants. The sun was like an invisible waitperson Windexing the tall windows, polishing the silverware on slate-topped tables, patting cloth napkins into place. In the late afternoon there would be a modern music ensemble playing the work of regional composers, and in the evening there might be someone singing Turkestan folksongs. It was the kind of city where there was always someone who knew Turkestan folksongs. It was the kind of city where people liked to eat hot fudge and raspberry ice cream sundaes while listening to Turkestan folksongs. But maybe it was also the kind of city where people got their books from the library.

There had been a celebration when he opened the addition. The alternative weekly newspaper had even done an article, with a photograph of Guy posed next to the cappuccino machine. The article talked about how the 1950s coffeehouses were the forerunner of today's community-center bookstores. READING, WRITING, AND RADICCHIO, went the headline.

Guy sits at his desk in the back room. He needs something to do, needs to do something. He decides to look through the catalogues that have piled up on the floor, a stack as high as the desk.

These catalogues tell him he doesn't have to restrict his ordering to books. There are many things besides books that a bookstore can sell. He can order T-shirts that say LABOUR'S MY LOST LOVE and sell them to exchange students from England. He can order T-shirts that say GIRL-COTT KNOPF and sell them to feminists. He can order T-shirts that say

SHEVARDNADZE FOR PRESIDENT OF THE U.S. and sell them to émigrés from the former Soviet Union. If he doesn't want to place orders, he can take inventory. He can take stock!

What he cannot do is tell her what he has to tell her.

He turns on the air conditioner. It is a small unit, somehow too delicate for the motor inside it, and it seems to be in a kind of pain, throbbing like a headache.

He opens the door and asks Teresa if she has some aspirin.

"I have Motrin," Teresa says, handing him a pillbox. It's pretty, this pillbox, a round silver kind of a deal with an eighteenth-century tableau enameled on the top, a bewigged gentleman in gold lamé tailcoat and breeches bowing to a bewigged lady in a periwinkle blue ballgown.

Guy flicks the top up with his thumb. The pills stare up at him like small eyeballs. "I thought these were what women take for their periods," he says, feeling obscurely threatened.

"Pain," she says. "They take them for *pain.*"

There is a sink in the room. He fills a mug with water and downs the pills. The mug is a promo mug for *The Wind in the Willows* and at the bottom is a ceramic Mr. Toad.

He can call his banker, but he would have to turn off the air conditioner before he could hear over the phone, and then Teresa and the customers would be able to hear *him.* He looks again at Teresa's pillbox, still in his hand. He can almost hear the harpsichord, something by Scarlatti or Mozart. The man and the woman beginning to dance, moving toward each other, moving away.

Guy loves his customers, the people he has grown up with and the students who stay the same age always because, as soon as they rush off into their adult lives, others, exactly like them, take their places. He loves his authors, both the calculating and the confused, both the ones for whom an audience is a mirror and whose gestures are choreography—a dance of seven veils but the last veil, torn away, reveals only a reflection—and those who look as if publication of their book had interrupted them at their typewriter (these would be the ones who still worked on typewriters, maybe even a few who clung, reactionarily, to pen and paper). *What am I doing here?* they seem to ask. *How did I get here?*

Jazz Piano, a cute young black woman with a purple streak in her hair who teaches in the art department at the University, had balanced precariously on a stool on the stage in the coffeehouse and performed a skit called "Is There Life after a Grant from the NEA?" Nina Bryant had read from her book of stories in progress. There was plenty of local talent, in addition to the roadshow, the visiting troupes of well-groomed minimalists, scruffy, myopic biographers, the occasional aging author of metafiction, and the poets, who were always, oddly, the best behaved, feeling, perhaps, that they had a past to live down. And at first, Jordan had been glad to call in a West High student to sit for the children and come down to the store on weeknights, proud to sit beside him during the reading, thrilled to serve the star of the night cappuccino and cookies after the reading, but then she started saying she'd heard enough, she knew how to read and didn't need to be read to thank you, and started spending the evenings with Dooley instead, who talked about sex as if he actually had it but Guy was sure he didn't, at least not anymore. In fact, the city was full of people who used to have sex but no longer did. It was one reason he got such a crowd at the store. They needed something to do, and rubbing shoulders was at least sort of like sex.

Dooley couldn't be more than five-five. He had hard, shiny eyes like birdseed, and a moustache like a brown sparrow perched on the clothesline of his upper lip. He did something with municipal computers—maps, traffic, Guy wasn't sure what, but it involved figuring out where things went. Guy had understood that much the day he and Jordan were introduced to Dooley at a wedding reception. He had understood, too, that Jordan and Dooley had made some kind of connection, one of those recognition things, though he can't figure out what it is based on. They aren't anything alike.

When he thinks about what Jordan is like, Guy rests his head on the desk, as if he is a first-grader at nap time, and hears the little air conditioner chugging away, working its fingers to the bone. He thinks there is still this first-grader inside him, and if he can just have some Quiet Time he'll be all right, he'll be ready for reading, writing, arithmetic, reading.

What's black and white and red all over? A newspaper.

Jordan's hair is straight as a ruler, dark red like a pencil a teacher would correct papers with. Three children, and she is as slim and pliable as she was when they were undergraduates. She packs Noah off to school on the bus and takes the twins, Dart and Zeke, in their two-seat stroller to daycare, and works part-time at the credit union, which is where he probably should have gone for the loan but he was embarrassed to go to her boss, and she always looks as if everything is running on schedule, except lately there's an edge, it's as if she's angry with him, and he doesn't know why. He tries to soften her up, he brings her a slice of Black Forest cake from his coffeehouse, he tells her silly riddles that he thinks will weaken her resolve, this resolve she seems to have made to be angry with him.

What do you get if you cross a canary with a lawn mower? Shredded tweet.

What he doesn't tell her is what he has to tell her.

He walks out onto the main floor. People are glancing at Tables of Contents in the Periodical Section, scanning blurbs on the backs of book jackets in the Fiction Section, picking up greeting cards and opening them and reading them and putting them back on the rack in the Novelties Section, the cards' edges tattering, the cards' envelopes blackening with fingerprints as if bruised, and he thinks he should be in VCRs.

On his lunch break, Guy drives to the daycare center to spend a half hour with the twins. He never wanted to be an absentee father. His own father had been close to him, breaking all the rules of fatherhood for that day and age. His father had read to him at bedtime, had sat in the bleachers for all the Little League games. His father had been, by midwestern standards, amazingly demonstrative, tattooing Guy's face with kisses before he left for his job at the Oscar Mayer plant each morning. He would embrace Guy's mother each afternoon when he arrived home, smiling a big, slow smile that was like a suspension bridge flung across a wide space. A smile like a safe passage. Except that Guy now knows, having watched death carry his own dad away, there is no safe passage for fathers.

What creature crawls on four legs in the morning, walks on two at noon, and stands on three in the evening?

Dart and Zeke roll up to him like tumbleweed, grab hold of his pant legs, endure the kisses he plants on the round garden plots of their faces. The center fixes lunch for the children, but he has brought them a treat from the coffeehouse—Black Forest cake.

They like the riddles better.

"Ugh," says Zeke.

"Ugh," says Dart.

"What walks on two feet and says *ugh?*" asks Guy.

"Zeke," says Dart.

"Dart," says Zeke, falling down on the floor and laughing. Dart falls on top of him, also laughing. At least they are not practicing sex.

It is possible, Guy thinks, that by the time his sons grow up there will be no such thing as sex. Or it will be historical, a thing people will talk about as having happened, once. It will be something people read about, a kind of fiction. It will still sell books.

Jordan would be by to pick up the twins in another hour. Guy brushes their hair back from their foreheads and says he'll see them at dinner. But when he stands on the front steps of the daycare center and feels a breeze on his face as if it is brushing the hair back from his forehead, he decides not to return to work. He goes for a walk instead, following the bike path that curves alongside the lake. The lake's surface is ruffled, like a skirt, and it dances in the light summer breeze, a lake with kick pleats, a lake that does the cancan! A lake that flirts.

When he gets home, he goes straight up to the attic. For the next few hours, he rereads the letters his father wrote to his mother from France. Cross-legged on the attic floor, his back aching and his throat dry and scratchy as if history is contagious, a cold or fever he's coming down with, he reads, and the sun advances across the afternoon like an armored division, a western front. He imagines these letters being read for the first time, by a young Geneva—so young her hair is in a pageboy, her smiling mouth is painted a bright billboard color, she is wearing bobby sox and oxfords with her long, slim skirt, and her sweater set is made of the kind of fuzzy stuff girls wash in Woolite. He sees how she is moved by his father's grief when a friend named Ferris Everly takes a grenade in his gut. Then he sees his mother and father, married, in their bedroom, and his mother, still so young, is in a blue gown that flows over her like water. He sees his father in tailcoat and breeches, the muscled calves almost bursting out of their white stockings, one leg extended forward, bowing to that young, so very young woman in her blue ballgown.

But it will take them a few years before they have a child. Him.

When his mother died, five years ago, he and Jordan transferred boxes of souvenirs to this house, which they had just moved into. "We've got more than enough room for you to come live with us, Mother," Jordan had said to her on the phone, but Geneva had been unbudgeable, refusing to leave the Victorian monstrosity on the east side, near the plant, and Guy had to admit that *Mother* never sounded quite right when it came out of Jordan's mouth, it had a premeditated sound to it, as if she started each sentence at the top of a ski slope and slid down it hoping to jump over the word *Mother* and slalom into the next paragraph. "I plan to die in this house," Geneva had said, making good on her word not long after.

He puts the letters back in the box and writes SAVE on the top and carries it down to the bedroom, where he puts it on the top shelf of the closet. When Jordan asks him what he's putting on the shelf, he says, "A box."

"I can see that," she says.

"Letters," he says.

"From the attic? But why not leave them in the attic?"

He knows he should tell her, but he can't. Not yet.

Noah is his firstborn, his favorite though of course he loves all three of his boys exactly the same amount, but Noah is the one who materialized from some place deep inside Guy. Jordan may have been the one they did the caesarean on, but it was Guy whose sternum split open, Guy whose heart the doctor pulled out in this new way of giving birth, a heart they named Noah.

As he pitches to Noah's bunt, the softball a sweet white shooting star in the lengthening light of early summer, Guy's heart catches better than he does, he feels as if Noah has hit the ball straight into his already scarred and tender chest.

All through the long spring and summer they play two-man softball like this, while the twins chase each other around the lawn and Jordan holds long, serious conversations on the cordless phone.

It seems to him that they play in the protective shade of a kinder, gentler house. The house is stucco, with a chimney on each side, and Guy and Jordan saved for years to buy it, or one more or less like it, in this neighborhood near good schools.

The first time Guy called her up for a date, she said, "Oh, yeah, you're in my Lit Survey class, aren't you. The one with the socks?"

Confused, he said, "I wear socks, I guess. I mean, I know I wear socks."

"No, if you were the one with the socks you'd know what I'm talking about. This character just wears socks, no shoes."

"He must get holes a lot," Guy said.

"If you're not the one with the socks, who are you?"

"I can answer that more fully," he said, "if you'll go out with me Saturday night."

He assumes it is Dooley she is talking with now. Or being talked to by, since she seems to be mostly just listening. He wonders what Dooley is telling her. He wonders what Dooley could have to tell her that he has to tell it to her so often, and for so long. If it is anywhere near as important as what Guy has to tell her.

The house is near West High. It is a dream of a house, even though they haven't gotten around to buying a fixture for the ceiling light in the living room and their furniture comes from garage sales. Arborvitae and a crabapple grow in the back, near the fence. There is a swingset that he has to take down and bring into the basement every fall and put up again every year when the weather gets warm. It is an American Dream of a house.

The house has four bedrooms, but the fourth serves as a guest room, since the twins share. When he tucks them in—*drumsticks,* he calls them, pretending to eat them up, *my little spare ribs, my pieces of peanut brittle*—they laugh at him and burrow deeper under the covers. Noah sits at the desk in his room, legs wrapped around chair rungs, concentrating on his geography book. "Name three principal products of Peru," Guy says to him, from the doorway, and Noah looks up at him, smiles, and turns back to his book.

Guy joins Jordan in their bed. She is wearing a gown the color of twilight, blue silk that stops short at her knees. Her hair is the dark red of the raspberry syrup on the ice cream sundaes on the coffeehouse menu. "You and Dooley seem to find a lot to talk about these days," he says.

"Is that an accusation? It sounds like an accusation."

"Of course not," he says, knowing it was an accusation. "I just wish you'd talk to me more." It occurs to him that this is supposed to be the other way around. The wife is supposed to be begging the husband to talk to *her* more.

"What do you want to talk about?" she asks him then.

But he can't tell her.

He is afraid something is opening up between them, getting bigger and bigger, becoming vast, like an ocean or the sky. Something that, if it gets any bigger, they won't be able to bridge. He does not think she can be having an affair with Dooley, because Dooley is both gay and celibate, but he thinks maybe she is having an affair with Dooley.

He starts to lose weight, worrying about this and other things. He takes two, four, six, eight, ten painkillers a day and his head still feels like something he has to lug around, a kind of bookbag, so that he is clumsy, and burdened with knowledge. He slides through spring this way, growing thinner and weightier at the same time.

A Famous Author—a Fresh New Voice, a Literary Light—comes to town and attracts a huge audience to her reading. Everyone is there, even Jordan and Dooley. Even all the local writers turn out to see this Famous Author. There is something a little religious about it, as if they want to touch the Famous Writer's hem, absorb some of the Famous Writer's success. What Guy thinks of as real people are there, too. Larry Adcock's wife, Lisa, is there with her husband's secretary, Billie. The Wallaces. Some of the academic types. Body heat is raising the room temperature. The air conditioner is off, because otherwise no one would be able to hear the Famous Writer. The natives, of Madison, are restless, and so are the transients, the students and visiting professors. The Famous Author is late. Perhaps this is a well-planned lateness. *The name of the game is Lit Biz,* the publishers told their writers. *Did you say you want to publish your next book with us? Get bigger advances? Signing books is not enough! You need your own, personal signature! You don't need just a style, you need style! Intense, jokey, whatever! And get a good haircut!* Twenty minutes after the scheduled time, the Famous Author arrives. Her hem is long, brushing against combat boots. She is only in her thirties but already imperious, not so much reading to an audience as addressing her subjects. Intense and jokey by turns, she reads a story about disorder and early sorrow.

A Short History of China

When China was a little girl, she seldom saw her parents, that she knew of, at least, because they were secret agents for the CIA. She spent most of her time in the big old house on Long Island with her grandmother. Sometimes her parents blew in just long enough to take her to the Tastee Freeze or throw a cocktail party. When the evening ended, and they tucked her into bed, their hands touching her hair, her shoulder, the blanket, lightly, like four-handed piano, or as if she were wet paint and might stick to them, they said, "Now look who's under-cover!" and winked at each other over her sleepy head. One day her grandmother died, while trying to change a lightbulb.

How many creative writers does it take to change a lightbulb? One to change the bulb and ten to workshop it.

After they buried her grandmother, China's parents came in from the cold, but she seldom saw them, because she was away at college. They had passed tests to become real estate agents. When she came home for Thanksgiving, they showed her her old bedroom, now redecorated and emptied of all her stuff, and said, "Look at all the closet space!" and winked at each other over her weary head. All weekend China just lived out of her suitcase, so they wouldn't feel the house had shrunk back to its former size.

After graduation, she got a job in the city, but she seldom saw her parents, because they had retired, at last, and moved to Sarasota. Her parents sent photographs of each other in front of the elephant on the circus training grounds. China fixed up her apartment, bought Wamsutta sheets and some scatter rugs and a floor lamp. She found a boyfriend, who dumped her for a florist named Betti with an i, and then another boyfriend, who dumped her for a market analyst named Tiffaney with an e, and then another boyfriend, who turned out to be married, so she seldom saw him.

One day her parents were trampled to death while trying to feed the elephant.

That night China lay in bed, incognito as a spy, feeling foreign even to herself. She felt like a stranger in the strange land of herself. She felt like a place where students were shot, although that could also have been Kent State, 1972. And she felt, too, like a crate, marked "Fragile," that had been tossed around during shipment and had gotten dropped and had smashed to smithereens.

As he sits there, observing the Famous Writer and listening to her story—and listening to the audience, also, in case there are whispered complaints or, as he hopes, murmurs of satisfaction, with the reading, his bookstore, his coffee shop—Guy thinks he sees a certain moistness filming the Famous Writer's expertly made-up eyes. He supposes it would be an occupational hazard for a writer—a tendency to empathize with one's characters. But then a tear, an actual tear, falls from one of those eyes onto the acid-free paper of the beautifully printed book, and a second tear follows, and Guy feels his back stiffening, senses backs all around him stiffening, as people begin to become aware of what is happening. The Famous Writer is weeping, a slow trickle of tears at first, and then—oh, the horror, the horror!—the *fascinating* horror of it—sobbing, her shoulders rising and falling under the black long-sleeved top. *No!* Guy wants to shout. *Don't have your nervous break-down here! Wait until you get to the Hungry Mind Bookstore in Minneapolis! The Borders Bookstore in Ann Arbor! Rizzoli in Chicago!* But it's no use, the Famous Writer has put her face in her hands and now as she takes them away the audience can see how her eye shadow has smeared, giving her a sooty look, as if she has recently cleaned a chimney, which reminds him that it is time to have his two chimneys swept.

Guy feels sorry for her. No one knows what to do, so no one does anything. The Famous Writer just keeps crying—bawling now, really—and the audience keeps on being polite and attentive, as if this is normal, as if this is, maybe, what Modern Literature is all about. You came to a reading, and the writer had a nervous breakdown at the front of the room, and you clapped and went home. It was a form of literary deconstruction.

Guy feels himself breaking out in a sweat half out of anxiety and half in a kind of sympathetic response to all those tears, water calling to water. He realizes he has to do something; after all, this is his store. This is not only not Rizzoli in Chicago, it is not even the bookstore at the other end of State Street, although life would be fairer, he can't help thinking, if it were. He pushes himself to his feet and swims—it feels like swimming, not walking, a progress through something viscous and muffling—to the podium. He smiles at everyone, everyone out there on the far shore. "I guess maybe we should call it a night," he says. "But hey, one free cup of cappuccino for everyone, okay?" He turns his back to the audience, deliberately, to give them a chance to get up without embarrassing the Famous Writer, whose heaving shoulders have sub-sided into a forlorn hunch, and thinks that this is what you would call saving somebody else's face, a rather engaging, if not exactly as attrac-tive as the publicity photos had made it look, face. He feels he has han-dled this pretty well. The Famous Writer reaches for the glass of water Teresa's always careful to place next to the microphone and gulps. Then she sets the glass down, looks at Guy, her photogenic face splotchy with emotion as if lit by a strobe light, and flings her arms around his neck and starts crying all over again. Teresa comes up and pries the Famous Writer's arms away and says, "There, there, everything's going to be all right, you'll see, why don't we just make you comfortable in this back room here, we'll just have a seat right here, shut the door would you Guy," and now they are all in the back office, with Jordan and Dooley, who have brought up the rear without saying anything.

"I have such a headache," the Famous Writer says, not looking at anyone, massaging her temples. Her nails are tipped with white in what Jordan calls a French manicure. Jordan's nails are cut straight across, but the Famous Writer's are caressingly shaped, ten little shells on a beach.

"Would you like some Motrin?" Guy asks.

"Guy," Jordan says, as if his name is a sentence.

He looks up at his wife.

As if it is a paragraph. A story. A chapter.

A minimalist novel.

"Motrin is for cramps," she says, staring back at him.

She is wearing a blue sleeveless sundress. Dooley has on a blue shirt. Guy decides they are so much alike that they match, like a pair of socks. He gets the Motrin and hands it to the Famous Writer with a second glass of water, except that for a glass he uses his *Wind in the Willows* promo mug. "There's a toad at the bottom of that mug," he warns her.

"I'm sorry," the Famous Writer says. "I don't usually do this. I mean, once I was so depressed I went to the Emergency Room at the hospital, but I just stayed there crying for two hours and nobody ever came over to ask what was wrong or see if I was dying or something, so finally I called a cab and went home. I've never cried at a reading before. It's so Anne Sexton."

"What are you doing with Motrin?" Jordan asks Guy. "Do you have a problem I don't know about?"

Teresa has gone to take up the folding chairs.

"I wouldn't want you to have to call a cab," Guy says to the Famous Writer. "I'll walk you to the hotel." He turns to Jordan. "Are you and Dooley coming?"

He thinks that he has been wanting to ask her this for quite a while, now.

Jordan shakes her head, and it's like something catching fire, igniting, that dark-red hair of hers. "Geri"—the baby-sitter—"will want to go home."

"I bet that's Geri with a G," the Famous Writer says.

"And an i," Jordan agrees.

"Oh, God," the Famous Writer says. "Oh, God. They're everywhere. They're taking over the world. They're like body snatchers, but they snatch only male bodies." Her voice snags and lurches and almost stumbles, but she manages not to start crying again.

Teresa will lock up after closing. Guy walks the Famous Writer a few blocks to the Edgewater Inn under a moon that, who knows, could be like the one hanging in the sky the night his father's friend, Ferris Everly, got blown away. Students mingle on State Street with the homeless. It's late enough that the mimes and guitarists and Vietnamese food stands have all put away their acts and vegetables for the night, and though there are voices and movement, it all seems like a shadow play, dark figures cast against a sheet behind which a different, more real world might be taking place. The Edgewater Inn hugs the shore of Lake Mendota, which means "gathering of the waters," as if many little waters came together there, for a convocation or a party, or to sign a treaty.

"Well," Guy says in the lobby, "good night, then." A tear peeks out of her right eye, as if not quite sure whether to come all the way out. It sort of tiptoes out onto a lash and stands there, shy and doubtful. "Don't cry," he says. "It wasn't such a terrible reading. I especially liked your riddle."

"I want to apologize. I need to explain. Please come up with me."

What, exactly, *did* publishers tell their authors when they sent them out on tour? Maybe they said, *Sell books any way you can!*

He follows her to the elevator. It was a dog-eat-dog world.

But he knows he can't actually sleep with her. There was no way of knowing whom else a Famous Writer might have slept with. It could have been anyone, even another Famous Writer. Even an agent!

"Relax," she says. "I'm not trying to seduce you."

"Oh." He feels let down, somehow, rejected, criticized, even though she has said nothing critical. He feels like a manuscript that has been turned down, and he has not even been submitted.

The Famous Writer sits on the double bed and tugs her boots off. "I hate boots," she says.

"Why do you wear them?"

"A person has to wear something on their feet. You can't just wear socks."

She's not wearing socks, he sees, but black tights, like a ballet dancer. Her feet are long and narrow. He wonders if her toenails, also, are like ten tiny seaside shells.

"I didn't mean to be presumptuous," he says now. "It's just that we all have to be so careful these days."

"Please, don't apologize. I'm the one who's supposed to be doing that."

He shrugs, as if all his writers cry all the time. "It must be hard," he says. "Getting remaindered, going out of print, stuff like that. A hard life."

"I'm so lonely," she says, and when she says this he sees it is true. Loneliness is written all over her face like a book no one ever reads. "Have a seat."

He lowers himself into the straight-backed chair at the desk, which has a blotter with hotel postcards tucked into its pocket and, the desk doing double duty as a dressing table, a mirror hanging on the wall behind it. "You must have friends," he says. "Other bratpackers." He knows this is what they call the young writers.

She glares at him. "They all have trust funds. Or they're married to movie directors. I have to *work* for a living."

It doesn't strike him that she has to work very hard. She goes to different cities and gives readings, gets interviewed, has her picture taken for *Vanity Fair.* It's not like she has to go around digging ditches, for chrissake. So he doesn't know how to respond to this. Instead he says, "The bank is foreclosing on my house. I took out a home equity loan, you see, to finance my bookstore, and not enough people buy books, and we're losing the house but I haven't told my wife yet because I can't figure out how to tell her."

"You have to tell her," she says. "How awful this must be for you! Oh, what a wicked, illiterate country this is!" And she seems so indignant on his behalf that he almost feels he could simply step aside and let her take care of everything. Even sitting down she's tall, her back straight, her breasts, he observes, hidden by her loose sweater, as if she's afraid they might get in her way.

He takes a postcard out of its pocket, gazes at the view of the pier, and puts it back. When he looks into the mirror he can see the Famous Author on the bed in back of him, her face, paler now that the makeup has worn off, like puffed rice, and his own, so close and stricken that it is a surprise, like an object nearer than it appears to be in the rearview mirror. *What did the balding man say to the street-corner Santa Claus? It is better to give than to recede.* He feels a little like Kevin Costner in a movie about Madonna: He thinks that the woman behind him is probably mentally sticking her well-cared-for finger down her throat, gagging at the very thought of him.

"Look at you," she says, and he *is* looking at himself, the confused image of himself looking at him. "You're what America is supposed to be about. A small businessman. An average guy."

When she says *average,* he knows she meant it when she said she was not trying to seduce him. That she really is a kind of Madonna of the book world, only without roadies. He turns around, straddles the chair. "Why are you so unhappy?" he asks, curious in spite of himself. "You've been so lucky. You have fame, fortune—!"

"I'm *tired* of people thinking I'm lucky. They try to take it all away, the fame, the fortune, by attributing it to luck. But I've earned everything I've gotten." Her face suddenly hardens, settling like Jell-O into a mold that he understands must be the expression it wears when nobody's around. What she wants, he thinks, is simply *more.* She wants to be admired for being admirable, praised for being praiseworthy. What she wants is to have the music turned up, loud, all the time.

His arms are resting on the chairback, and she places a hand on the top arm. Like Wite-Out, he thinks, looking down at the French manicure, like Liquid Paper. "What about you?" she whispers, returning his question to him. "What do you want out of life?"

If she is alone, he thinks, it must be because there was a boyfriend and she has broken up with him. And she hates the boyfriend for dumping her, but he feels sympathy for the boyfriend, because sleeping with a Famous Writer would be a lot like going to bed with a book. It would be Intertextuality.

Guy realizes that for him love means never having to say your story.

And afterward, it would mean having to listen to her revision of it, the way she would steal it and make it her own, changing the way it really was. He would like to tell her how important it was to him to leave the east side for the west side and that when he and Jordan moved into the house on the west side they celebrated by making love on the floor, but he doesn't want his life turned into fiction.

What he wants, what Guy wants, is to have everything back the way it was. He wants his bookstore back the way it was before he put his house up as collateral, before writers started having nervous break-downs in his store. He wants Jordan the way she was before she started practicing sex. He wants his father and mother back, too, and he wants Ferris back even if it means having to fight World War II all over again. But he doesn't want to lose what he has now, either. He doesn't want to give up his children to get his parents and their world back, he doesn't want to give up his coffee shop and readings series to get his house back. He thinks that it is no wonder he has a headache all the time. He tries to find a way to say all this, to say how much he misses his dad, but, finally, he is not a writer, he's just a bookseller, and he doesn't have the words. "What I'd really, really like to do sometime," he dis-covers himself saying, "is take my boy, my oldest son, to see the Cubs play in Wrigley Field."

"Here," she says, withdrawing her hand to reach into her purse. "Two tickets to Wrigley Field." She holds them out to him. She says, "I have to do a reading at Rizzoli in Chicago, so someone gave me these to use while I'm there. But I don't have anyone to go with, because I broke up with my boyfriend."

He is still in a daze as she shows him out her room. "You're a riddle yourself, do you know that?"

"Let me give you a piece of advice," she says. "Don't ever call a woman writer you want to sleep with a *bratpacker.*"

He has to pick up his car at the store before he can go home. At this time of night, he can hit green lights all the way to the house, a clean, straight shot as if he were driving a cue ball instead of a Subaru. He leaves the car on the street, because Dooley's is in the driveway. The overhead light is on in the living room, and through the window he sees Jordan and Dooley dancing, the kind of dance people do in which their bodies talk to each other without touching, and he thinks that his wife understands the music of sex. When he steps inside, Dooley stops moving, but Jordan is lost in the beat, and she sways to the music, which is lowdown and sexy, and not too loud, so it won't wake the kids.

"I have something to tell you," Guy says to Jordan.

"Oh, say, look, I'd better be going," Dooley says, in a mumble that is itself like background music. "I'm outta here."

Guy hears the door closing behind Dooley; Jordan is still dancing, by herself, in the periwinkle blue dress, a dress of purplish-blue redder and deeper than lupine or zenith.

"Later," she says, either to him or the vanishing Dooley, Guy's not sure which. "Dance with me."

He moves toward her.

"How did it go?" she asks.

"You can guess. What does a jigsaw puzzle do when it gets bad news?"

"Goes to pieces." She smiles, a smile like a safe passage. "I really can't stand writers," she says. "They're like children, and I already have three. I swear I wish you were in VCRs."

It seems to him as if the overhead light has become a chandelier, because there are sparks and shadows flickering around the room, and the music sounds like crystal ringing against itself. If he doesn't look too closely, he can imagine that the furniture in the room is rosewood and mahogany. He can almost hear the harpsichord, something by Scarlatti or Mozart.

"Dooley's the best friend I ever had," Jordan says. "He's so much fun to talk with. Do you understand what I mean? A friend is someone you talk with. And a person can have many friends and a best friend and still be married to a friend."

As he dances with her, he can see, down the front of Jordan's dress, that her breasts are shaped by light and shadow, as if by a corset, a bodice, into a lively fullness.

Guy thinks of all the friends he, too, has, as the music shifts, becoming something slow and easy. He puts his arms around his wife. The man and the woman beginning to dance, moving toward each other, moving away.

The Society of Friends

Whenever my small dog misbehaves—mostly this means when he lifts his leg on the living room couch—he punishes himself by retreating into the traveling case that sits in a corner of the kitchen and serves as his house. Recently my child has decided to imitate him. Now when she does something that she knows is wrong, she doesn't wait for me to find out about it. She marches herself off to a corner of the living room and stands staring fiercely at the wall. The only hitch is that both my daughter and my dog seem to think that as long as they punish themselves it is all right to misbehave. I suspect they have been reading Thoreau on civil disobedience.

Sometimes, when she has done something *very* bad and figures she deserves to be punished for a *long* time, my little girl pulls her tiny rocking chair up to the wall and takes a seat. Usually she has her teddy bear with her. "Bad bear," she says, scolding him. She will even spank him, though I have never spanked her. What a stern taskmaster she is! Already, at three, she reminds me of my mother.

The rocking chair was a gift from Rajan, a toy designer whose largess we largely depend on. She loves this man—his jewel-in-the-crown good looks, his Midwest accent. He's been the closest thing to a daddy in her life. So when he stopped by to tell me he was marrying Lucy, his supposed-to-be-former girlfriend, I was deeply unhappy, on my child's behalf as well as my own. She didn't know what his getting married meant, of course. He explained that he was going to live with

Lucy. He picked up my daughter and swung her over his head—his sleeves rolled up, the tendons of his arms standing out sexy as hell, as if his whole body were a system of ropes and pulleys. "You're my best girl," he said to her. "You know that?"

She was squealing with pleasure. Her long hair flew into her face, across her open mouth, and the world rushed away from her like childhood itself.

He set her down. The dog was waiting for his turn.

Over her head, he said to me, "I would have loved for her to be the flower girl but— I mean, you can understand why Lucy wasn't wild about the idea."

Flower girl? Rajan is forty-three, he's got two handsome boys in college, he's been divorced for a decade, the city of Madison is like a patchwork quilt of women for whom the common thread is Rajan, and he's talking *flower girl*?

From where we sat in the Quaker meetinghouse on their wedding day, I could catch only glimpses of Lucy and Rajan. She was wearing seed pearls in her short dark hair. She carried a bouquet of wildflowers, and her dress was ivory satin. Light from the long windows chuted in; it fell in a slant, the hologram of a playground slide. Rajan looked both scared and elated.

During the ceremony people began to get up and speak. This was because, my neighbor to my left whispered, they had been prompted by the Spirit. Someone would stand at one end of the church and tell a story about when Rajan or Lucy was a teenager, and then someone else would stand up on the other side of the room and offer his definition of a good marriage, or perhaps he would just give his blessing. You never knew who was going to pop up where or say what, and at first those of us who were not Quaker were filled with apprehension. We didn't know if everyone could be trusted to say things it was okay to say. There were things in our own hearts we might have told with just a little prompting, but would the world be well served thereby? But then the process took on its own rhythm. The people speaking seemed to form a continuum with the silence, and it was all part of the same thing, the peacefulness of the afternoon.

I lost myself in the reflective grace of a summery day. It seemed to me that the bright green leaves were an alphabet—nature's book. Looking out those windows during the lazy service was like reading the story of your life, both familiar and strange. I was scanning the chapter on Rajan when I discovered that my daughter had slipped down from her seat beside me and even now was wandering toward the front of the room. Maybe she wanted to say hello to Rajan.

I stood up to get a better look at her and then realized that everyone had turned in my direction and was waiting expectantly to hear what I had to say.

Oh God, I thought. Deliver me.

I was blushing—I could feel the warmth radiating from my face. On that warm day, my face was as red as a furnace.

"I just want to say," I said, "that I hope Rajan and Lucy have many years of happiness together, and could someone please grab hold of my daughter?"

It was too late. She had reached the front of the room, and there, as I could now see, was the flower girl, a perfectly innocent, well-behaved child who was not in the least prepared for a strange kid to come right up to her and kick her on the shin. She started to wail. She was wearing an apricot dress with an embroidered bateau neckline and a sash, and she plopped straight down on the floor, as if her legs had been kicked out from under her, crying.

I raced up the aisle, clutched the relevant child's hand and pulled her out into the lobby.

"Don't think you can fix this one by sitting in the corner," I said. "Why did you do that?"

"Rajan mine," she said.

"Rajan Lucy's," I said.

"N-O," she said, spelling the word out the way the boy down the street, Jason, had taught her to.

"Y-E-S," I said.

She put her thumb in her mouth. She is so pretty, so bright. When she frowns, it is like a light being turned off. I took her thumb out of her mouth. She put it back in. I sighed. The service had ended and Rajan and Lucy were walking up the aisle, out to the hallway, where we were. I rose from my knees, catching my kid's free hand in mine. "I'm so sorry—" I started to say, but then noticed that neither Lucy nor Rajan was particularly interested in an apology just at this moment. Lucy looked gorgeous. Rajan looked crazed. Before any of us could think what to say, the doors opened and the crowd flooded out. People wanted a breather before lining up to affix their signatures to the marriage document. According to the Society of Friends, it had been explained to us, we were to sign, all two hundred of us, because we were all witnesses to the ceremony. Rajan and Lucy are married to each other not only in God's eyes but ours. That means mine too, I pointed out to myself.

Rajan is not the love of my life; he's a good friend who, had it been up to me, I would have nominated for that other office—but it wasn't up to me. He is, however, the love of my young daughter's life.

When we got home, I helped her into her leotard so she could rehearse her role in the Tiptoe Toddlers' ballet recital. She had been cast as a bee. Her role consisted principally of a series of swooping whirls. Where the butterflies would rise gracefully on their toes and take light little steps in a row across the stage, their colorful gauze wings a rainbow in the spotlight, my child was slated to buzz busily about, twirling dervishly in her black-and-yellow leotard, antennae waving from her forehead, which would certainly be furrowed in concentration. Daily she threw herself into this role with the true dedication of an artist, scowling in deep seriousness. The waistless slope of her torso seemed remarkably beelike.

As she buzzed around the living room, landing momentarily on various pieces of furniture, our dog at her heels, I fell into a kind of trance, watching her motivated but miniature limbs express such a complicated authorial intention: To bee or not to bee, that was the question, and she had answered it from the beginning by saying yes, art is a worthy receptacle for human energy. I thought about my parents. Night after night when I was a child, they had practiced the Beethoven string quartets, the room so dense with cigarette smoke it was like living in the middle of a cloud, the music so celestial that a cloud seemed a down-to-earth thing, a flat-footed fog, by comparison. And I had loved it, more than anything—that music, and my parents' devotion to it. It was many years before I acknowledged that there were other reasons for living. My mother never did find another reason, not really.

The Tiptoe Toddlers gave their end-of-summer performance in Randall Elementary, not far from the meetinghouse where Rajan and Lucy had been married two months earlier. I had asked Rajan to come, knowing how much he was missed. He arrived at the last minute, with Lucy, and took a seat at the back of the auditorium.

As the curtain lifted—the phonograph starting with a sickening slide of needle as the child in charge of music searched for the right place—the Tiptoe Toddlers gave us a brief tableau of true Augustan charm: The littlest children sat or stood in their assigned spots, waving their arms, green leaves. These were the sunflowers. Butterflies flitted across the stage on languid currents of bright summer air. The heroine, a four-year-old, strolled through this flower-strewn meadow and lay down to dream beside the painted stream. And my bee made her entrance.

Swooping in circles—not a beeline—from stage left to stage right, she hovered a mere terpsichorean instant over this flower and that one, before buzzing to the next. How intense she was! A dynamo, a piston, a small energy field—oh, she was all erg, my baby, my honeypot. Her eyebrows were drawn together under the waving antennae in deep balletic identification with her subject. But what was she doing now? She had zeroed in on the prima ballerina, our lady of the lake, and, with a loud hornety buzz, jabbed her forefinger into the girl's side and, evidently, pinched her. The girl yowled. My baby buzzed to the other side of the stage; she had her head and arms stretched out and down in front of her, as if she were diving, or boring a hole through air. The yellow crepe paper I had attached to her leotard was coming loose. The butterflies forgot to stay on tiptoe. One of the sunflowers began to scream for his mother. The prima ballerina, a trouper, tried to carry on as if nothing had happened, but it was too late—all the sunflowers were screaming for their mothers, the butterflies were running wild, they had a bee in their bonnet.

I wanted to disown her. That kid? I don't know who that kid belongs to! I wondered what I was going to do when she grew up and got sent to the penitentiary. What would it feel like, visiting her on Thursdays, talking to her through a transparent partition via walkie-talkie while the guard looked on?

On this pandemonium, the ballet teacher brought down the curtain. She stepped out in front of it. "Ladies and gentlemen," she said, "we'll have an intermission while the Tiptoe Toddlers take their places in the audience, and then the Preschool Pirouettes will perform."

Parents gathered their offspring; my child, hanging her head, followed me out front. After the show, Rajan and Lucy joined us. "You were a wonderful bee," Rajan said. "I admired the way you buzzed. It was so realistic."

"Oh yes," Lucy said, seconding his enthusiasm.

But my bee-loved wouldn't speak to Rajan; she disappeared behind me, clinging to my leg, her face crushed against my dark cotton skirt.

"Peekaboo, I know you," Rajan said. When she wouldn't come out, he said to me, "I'm sorry, Nina. I don't know what to do about it. I feel so guilty—but she has to learn that not everyone can love her the way she wants to be loved." There was a rushed, breathless note in his voice, as if he were defending himself against all the women he had had to disappoint, as if he knew the burden of all that unrequited love could not be his alone to bear and yet part of him feared it might be.

His thick hair, his knowing eyes—lined now at the corners—his body, like a racing car that could take the most complicated turns effortlessly, stung me into a sense of nostalgia. This would probably never be mine again—male beauty, sexual love. I had missed my chance (which was not with Rajan anyway). Circumstance and choice were such an old Odd Couple, I thought to myself—always around, always together. Like married people, with time they began to look like each other. After a while it became difficult to tell them apart.

"It's okay, Rajan," I said. "Don't worry about it. We'll be all right."

I was using the royal *we*. As far as I was concerned, my daughter was the queen bee. But perhaps he thought I meant to include myself.

Rajan and Lucy said good night and went on ahead to their car.

"Are you sleepy?" I asked my daughter. "Ready for bed?"

She shook her head. "N-O," she said, but she was asleep in the back seat by the time I got her home. I carried her inside. Her antennae, sewn to a headband, had gotten turned around and were dangling limply over her left ear.

In the morning she was inconsolable, hating herself: She had wet the bed. I pulled her damp nightgown off and scrubbed her in the tub. I soaped and rinsed the bee's knees. I described little circles in the air with my forefinger and made a buzzing sound between my teeth, a bee aiming at the sweet nectarean bloom of her belly button. She giggled and splashed, trying to keep my finger away, and laughed when it delved into her belly button. I let her dry herself, droplets springing everywhere, and then stripped her bed. I carried the sheets and her nightgown down to the basement and started the washer. When I was a child, I had wet the bed long past any excusable age. I remembered the rubber sheet spread out over the radiator, the acrid stink of sizzling urine, my mother having to wash the sheets by hand on a washboard in the bathtub until we got a small portable washing machine that sat on the kitchen counter next to the sink and did a little jig across the Formica whenever it was turned on. How hard she had worked— typing, cleaning, cooking and, of course, rehearsing. If that music had meant everything to me, it must have meant even more to her.

The basement's spidery darkness seemed to have wound itself around me in an invisible web. I had boarded up the basement win-dows to make the house less vulnerable to burglary, and as I stood there in the dark, listening to the washing machine fill and start to chug, I became aware of how *occupied* everything was. Nature really did abhor a vacuum. The metal bookcase overflowed with old clay pots and plastic drainage saucers. Dismantled motors from various items of broken machinery lay lightly scattered, like flotsam, on the damp floor. My mind was cluttered with stray memories. Even the blank place under the basement stairs seemed to pulse with forgotten meaning. Dazed and suddenly anxious, I looked at the overhead water pipes sweating with condensation, and then I couldn't help myself, I raced upstairs; I raced up more stairs to the second storey where she was sitting on the floor quietly turning the pages of a Golden Book, showing each of the pictures, like a docent, to Teddy, and before she could say anything, I scooped her up and hugged her tight, burying my nose in her neck. "I don't want you to punish yourself anymore," I said, forcing my voice as low as it would go, as far as possible from the high peaks of hysteria, speaking carefully and calmly. "Mommy will punish you when you do something bad. You are not to punish yourself ever again."

I wonder where I've gone wrong, what I've done to give her the idea that she must monitor and chastise herself. Does she not know that I cherish her rebellious spirit, the single-minded determination with which she gets into trouble day after day? Who was this saintly child, muffin-fresh in a ruffled pinafore, sweetly regarding me with pity and compassion?

I try to imagine my mother this age. My mother, self-willed and en-ergetic, seeking to find a way to fit her being into a world already traffic-jammed with bigger beings, most of them with proscriptive ideas about how a girl of her time *should* fit in. When I hugged my daughter, I imagined, just for a moment, that I was hugging my mother, who, of course, would have hated any such display of emotion—but maybe not when she was three.

My daughter didn't say anything. I put her down on the changed bed and sat next to her. I turned her face toward mine, holding her chin between my prayerful hands. "You are my song, my symphony, my string quartet," I said.

Now I knew what it meant to *speak from the heart.* My heart was punctuating every phrase, a systole and diastole of grammar, a ventricular Strunk and White. As I spoke, I felt every word like love, like my heart beating, as if I were being moved to witness to friends.

Today, on our way back from our walk with our dog, my daughter and I stopped at Sam and Mary's.

Sam and Mary and I were lounging around the picnic table at the back end of their driveway and my daughter was making mudpies, shaping each pie carefully and setting it to dry in the late-afternoon sun, when we heard voices calling from the sidewalk.

It was Ian and Shelley Wallace, my neighbors from across the street in the opposite direction. How lucky I am to live in this world, with this dog, with my child, in a house set among the houses of my friends. There is my house, across the street, the brick facing of it rosy and cheerful, the white trim like a shirt collar. Before Tavy joined us, I would come home to find my dog curled up in his little house in the kitchen as if he were a ribbon tying itself into a bow. I love this dog, the ongoing gift of him.

"Hello, Miss Mudpie," Ian said, arriving at the picnic table and addressing my daughter.

"*I'm* not a mudpie," she said.

"But you make mudpies, don't you?"

"Y-E-S," she spelled. Which, to a mother, is like higher education.

"Same difference," he said. "Here, I'd better pat you into shape."

She shrieked and ran to the other side of the picnic table. He pretended to come after her. She pretended to think he really was coming behind the table for her and ran in front, where he would be sure to catch her. He caught her around the waist and pretended to eat her. "Yum, yum, what a good mudpie," he said.

"You don't eat *mudpies,*" she said. "That's *stupid.*"

"It is? Oh, well, that's mud in my eye, I guess." He stood up. "Shelley and I are walking up to the store. Anybody need anything?"

As they strolled off, I thought how amazing it is that each day brings with it something new. We sit in our driveways and someone stops by, a local flurry of activity, a contained, neighborly turbulence, and out of these moments we construct our histories. Our lives are what we do to each other.

The Wedding Cake in the Middle of the Road

It was white cake with white icing. There were tiers of it, layers stacked like a ziggurat or Mayan ruin, so that if you had been very small, the size of a clothespin, say, and light enough on your feet not to sink into the frosting you could have climbed from the bottom to the top. You would have encountered pink sugar roses with green mint leaves, and curlicues of the white icing that looked somewhat like tracks or skid marks in snow. You might have thought that someone had been skating on the icing, doing figure eights and crossovers, and gliding along in a straight line around and around. And there are worse ways to spend one's days, you might have thought, than drawing a straight line in a circle. On the second layer, there were white swans, probably of marzipan, floating on a lake made from a pocket mirror. As they swam, they could see their reflections, like Narcissus. A ballerina in a white tulle skirt with satin bodice danced *en pointe* at the edge of the lake, her stretched neck repeating the pattern of the swans' necks, one arm arched over her sculpted head, one extended like a wing. If you had wanted to, you could have watched for a while; you could have stayed to the end and applauded, applauded not only for her graceful, complex performance but for the long-ago days she had reminded you of, when you, too, were poised for the curtain to rise, on your own life, which, you thought, would surely be graceful but which had only been complex. Another tier, and there were tiny white dogwood trees, all in flower, the blossoms bearing the narrative of the cross all around the lacy edge of the cake. Buttery butterflies slept

dreamlessly in the dogwood branches, occasionally fluttering, as if
about to wake, and causing a blossom or two to break off. Blossoms
kept falling off and drifting to the layer below, suspended for a moment
on Swan Lake and then sinking to the bottom of the mirror. Perhaps
these blossoms had been fashioned from Tic-Tacs. The penultimate tier
was rather celestial, with white clouds of sugar wafers. Sometimes it
snowed, and then confectionary flakes fell on the dogwoods in bloom,
and on the butterflies hidden in the branches, and on the dancing girl
and swimming swans, and on the fiercely single-minded ice skater,
who went on gliding even while snow covered up his tracks. At the
very top of the cake there were two figures, one male and one female,
both about the size of clothespins. They were groom and bride, and
wanting to wish them well, you would surely have gone up to them—
Best wishes go to the bride, congratulations to the groom!—and you
would have been so surprised, then, seeing them close up, to realize
that they were your parents on their wedding day, your mother brilliant
in her stern beauty, your father naively handsome in his early twenties.
They were there at the top of the cake, waiting for you, waiting for you
from the beginning of time—if you had been as small as a clothespin,
and able to climb a cake without making a mess of it. You could have
looked into their faces and seen what they saw, or what they failed to
see. You would have been able to see the world before its creation. And
then you would have wished them well, because that was what you had
always, always, always meant to do, and you would have descended
again, through blizzards and springtime and music and the astonishing
facts of intention and determination, and when you leapt off the last
mysterious ledge, like a leap of faith, like leaping from a Babylonian or
Mayan mystery into the light of day, and landed at the bottom, what
you would have seen, which you could not have seen before, was that
on one side of where you were the road ran north, and on the other side
south—or maybe it was east and west—and all along the way there
were trees, and houses, and telephone poles, and people going places
and coming back from them.

Not the Phil Donahue Show

This is not the Phil Donahue show; this is my life. So why is my daughter, who is twenty years old and, to me, so heartbreakingly beautiful that I think that for the sake of the health of the entire world and probably universe she shouldn't be allowed out of the house without a cardiologist at her side, why is my daughter standing in my doorway telling me she's a lesbian?

She hangs in the doorway, her face rising in the warm air like a bloom in a hothouse. (I have been cooking.) She has chin-length blonde hair, straight as a pin, side-parted. Her skin is bare of makeup. Her blue eyes are like forget-me-nots in an open field. She has a superficial scratch on her cheek, a deep resentment that pulls her head down and away from me.

I'm standing here with a wooden spoon in my hand like a baton and I feel like there is some music that should be playing, some score that, if I only knew it, I ought to be conducting.

If I say it's a phase, that she'll outgrow it, she'll peel herself from the wall like wallpaper and exit, perhaps permanently, before I can even discern the pattern.

If I say honey, that's great, nonchalant and accepting as history, I could be consigning her to a life that I'm not sure she really wants—maybe she's just testing me. Maybe this *is* just a phase.

I can't help it, for just a moment I wish her father were here. I want him to be as shocked and stuck as I am, here in this blue-and-white room with steam rising from the stove, enough garlic in the air to keep a host of vampires at bay. But I remind myself: He would have been glad to be here. I am the one who walked out on him. As Isabel, in her posture, her sullen slouch, her impatient, tomboy gestures, never lets me forget. *Daddy would know how to handle this,* she seems to be saying, defiant as a rebel with a cause. *I dare you to try.*

It is five o'clock. It's already been a long day, which I have spent as I spend most of my days—nursing patients to whom I have let myself get too close. And sometimes I feel a kind of foreclosure stealing into my heart, sometimes I feel like an S&L, sometimes I feel overextended. But I'm always home from my shift at the hospital by four-thirty, while Ian stays late after school to devise lesson plans, tutor the sluggardly, confer with parents.

Now the front door swings open and it's Ian. He's taller than I, who am tall, so tall his knees seem to be on hinges, and he unlatches them and drops into one of the dining-room chairs. I can watch him over the dividing counter that connects the dining room with the kitchen, one of the results of our renovation last summer. Isabel has not moved from her post in the doorway (there's no door) between us.

"Hi, Shel," Ian says to me. "Hi, Belle," he says to my daughter. "Nice to see you."

He wants so much for her to let him enter her life. He has no children of his own—he wants to be, if not a second father, at least a good friend. "Shelley," he says, "what are we drinking tonight?"

"Isabel has an announcement," I say, waving my wooden wand. I turn around and start stirring, the steam pressing the curl out of my hair like a dry cleaner.

"I'm in love," I hear her say behind my back.

"Hey, that's great," Ian responds and I realize how unfair we have been to him, we have set him up for this.

"With a woman," she says.

Girl, I want to correct her. With a *girl.*

Marlo Thomas would kill me.

"Oh," Ian says. "Well, why isn't she here? When do we get to meet her?"

And I remember: This is why I married him. Because he puts people ahead of his expectations for them, even though his expectations can be annoyingly well defined. Because he doesn't create a crisis where there isn't one.

But this is a crisis. If she were *his* daughter, he'd realize that.

❧

Entirely without meaning to, entirely illogically, I am suddenly angry with Ian for not being the father of my daughter. Why wasn't he around when I was twenty—her age, I realize, startled—and looking for something to do with my life, which I had begun to understand stretched before me apparently endlessly like an unknown continent, one I was afraid to explore by myself? Why did I have to wait for most of my life before he showed up?

We are seated at the table from my first marriage, now located under the dining-room window overlooking the leaf-strewn front lawn and Joss Court. It is September in Wisconsin, and the home fires have begun to burn, smoke lifting from the chimneys like an Ascension. The maple and walnut trees are a kaleidoscope of color; the bright orange-red berries of the mountain ash are living ornaments. Soon it will be Halloween, Thanksgiving, Christmas. Across the street, abutting Joss but facing Highland, is my friend Nina's house, in which I lived for a year while making up my mind to divorce Isabel's father. Directly across from me, behind Nina, lives Sophie, recently widowed. She pushes a hand mower, the last lawncut of the season before raking starts.

"You should go over and offer to rake for her sometime soon," I say to Ian.

"I will," he agrees, drilling a corkscrew into the unopened wine.

Isabel says, "I think she likes doing things for herself."

"I can still offer," Ian says. "She can say no."

During this conversation, a fourth party has been silent: Judy, Isabel's friend. As soon as Ian suggested we meet, Isabel raced out of the house and brought her back for supper.

Judy is not what I expected. For one thing, she's pretty—almost as pretty as my daughter. She has long wavy honey-blonde hair so perfectly cut it falls with mathematical precision, like a sine-curve, around her glowing face. She has this generation's white, even teeth, a kittenish face. It is easy to see why Isabel has fallen in love with her; in fact, I don't see how anyone could *not* fall in love with either of them—so why shouldn't they fall in love with each other?

Thinking these thoughts, I am swept by a sense of déjà vu. I have lived this scene before—but where? In another life?

Then I figure it out: not lived but read, in all the contemporary novels Nina lends me. Again and again, a mother is visited over the holidays by her college-going son, who arrives with a male lover in tow to explain that he is now out of the closet. Sometimes the father seizes this opportunity to declare that he, too, has all along been a homosexual. I glance at Ian suspiciously. He is in his gracious mode, entertaining the two girls with tales from his life in the Peace Corps, following the fall of Camelot. These stories now have the luster of legend about them; they are tales from far away and long ago. The girls listen to them, enthralled and cynically condescending at the same time, in both their lovely faces the question, *But how could anyone have ever been so innocent and hopeful?* And I am filled with the furious rush of my love for Ian, my heart pumping, powerful as hydrology, and I want to say to them, *That's the kind of innocence you learn, it takes age and experience to be able to shake off your self-protective defenses and give yourself over to helping someone else.* But I don't say anything, I just look at Ian, reminding myself that later the girls will be gone and we can indulge our heterosexual sexual preferences on the water bed, and he says, "Passez-moi le salt, s'il vous plait."

Ian teaches French at West High.

Two sky-blue tapers burn driplessly next to wildflowers I brought back from the farm a few weeks ago. The wildflowers have dried—it was a delicate transition from life to death, so shaded it would have been impossible to say exactly when death occurred: At what point did these flowers become what they are now?

The candlelight projects a silhouette of the wildflowers onto the wall; it polishes the real gold of Judy's hoop earrings, casts a mantle of light over Isabel's bent head.

I'm not losing a daughter, I tell myself, I'm gaining a daughter.

"They are children," I say to Ian in the kitchen, after they have vanished into the night.

I remember those college nights, full of adventure, philosophy, midnight desperation in the diner over coffee and cigarettes. I had two years of them before I decided to go to nursing school, where nihilism was not part of the curriculum.

I peer out the window as if the children, or my youth, might still be out there, in the dark.

Through the window, which we have opened slightly to cool off, comes an autumnal aroma of fallen apples, bitter herbs. Already, the birds have started south.

"Isabel's almost twenty-one," he says. "You've got to start getting used to the idea that she's grown up. She has her own life to live."

But when he says "life to live," I of course think of one of my patients, only a few years older than Isabel and like her gay, who, however, has but a death to die.

Noting parallels and contrasts to patients' lives in this way is, I discovered a long time ago, an occupational hazard of nursing, and I don't allow myself to be sidetracked. I just say, "That's easy for you to say."

He slams the silverware drawer shut. "No, it isn't, Shelley. As a matter of fact, it's very hard for me to say, because I know you're upset and you're going to take it out on me. It would be much easier for me not to say anything, but someone has to keep you from making a big mistake here."

He's right, but I don't have to be happy about that.

I'm elbow-deep in hot water—literally. I rinse the last dish and he hands me a dishtowel. When we remodeled this kitchen, we made it comfortable for both of us to work in at the same time. We both like to cook. When I think of Ian, I naturally think of spices—"a young stag upon the mountains of spices." Old deer, I have called him, teasing; old dear.

Sometimes he sits at the dining-room table, marking papers, while I make something that can be stored in the freezer for the following day, and as I scoop and measure, doing the Dance of the Cook, I look at him through the rectangular frame created by the counter and cabinets. He is a year younger than I am. His eyes are small, his cheeks ruddy. He would have made a great British colonel, except that he would have liberated all the colonials, at the same time forcing them at gunpoint to call in their pledges to public radio. He is a born-and-bred Wisconsinite, and I love every contradiction his un-French mind so blithely absorbs. For him, I left a husband who was equally good-hearted but incapable of such contradiction, paradox, surprise.

"Maybe I'm not the one to do that in this case," he continues. "Call Nelson. Maybe *he* can keep you from going off the deep end."

I look at Ian; I pick up the phone; I dial. It rings. "Nel?" I say.

"Shel."

God, we were young. We were young for so long—longer than we should have been. We were still so young even by the time our daughter was born that we thought, amazingly, that the family that rhymed together would stay together.

"I need to talk to you. Can you meet me at Porta Bella?"

"In twenty minutes," he says. "Listen, I know what it's about. Everything's going to be all right."

"She told you first?" I ask. I can't help it, I'm hurt.

Nelson leans back in the booth, and the leather seat creaks. His white hair—it started turning white when he reached forty—looks pink in the red haze of the table lamp, a stubby candle in a netted hurricane shield.

At the bar, male and female lawyers and professors bump against one another, pushing, as if hoping to annoy someone into noticing them. When you are young, you're a sex object because you're *sexy,* but then you reach an age when you have to make someone aware of you as an *object* before it will occur to him or her that you just might possibly be a *sex object.* This is one of the few places near State Street that the students tend to leave to an older crowd.

Nelson's pink beard looks like spun sugar, and for a moment, I re-member being a child, wanting to go to the circus and buy cotton candy. My parents said no. It was the polio scare—people thought per-haps children contracted polio from being in crowds. No circus, no swimming lessons, no—

"It's hard on her, our divorce," he says. "I'm happy things have worked out for you with Ian, but you must realize she senses a barrier there now. There's not the same unimpeded access to you that she had."

Unimpeded access. Do I detect smugness in his voice, the way he drapes one arm over the back of the booth like a long, sly, coat-sleeved cat?

"Do you think she's doing this just to get back at me? Will she grow out of it?"

"I think it's the real thing, Shelley," he says. He smiles. "As real as Coke." He means Coca-Cola, I know. We are not the kind of people who would ever mean anything else, I realize, wondering if this is in-sight, boast, or lament. It could be an elegy. "I think she's in love."

He has brought his arm down, shifted closer to the table. Whatever he wanted to say about my behavior, he feels he has said. Now we can talk about hers. "She's still our little girl," he says.

"She always will be," I agree. "And she's *free to be herself.*" I start to tell him that I'm quoting Marlo Thomas, then don't. The guy has enough to deal with without his ex-wife quoting Marlo Thomas. "It's just that, well, weren't you counting on grandchildren someday?"

"I wouldn't rule out the possibility yet," he says. "A lot of lesbians have children, one way or another. I think she wants to have children someday."

He leans back again, the thick, pink beard like a strawberry milk shake glued to his face. "That wasn't the only thing I was counting on," he says sadly.

We wake to FM. Ian and I lightly touch our mouths together on the corner of Joss and Highland, walking in opposite directions to our respective places of work. All night I dreamed memories, dream-memories of being pregnant with Isabel. That swimming heaviness, that aquatic muffle. Followed by life on land.

All day at the hospital, I dispense meds, take temps, rig IVs. I draw blood, turn or ambulate patients, record BPs. It's an unexceptional day—people are dying. September sunlight, that last hurrah of brightness already muted by the foreknowledge of winter, slips across the islanded rooms, making watery squares of shadow on the white sheets of so many, many single beds, in all of which people are dying. Some will go home first; some will have remissions; some will live long lives; all are dying.

In the hall, I pass Nelson, his white coat flapping behind him like a sail, a tail. If he hurried any more, he would lift off, airborne, a medical kite, a human Medflight. We nod to each other, the way we did before we were married, while we were married.

In the fluorescent glow of the hospital hallways, his beard no longer looks like peppermint. It is as white as surgical gauze.

Gloved and gowned, I duck into Reed's room.

Reed has AIDS. He has been here before, during two other episodes of acute infection. This time he has pneumonia. This time, when he leaves here, he will go to a nursing home to die.

It seems to me that his single bed is like a little boat afloat in the sea of sunlight that fills the room. Reed lies there on his back, with his eyes shut, as if drifting farther and farther from shore.

"Reed," I say to call him back.

He opens his eyes and it takes him a moment to process the fact that I am here, that it is I. I believe the dementia that occurs in eighty percent of AIDS patients has begun to manifest itself, but it's hard to say. I don't know what Reed was like before he became an AIDS patient.

I pull up a chair and sit beside him. The skinnier he gets, the more room his eyes take up in his face. He winks at me, a thin eyelid dropping over a big brown eye that seems, somehow, just a little less sharp than it did the last time he was here.

"Hello, Shelley," he says.

"I thought for a minute you'd forgotten me."

"I still have my *mind,* Shelley," he says, too quick, I think, to assume I mean more than my surface statement. "It's just my body that's going."

I don't contradict him. He knows everything there is to know at this point about his disease. He knows more about it than I do—like many AIDS victims, he has read the research, questioned the doctors, exchanged information. At the limits of knowledge, the issue becomes belief, and I figure he has a right to choose his beliefs. Reed believes he will lick his illness.

I look at the *body that's going:* He has lost more weight since his last hospitalization, despite a rigorous fitness plan. His cheekbones are as pointy as elbows. His brown eyes have lost some of their laughter. When I pick up his hand to hold it, it doesn't squeeze back. There are sores on his arms—the giveaway lesions of Kaposi's sarcoma. K.S., we say around here. I take his pulse, the wrist between my fingers and thumb not much bigger than a sugar tube.

"Reed," I ask him, "are you sorry you're gay?" I almost say *were.* As in *were gay.* Or *sorry you were gay.*

"Because of this?" He withdraws his hand.

"No. Just—if there were no such thing as AIDS, if nobody ever died from it, would you be glad to be gay?"

"How can I answer that? How can I pretend Eddie never died?"

Eddie was his lover; he died of AIDS two years ago, in California. Reed came back home, but his parents, small dairy farmers in northern Wisconsin, have been unable, or perhaps unwilling, to look after him.

He's not having trouble talking; his lungs are much better now, he is off oxygen, and he'll surely leave us in a day or two. I'll never see him again—this former social worker, still in his twenties, now dying more or less alone, whose gentleness is reflected in the sterling silver–framed photo portraits of Eddie and his parents and sister that he brings here with him each time and props on the night table, next to the tele-phone and water tray.

In my imagination, I try to read—Reed!—the dinner scene from the story of *his* life: His parents are seated at either end of the old oak table that has been the heart of their family life for twenty-five years. Would they place Reed next to his sister, across from Eddie? Or would they put the two boys together, facing their only daughter? The former, I think; Eddie is an outsider in this scene.

I know what they look like, gathered around that table, because of the portraits. Reed's sister is dark, a little overweight; she is the media-tor, the one who tries to make all the emotional transactions among the family members run smoothly. His mother looks like a blueberry pie— dark and creamy-skinned, round-faced, plumply bursting out of her Sears slacks and top. His father is shy, turning away from the camera, turning away from Eddie not out of any dislike in particular for him but because he always turns, always has turned, away from even the merest implicative reference to sex, and Eddie's presence is an implication. And Eddie—Eddie is healthy. Eddie is broad-faced and big-shouldered, Eddie is the one who looks like a farmhand, who looks like he could do chores all day under a midwestern sun and drink Stroh's at night, fish for muskie and shingle the roof on Sunday. He does not look like he will be dead anytime soon.

I wonder how the family took it, how explicit Reed was or how much they guessed or refused to understand. Reed would have been sensitive about everyone's feelings, wanting not to hurt either his par-ents or his lover, wanting his sister not to be disappointed in her big brother but eager for her to understand Eddie's importance in his life. I wonder how Reed felt when, after dinner, they all rose from the table and said, not impolitely, good night, taking him and Eddie up on their offer to do the dishes, and retired to their rooms—not condemning him but also, not, not—what did he expect from them? he asked himself. Had he hoped they would embrace Eddie as their own, that they would feel, when they looked at Eddie, the warmth of emotion that sometimes suddenly welled up in him so intensely he could almost cry, a cup over-flowing? When he turned the dial on the dishwasher, a red light came on like a point of reference.

While I am musing, Reed is busy fighting off an invisible force that wants to pull his mouth down, wants to yank tears out of his eyes.

When he wins, his face falls into place again, at rest, the exhausted victor of yet another round in an intramural boxing match against grief.

"How are Ian," he asks me, "and Isabel?"

We are talking together in low voices, telling each other about our lives, when Dr. Feltskog stops in with a couple of residents following in his wake. They are all using universal precautions. This is a teaching hospital. He introduces them to Reed, explains Reed's situation, the presenting pneumocystic pneumonia, our methodology for managing the disease.

Dr. Feltskog finishes his spiel, and I am looking at Reed, trying to measure its impact, when one of the young doctors steps forward. "Reed," she says—even the youngest doctors no longer use patients' last names—"how do you feel?"

Reed winks at me again, though so slowly I am not sure the others in the room recognize it as a wink. They may just think he is tired, fighting sleep.

"Okay," he says.

The young doctor nods as if she understands exactly what he is doing: He has said that he feels okay because he doesn't want to burden them with details about how he really feels. It doesn't occur to her that maybe he just doesn't want to burden himself with the attention he can tell she is dying to give him.

"Now, Reed," she says, leaning over him so close it is as if he has no boundaries at all, leaning into his face, "we know you have feelings you want to talk about. It's natural. If you like, we can ask a staff psychiatrist to stop in to see you."

There is a silence in which I learn to feel sorry even for her—not just Reed, not just Isabel, not just Ian and my ex, and not just myself but even this jejune, over-helpful (and unconsciously manipulative), too-well-intentioned doctor in pearls and Hush Puppies, the white coat, though she doesn't know it, a symbol of all that she owes to women my age, who made it possible for her to do what she does, have what she has—as I watch Dr. Feltskog register, on his mental ledger sheet, her lack of sensitivity.

To Reed, the suggestion that he see a psychiatrist means he really is losing his mind. It means he will be defeated after all: If his mind is not on his side, how can he combat what is happening to his body? It means he really is going to die before he has had a chance to live.

"I don't want a psychiatrist," he says softly, the tears he had beaten back earlier now overtaking him.

They leap to his eyes, those tears, and others to mine, as he says, with as much exclamatory emphasis as he can command, a look on his face like that of a child who has been unfairly trapped into protesting his innocence even after he knows that everyone knows he is guilty, "Why are you interrogating me about my feelings like this? This is not the Phil Donahue show! This is my life!"

When he says this, I lose track of which one of us is me. It seems to be *me* in that bed, it is *my* body going, *my* mind that's no longer to be trusted. This is the opposite of a near-death out-of-body experience, this experience of being in *someone else's* body near *someone else's* death. Those are my tears on his face, surely; surely, these are his tears on mine.

At first I think he has read my mind. As I begin to regain my onto-logical footing, I understand that, all over America, people are struggling to prove to themselves that their lives are more than television, that their lives are real, the real thing.

Assembled like this, we have all entered a world outside time, it is as if a collective catastrophe has carried us into a place of silence and immobility, we are a mass accident, a tragedy.

Thus: A moment of stasis, a moment like cardiac arrest, and then we all come to life again, a jumpstart, a fibrillation. And a fluttering, too, a fluttering is going on here: a fluttering of hands, of hearts, of eyelids too nervous to lift themselves all the way up. There is this swift, gener-alized occupation, and I have a sense as of tents being taken down and away quickly and quietly, a stealth of tents, and yes, now everyone has scattered and I am alone again with Reed. I think of all the things he might have said, the true profanity of his condition, and it seems to me that no words could ever be as shocking as "Phil" and "Donahue" and "Show," words that have brought America into this hospital room, the dream of an essential empowerment so at odds with the insomniac knowledge of our own helplessness, our midnight desperation over coffee and cigarettes.

"Please," I say to Reed, and I am intrigued to note how my voice supplicates, my voice, which is, really, pretty good at both giving and accepting orders and not accustomed to hovering in between like this, "get some rest now, Reed."

He doesn't answer. He turns his face away from me and I wait, but he still doesn't answer or look at me. I am left staring at the back of his head, the bald spot that is the tonsure of early middle age and was once the fontanelle of an infant, and I think—what else could I think—that I don't care what kind of life Isabel leads, so long as she gets to lead one.

I think of my beautiful daughter, her grumpy spirit caged by the circumstances of her own sexuality and her mother's, and of how it will one day—soon, I think—be freed, *free to be itself,* and how, when it is, her sweetly curved profile will disclose the inner strength I know is there, how her blue, blue eyes, deep and true as columbine, will sparkle with the triumph that integrity is.

Not that I wouldn't prefer things to be otherwise; not that I am exactly happy about my daughter's choice. I wouldn't go so far as that—not yet. But what I know, almost annoyed with myself for knowing it because I wish I could surprise myself, but then that is why I married Ian, isn't it, to be surprised, is that I'm going to. I love her too much not to know that the day will come when I will feel however I must feel in order to keep her in my life. This, I realize, was never in doubt, no matter how much I may have been in doubt. The issue always becomes belief.

But back out in the hallway I stop short, confused, almost dizzied, feeling I have lost my place in some book or other. They are paging Nelson—*Dr. Lopate, Dr. Lopate!*—and I remember how I used to call him that our first year together in Detroit. We were the same height, and I'd launch his newly earned title in a low whisper from the rim of his ear, a little raft afloat on the sea of ego. And he loved it, at least for that first year.

I find my way to the locker room and change out of my work shoes into Nikes. Walking home on Highland, I see that we are having what I secretly think of as a Code Blue sky—alarmingly bright, the kind of sky that can galvanize you. A sky like emergency medicine, needing to be attended to on the spot. So when I get home I call Ian at the school. The secretary has to go get him, of course, because he's in his classroom, grading papers. *Nous aimons, vous aimez, ils aiment.*

Elles aiment.

"Let's spend the night at the farm," I tell him. "I'll swing by and pick you up."

After supper we go for a walk and wind up down by Beaver Pond. The pond is as round as a smiling cheek, the setting sun a blush on it like rouge, and in the sky a thin crescent moon, the squinty eye of it, the shut eye of it, is already risen, as if it just can't wait, it has things it wants to see, it won't be kept in the dark any longer. Ian and I straddle a log, and we're glad, given the late-day chill, that we are wearing flannel shirts.

Let's face it, things are not exactly quiet out here in the country. Things are going on even out here. We can hear the beavers working away in a scramble against winter. Every so often, there's a crash or a cry, and no way of knowing whether the sound means life or death. There are so many creatures out here, deer and owls and just so many, and the prairie grass, and the abandoned orchard, and wildflowers.

Sometimes I think of the whole world as a kind of hospital, the earth itself as a patient.

There are days, now, when so much seems to be slipping away. Even the things one tends not to think of, like the walnuts. The walnuts are slipping away, going off to be stockpiled by squirrels. The green of summer is slipping away, hiding its light under a bush or a bushel of autumn leaves. There are dreams that slip away in the middle of the night, losing themselves forever in some dark corner of the subconscious. There are stars that are disappearing even as we look at them. There are mothers and fathers and children, all of them slipping away like the fish in the pond, going down deeper for winter. And you reach out to hold on to your child, and she is slipping away, going off into some life that is not your life, and you are afraid to see her go because you know, you know how far it is possible to go, how far it is possible for things to slip away.

"You're thinking," Ian says. "What about?"

But I don't know how to say what I'm thinking, because it seems to me I am thinking of everything there is to think of and of nothing at all, at the same time. "I don't know how to put it into words," I confess. "You have to remember, I had only two years of Liberal Arts."

"I've often wondered," Ian says, "what the Conservative Arts would be. Anything Jesse Helms likes, I guess."

We hear a noise like a senator. "Did you hear that?" I ask.

We listen to two or three frogs bandying croaks back and forth. They're more subdued than they are during the spring, but they still have something to say. "There are throats in those frogs," I say. "Those frogs are talking to one another."

"In French," Ian says. "Frogs always talk in French."

I let out a whoop and get up from the log, but when I do I trip and Ian jumps up to catch me, and he holds me, and my face is buried against his left arm, and my left ear is over his heart, which is making its own happy racket through the walls of his chest, as loud as a neighbor living it up.

Chores

Conrad hired a Czech to shovel his snow. She is a graduate student in mathematics, still in her twenties, with dark, revolutionary eyes that shine bright against her absolutely clear, un-made-up skin. She enlisted her mother, and now he has two Czech women, one in her fifties, scraping and shoveling his sidewalk. He watches them from his bedroom window, peering between the slats of the blind. When Milena answered the ad, he realized she needed the money. He wanted to help. Now he feels like a shit. This is not how he wants to see himself: as landed gentry, an overseer. He wants to be kind. He wants to make broad, humanitarian gestures. He wants to be Václav Havel.

There is a lot of snow. He has a lot of sidewalk, a driveway. Next year, he thinks, he will shovel the snow himself (but how will Milena pay her tuition? he wonders). It is good to have things to do, chores to occupy your time.

Fortunately, there is no end of things to do in a house you have only recently moved to. There are floors and walls to clean, shelves to build. He buys books—it is his one indulgence—and he needs to put them somewhere. He has designed cabinets for the study. The cabinets are to have glass doors and will take a long time to construct. Many of the books are first editions—not old, but someday they will be *you can say that about an object not always about a person,* and so they deserve a certain respect. And anyway, it is good to have something to do with your time.

In the evenings, he sits in his study and tries to read. First editions, alas, are not necessarily more riveting than subsequent ones, but there is always the possibility that a new book will jolt him out of his despair—if he can just concentrate on it long enough. He has taken to reading Czech writers—Kundera, Kafka, Čapek. Havel.

Eventually he puts the book down, marking the page with a small copper clip someone had given him. He is not an old man, not even middle-aged—he's only thirty-five—but at this point in the evening he sometimes forgets, for a moment, where he is, what he means to do— go to bed—even who he is. He will discover, a few minutes hence, that he has been staring at the wall as if he were watching a slide show *their faces like works of art not life their marvelous postmodern, oh, god, post-everything faces.* Then he will be annoyed with himself, and a little frightened as well, and he will say to himself, harshly, Snap out of it, and sometimes he will actually snap his fingers, too, as if he were accompanying himself in a rendition of some well-known refrain, backup to his own band.

Lying in bed, upstairs, the blinds turned against the night and snow—he knows it is snowing again because traffic sounds are muffled, reaching him only as strangled cries, as if automobiles were coughing and dying all up and down his street, as perhaps they are—he draws up a mental list of everything he must do the next day. There is dry cleaning to drop off and pick up. He needs to put salt in the water softener. The list is endless. There are always things to be done.

In the wintertime, there is snow to be shoveled—next year he will do that himself (unless, of course, Milena is still as much in need of the money as she seemed to be when she answered the ad, her eyes bright with opportunity, her skin flushing with shame). In April and May, there'll be chores to do in the lawn—the hedge to be trimmed, a crabapple tree to be planted, shrubs and flowers to be mulched. In the summer he will mow the grass every Friday afternoon after work, unless it is raining or promising to, in which case he will stay inside, fix himself a drink, and pick up around the house. (The pizza boxes from Domino's will have to go into the trash, he can wash the week's dishes while listening to MacNeil-Lehrer.) The rain will hurl itself against the house, angry at being shut out. Wisconsin seldom has the kind of rain he grew up with, steady all-day downpours. In Wisconsin, the rain lurches across the sky, a stumbling drunken rain-god. It'll be raining but it'll be hot in the house and he'll run a fan even though the windows are closed and he'll work on his drink and read and send out for ribs instead of pizza and there will be the continuous low whoosh of the fan and the rattle of rain on the roof.

By then, the house will no longer seem so strange to him. A little strange, maybe, the way any place he could think of would now be strange to him *because without them he is a stranger to himself he no longer knows who he is he is certainly not Václav Havel,* but not so strange. He'll have grown used to it, the way you grew used to being yourself even if you couldn't say, and who could, who that was. In early September, while the house is still dreaming of summer (winter will wake it soon enough), he'll mow the lawn. Quite likely, he will buy a headset and listen to music, undisturbed by the roar of the mower. He will listen to Smetana.

When she answered the ad, she said, "My name is Milena. The accent is placed at the beginning. It is on the first, the first— Do you see?" Her cheeks were red with a kind of revolutionary fervor, her lashes dark even without mascara, glistening from melted snow like animal fur.

It was a soft "i," almost an "e"; a soft "l." "What an unusual name," he said, smiling, though he knew it might not be unusual at all in Czechoslovakia. "You must be very *bohemian.*"

Before he knows it, it will be the time of year when mice find their way into suburban basements—he'll have to call an exterminator. He'll worry about chemicals, the environment, himself. He'll worry about the mice, their eating poison and crawling off like tiny furry French legionnaires in search of water, dying horrible, lingering deaths in the laundry sink. He is such a shit, he knows it. Would Havel call an exterminator? Would *Kafka*?

As winter approaches, he'll have to put up the storm windows. This is a major job, requiring several hours. He'll have to take the screens down, then bring the storms up from the basement. He'll have to hose the storms down and wipe them with Windex, and then fit them into the frames—which can be tricky, especially on the second floor. Then he'll have to rope-caulk all the windows—more hours. Some chores are major, some are minor, but there are always plenty of things that need doing in a house.

After it happened, people said Why don't you get an apartment it's not as if you need, and then they stopped while he finished the sentence for them, but silently, to himself, so much space, and he said to them, I thought I'd look for a house.

At about the same time, there will be leaves to rake—the leaves fallen from the black walnut tree, the maple seedlings, the locust tree, the newly planted crabapple. He'll like the heft of the handle in his gloved palms, the deep draughts of bright air, the feeling of being alert that you get when you attend to the changing of the seasons. He'll stand in his lawn, leaning against his rake as if it were a staff, and the November sun will slide across his shoulders without really warming him, and he'll be surprised at how fast time goes when you have things to do. The gutters will need cleaning, the outside faucet must be turned off. He may have to call a chimney sweep, a cement contractor. He could plant bulbs and in the spring there would be tulips and hyacinths. He will definitely buy a tape of *The Moldau* and listen to it via earphones as he mows the lawn, and the tulips and hyacinths, if he has gotten them in, will stand tall and straight, as if they were listening also, just waiting for the proper moment to applaud.

In the evenings he'll read, opening glass doors and taking from the cabinet some book or other and settling into the chair in the study. Sometimes he'll forget, for a moment, who and where he is, and when he remembers these things—that he is head of a medical library, that he is in the house he bought because it is within easy walking distance of work *if they'd been walking not driving; the freezing rain turned the Subaru into a bobsled,* that he is still a young man—when he remembers, he is stunned to realize how easy it is to lose track of everything, to let go. Suppose you could forget to live in the world. Suppose you could forget to eat, to sleep, to wake up, ever. You could wander through your dreams forever, an echoing hallway lined with candles in sconces, the flames blurring into the jittery darkness, shadows of varying depth, some as deep as time.

In his bedroom, he'll empty his pockets, dropping the loose change into a small brass tray on the bureau. He'll turn the blinds against the snow and the night. By now, he'll know the couple next door—the Wallaces—because she is a nurse at the hospital, and he has met her, walking to and from her shift, and they have acquaintances in common. He will know the woman with the dog who lives across the street. He will be a fixture in the neighborhood.

If he runs out of things to do around the house, he can offer to help out. There is a widow who could surely use some help. He can mow her lawn, he can shovel her snow if the boy she hires fails to show up.

The kids in this city—they turn sixteen, they get a driving license, they can make much better money at McDonald's. Only third-year graduate students in mathematics are desperate enough to hire themselves out as snow shovelers. Only women from Czechoslovakia are willing to get out of bed at six in the morning and walk several blocks to shovel snow. When he wakes, he hears them scraping and shoveling, Milena and her mother, it is what calls him back from the mysterious place he has been, the hallway lighted by candles in sconces, their shape-shifting flames. When he wakes . . .

He tries to think of everything he knows about Czechoslovakia—anything. King Wenceslaus. Or Alexander Dubček. Though he was only twelve, he remembers television images of Dubček on a balcony, he remembers the words *Prague Spring* like the title of a song. The tanks lumbered through downtown Prague, stiff with arthritis. The soldiers, boys who would be middle-aged now, but he remembers them as younger than he is, remembers their confusion, their haircuts that made them look overexposed, as if they were not flesh at all but just pure film . . .

He lies there, listening to Milena and her mother, and he feels like a totalitarian government, but all he wanted to do was help. He expected a teenage boy to answer his ad, but it was Milena who called, Milena who came by to look at the sidewalk and driveway and say yes, she could handle it. Her eyes were dark, shining with an inner light, and her skin, bare of makeup, was like a part of the world he had never visited, full of points of interest (her cheeks as red as *The Communist Manifesto,* her mouth as mobile as America).

He hired her. He didn't want to be sexist. She straightened her shoulders and raised her arms as if she were flexing her biceps but of course she had on her coat and so it was only a gesture, not for real, and said, "I am *very* strong."

He had never meant for her to put her mother to work too. "It is good for her health," she said, speaking for her mother, even though, he knew, her mother spoke English. At least some. Milena and her mother worked in concert, a New World symphony.

Downstairs, in the kitchen, he confronts the pizza box that he left out last night and that now smirks at him from the vinyl-cloth'd table, gaping like a mouth, dried tomato paste clinging to the sides. He stuffs it into a Hefty bag and ties off the bag with a blue twist. He has dry cleaning to drop off on his way to work, to pick up on his way home. He must go to the grocery store. He needs milk, bread, salt for the front stoop.

There is so much he has to do. He never understood just how much there is to do *she had done so much of it, cheerfully, efficiently, never complaining, she had been on the way to the store when it happened Caleb not yet five.* He realizes now that there are baseboards to be scrubbed, floors to be waxed, moldings to be dusted, radiators to be vacuumed. There are toilets that want scouring, wastebaskets that want emptying, sheets that want changing, walls to contemplate painting. He is building bookshelves, cabinets with glass doors, doors that will open and shut with a polite, satisfying click, the sound that things make when they acknowledge their gratitude, knowing they have their own place and are safely in it.

As he has and is, here, in this house that is within walking distance of where he works. But how dark it is when he arrives home, in the evening! How terribly, dreadfully dark! He turns the key in the lock and enters the hallway, his shoes leaving a Hansel-and-Gretel trail of salt and melting snow. He hangs the dry cleaning in the hall closet. He hangs his anorak in the closet, slipping the loop inside the collar over a hook on the wall. He finds his way in the dark to the lamp in the living room, and when he turns it on, the light is as sudden as accidental death.

For a moment, he forgets where he is, who he is. He stands there blinking, his shoes as heavy as chains, a worker's chains—the chains of a man whose life is a chore—the room dancing in and out of the lamplight. Then he remembers, and he goes to the study, picks up a book, and settles down to read. This book could be by Hašek, Seifert, or Škvorecký. From time to time he looks up from the book and stares out the window. It has begun to snow again—he can see it tumbling around the streetlight, a busy snow, a well-traveled snow blown this way and that (up from Iowa, down from Minnesota) by a no-nonsense midwestern wind. Now the whiteness is everywhere. It has filled up the rectangle of window like milk poured into a glass. Upstairs, undressing, he turns the blinds against the snow and the night, but then he pulls two slats apart and peers out between them. Milena must come in the morning, with her mother; the shovels are waiting for them, on the front stoop.

"Mathematics?" he'd asked, startled, impressed. Her eyes shone like candles in sconces, her lashes were as dark as shadows. Color bloomed in her face, a kind of warmth, like springtime, though it was snowing and she had on her coat, a fur hat. "I can't even balance my checkbook," he said, becoming aware of what he had said only as he said it, and then he was blushing too, while she looked at him with a mild pity, perhaps the way she regarded all Americans, as a weak people with money and bad puns. She is strong and beautiful and smart, a worthy compatriot of Václav Havel.

Sometimes he forgets—himself, everything, almost everything—and then he is annoyed with himself, and a little frightened as well, but he is also a little proud of himself, amazed by his own great weakness, his enormous weakness, for he is capable of far more weakness than he ever suspected might be in him. He never knew how easily he could be defeated. The snow dashes across the street in drifts; the sky seems to have dropped, and clouds lie over the street, the sidewalk, the driveway. Who is he? What did he mean to do? Wasn't there a dream, a dream he woke from? These are questions he asks himself when he has time on his hands, when he has nothing to do, nothing to keep him from thinking about a future as oppressive as the history of a small Eastern European country.

As It Is in Heaven

After my father had been dead for about nine months, he began to appear in the kitchen. I'm referring to the kitchen in England, where my parents had chosen to live in their retirement. They were musicians, and what they wanted to do with their retirement was listen to music, and England is a place for that. They bought a small red-brick house in a village outside Reading, within commuting distance of London. After six months in quarantine, their dog was allowed to join them. They had been careful to buy a house with a fenced-in backyard, the fence hidden by a hedge ten feet tall. A munificent oak held court at the far end of the property, scattering a largess of acorns for those squirrels willing to brave the dog.

The day came, of course, when the dog could no longer chase the squirrels and my parents could no longer make the long trip to London. My parents now watched telly most of the day; at nine o'clock at night, they moved to the kitchen for ice cream. My father scooped up three dishes, setting one on the floor for the dog. The three of them were crowded into a kitchen barely big enough to hold the appliances. The furnace was in there too, inside a cabinet, warm as a hand, so that being in the kitchen felt like being held in somebody's palm. Whenever I visited them, I ate the mandatory bowl of ice cream and had that feeling of being held, being clasped and enclosed.

When the dog died, and my father no longer felt needed, sadness took over the house. Such sadness is not unlike what the English call "rising damp," a pervasive mold in rainy climates. My father declined rapidly. He was diagnosed as having Alzheimer's, and within a year, he was dead of a stroke. My mother weighed seventy-eight pounds and had lost the use of one of her legs. She had end-stage emphysema. She could no longer manage the stairs. On my last visit there, which I had made wanting to see my father while he could still recognize me, I had gotten them a replacement for Blaze, the dog that had died. Oscar was a Shih Tzu who'd been born with a hernia that rendered him ineligible for breeding and who, at six months, was just a bit too old for consignment to a pet shop. Now he and my mother slept together on a single bed that had been set up downstairs in the dining room, next to the kitchen. When my mother wrote to me that she had seen my father sitting in his chair in the kitchen, I wondered if her mind was going too, and perhaps it wasn't even Alzheimer's—I knew from experience that losing someone you love can sensitize you to every memory of him, so that his memory is as present to you as he used to be. It would surely not be difficult to confuse the presence of the memory with the man himself. "Dear Nina," my mother wrote back, when I suggested this, "don't be a dope. I do not have a sentimental bone in my body, and if your father is not in the kitchen, who the hell is sitting in there scarfing ice cream every night?"

I was, myself, when I read this letter, ensconced in my Green Bay Packers chair—a club chair I'd bought years ago, that had a Green Bay Packers emblem on it; the department store was eager to unload it because even in Wisconsin nobody had been a Green Bay Packers fan since the days of Vince Lombardi—with my own little dog curled up beside me. My daughter was rocking in her rocking chair in front of the radio. Madison, which is so relentlessly populist that it feels that every musical faction, like every political faction, must be served even if it means that everybody winds up feeling shortchanged, refused to have an all-day classical station, and just then, the afternoon jazz program began. My little girl will tolerate nothing but classical. "N-O!" she shouted, stamping her foot on the floor. It was clear that if she had been old enough, she would have retired to England.

I got up and turned the radio off. She had never met her grandmother—who was also her great-grandmother, since her biological mother was my brother's daughter. I had adopted her.

"How would you like to fly in a big plane across the ocean?" I asked her.

"Can Teddy come?" He was sitting in her lap.

"Yes," I said, "Teddy can come, but this little piggy will have to stay home." I picked up my little dog, and he looked straight into my eyes as if saying, How can you do this to me after all we've meant to each other? "It's only temporary," I said to him. "I'll be back."

We Bryants clung to our animals as if they were our lovers, our life-lines. They helped us to have faith in ourselves. Maybe they *were* ourselves, or the most generous parts of ourselves. As the morning sun broke over the wing of our plane, light spilling ecstatically across the horizon, Tavy held Teddy up to the Pan Am window, pressing his button nose against the pane, showing him the sky, the clouds, the flashing blue-and-silver sea. "My nose is cold," she said in what appeared to me to be some kind of sympathetic confusion, falling back into her seat.

"You mean Teddy's nose, don't you?" I corrected her.

"Teddy's nose is a *button,*" she said, amazed by my stupidity. She looked at me as if I was crazy. She didn't know I used to be. I smiled at her. "A nose by any other name would smell as sweet," I said, pretending to catch hers between my fingers, making the tip of a nose with my thumb.

My mother, who had been tall and beautiful, slender and strong, was now a wrinkled doll propped on pillows. She was an island in a sea of cigarette wrappers and ashtrays, Kleenex and toilet tissue, Rollo chocolates in gold tinfoil and half-full cups of cold cocoa, and the complete works of Dickens. Oscar, all gold fur, a live Rollo, sat at her side. I tried to straighten up the mess at the same time I embraced her and introduced Tavy.

I had been worried about this introduction.

As she gazed at her grandmother, Tavy's eyes grew rounder and rounder. They were green eyes—after the blue period of infancy, her eyes had turned green, though still a blue-green, elm-leaf eyes. My brother and my niece had both had true-green eyes, deep-green off-the-coast-of-Cozumel eyes; my mother's eyes, now weak and cloudy, had once been hazel-green, sometimes golden, sometimes gray. These subtleties of hue may mean nothing to anyone else but I had observed them with fascination. It was as if there were two branches to the family: the bold branch, with green eyes and outrageous energy; and the quiet brown-eyed branch, the observers.

"Why are you staring at me?" my mother asked Tavy. She'd had a minor stroke a few years earlier and the left side of her mouth seemed to resist any attempt at speech, so that her words came out slightly scrunched, determined but fugitive, softly slurred.

Tavy said, "You're so old."

"Ha," my mother said. "You will be too, when you've lived as long as I have. And maybe by then you'll have something more interesting to say."

My mother had never liked children. Sometimes she would act as if she did, for the sake of her reputation among neighbors or coworkers, offering congratulatory comments over snapshots of newborns or reports of grade-school genius, but she would tell her own children, speaking about children-in-general, "They're more trouble than they're worth. After all, what are they going to be when they grow up? People!" Her dislike of children was minor compared with her contempt for adults, to which it was teleologically related. She would have liked it better if human beings could have grown up to be dogs or dolphins.

This was one reason I'd been worried about this introduction.

I was used to my mother's ways but Tavy wasn't, and I didn't want her feelings to get hurt. "I'll take Tavy upstairs and get her settled in," I said, standing behind my adopted daughter. And with a protective hand on each small shoulder, I tried to steer her away.

Tavy twisted free, turning back toward the bed. "Are you going to die?" she asked.

I watched my mother's parchmenty face crumple like a piece of paper history had wadded up and tossed into the trash can of time. She had had such plans. Once upon a time, she had thought she would outlive my father by enough years to have a second, single life. She would travel to Scotland, take a boat trip through the Norwegian fjords; she would read every novel published before the twentieth century (twentieth-century novels being by and large not worth reading), have affairs for adventure's sake even if the sex was uninteresting, become a CEO, quite possibly an astronaut as well, and in short, live the life she had never had a chance to live. Instead, she was an unhappy invalid, confined to her downstairs, and so far from being single that her late husband was still hanging around the house.

"Take Teddy upstairs," I said, pushing my daughter out of the room.

I sat on the bed and held my mother's hand. Oscar growled.

"I don't know what's wrong with me," she said. "All I do is cry. It's so stupid. I think maybe I've got Alzheimer's."

"It's not stupid," I argued. "On the contrary, it's completely logical.

When your husband dies, you're supposed to feel sad." I said this knowing that it was a statement that would not carry much force for her. She thought sadness was a waste of time—if not precisely a fungus.

"I'm worried about him," she said. "Why is he hanging around here unless it's because he's not happy *there*?"

"Maybe he misses you," I said, "the way you miss him."

She sank back onto the pillows. I pulled the afghan up and tucked it in around her arms and sides. "Yes," she said, frowning, "that would make sense. Your father was never any good at being on his own. I always had to take care of him. But sometimes I got sick of it," she added. "The responsibility." She had closed her eyes; now she opened them again. "It's lucky for him he was a good fiddle player." She meant she wouldn't have loved him so if he hadn't been.

In the life she had actually lived, she had played second fiddle to his first in a succession of string quartets.

"Take a nap," I urged. "I have to unpack and tend to Tavy. She's worn out from the trip."

"She's a cute kid," my mother said, but then she couldn't keep from adding, "as kids go." She closed her eyes again.

I stood there a moment, looking at her—my mother, a creature of such complexity that it had taken me years even to begin to figure out how to untangle my self from hers.

She had set standards of self-discipline, hard work, and sound reasoning that had for years seemed, no matter how I drove myself, beyond my reach. Yet now, to my surprise, they didn't seem high *enough*—they were predicated on a need to disown everything human, and so were still dependent on everything human, whereas I had arrived at a point where my ambitions simply grew out of my work. I had an inkling of where it might go, my work, and the world's opinion of it or any art had become irrelevant.

I wished she would consent to understand this. I wanted her to believe, with me, that in adopting Tavy I had not been betraying her or her ideals, that I was merely being true to myself.

Oscar was a little larger than a caramel-covered apple, and about the same color. His coat was a heart-meltingly beautiful gold with light and dark streaks. His squashed-in face resembled that of an ancient Chinese emperor or sage. He glared at me.

❧

By the next day, Tavy and I had recovered from our jet lag. I put Tavy out into the backyard, the same way my father had let Blaze out for his morning constitutional. Oscar went out with her but he was back in seconds, his fur fringed in dew; he refused to leave my mother any more than was absolutely necessary.

When I wasn't there, my mother managed with a patchwork system of part-time nurses, helpful neighbors, and a cleaning woman who came in mornings. In my honor, she had dismissed most of these. I spent the day plumping her pillows, fixing meals, helping her to the commode chair, emptying the commode chair, washing dishes, answering the telephone, handling business correspondence, bringing in the milk, doling out pills—and then there was Tavy. I hadn't a minute to myself, and before long, I was exhausted. So when I bumped into my father in the kitchen, I told myself I was seeing things. The power of suggestion coupled with repressed hysteria and total tiredness was causing me to hallucinate. My father just shook his head, slowly, sadly, the way he'd always done when he was feeling pessimistic.

"It's true," he said. "I'm really here." He sighed heavily, as if this was not only unlikely but lamentable.

"But why?" I asked.

"Search me," he said, shrugging his shoulders. "I don't have any idea what's going on. I've got a hunch it's like what Satchmo said about jazz: If you have to ask, you'll never know."

He was nicely dressed in a pale green long-sleeved shirt and gray slacks. He had always cared about clothes, although he'd rarely spent any money on them for himself.

He was thin, with dark, thinning, but attractively unruly, hair that had the right amount of gray in it. He looked stronger than he had in his last year of life, but he was still frail. When he took off his glasses to rub the bridge of his nose where they pinched, I could see, in his large brown eyes, the intelligence that had made him who he was, before Alzheimer's disease had come along like a thief, some sort of mental mugger, and snatched it away, leaving him someone he wasn't. In other words, I realized, this was indeed the ghost of my *father*—not the ghost of the pitiful physical envelope that had contained an Alzheimer's victim.

I wondered if something had happened to him that I was supposed to exact revenge for so his wandering spirit could find peace. I wondered if this kitchen were the modern equivalent of parapets and that was why he was here. Was he restless? Had he been wronged?

I sat down at the table. My mother had dozed off in the living room, in front of the telly, after the seven o'clock news. "I don't understand," I said, facing him. "I thought ghosts, if there were any, would be the residue of souls who died violently or at any rate before their time. You were seventy-eight. You had emphysema almost as bad as Mother's. You had arthritis. You had Alzheimer's. A stroke was probably the best thing that could have happened to you."

But even as I was saying this, I was remembering how alone he had been when he died.

He had been at the rest home for a week—not for his sake but to give my *mother* a rest. She could still walk unaided then, though barely, and she wore herself out day after day trying to take care of him. He thought that by going into the home for a short stint, giving her a respite, he could put off the day when she might feel compelled to send him there forever.

The day before he was to come home, she slipped in the bathroom and fell, hitting her head on the sink and also hurting her back. This was the bathroom she had tiled herself, a dark green paragraph of tiles punctuated here and there with the odd Dutch scene, Jack and Jill carrying pails, or a windmill in a tulip field. Confined to bed, she was unable to look after her husband, but his room in the rest home had been spoken for, so the doctor arranged to have him moved to a second rest home.

It wasn't far—a few blocks down the street from the little red-brick house. His room was at the back and had a view onto a duck pond. It was Christmas Eve, and that afternoon the Salvation Army threw a party in the lounge for the "guests." Every so often, my father, the musician, would recognize one of the carols and shout out a word or two—a kind of rudimentary singing.

After the party, back in his room, he was sitting in the chair by the window, gazing at the ducks, perhaps trying to comprehend how it was that he'd once been a small, obedient boy in Rock Hill, South Carolina, and then was a shy, intense young man in Chicago and Louisiana and New York, and then a middle-aged man in Virginia, and now had become a dotty old fool in a rest home in England, separated by illness and accident from the woman with whom he'd lived for over fifty years. Perhaps this would have been difficult to fathom even if he had not been senile. The ducks in the pond were so bright, as bright as paint. The sky was as gray as a goose, with pinfeather clouds.

Suddenly his heart seemed to double over, and his left arm, which had for most of his life been a kind of mast, holding his violin aloft in musical light, crashed against his chest with a killing weight.

He could still think, images were still vividly present to his consciousness even if the connections among them were sometimes scrambled, and what he thought about at this moment was his wife. "Is Mother all right?" he asked in the ambulance, on the way to the hospital. He pictured her at home, alone, ill and worrying about him.

But right after he asked about her, even before the ambulance had reached the hospital, the walls of his brain gave way too—it was a general collapse, his entire body falling apart section by section, being demolished by the great wrecking ball of age. "The walls of his brain were incredibly thin," the doctor said. "There was massive bleeding."

His lungs and legs were still working. The doctor had said my father would die before daybreak, but Christmas afternoon, a nurse found him wandering the hallways. "A reflex action," they said; they said he could not have thoughts or feelings anymore. What did they know about his thoughts and feelings? He could still refer to himself as "I," as in "I'm thirsty." They decided not to give him water or food; he was starving to death. On the twenty-seventh, he died, unattended even by machines.

And so, he must have come back because he was lonely. I'd been right, I thought—he missed my mother. He nodded. "I never liked that little dog, though," he said. "I couldn't get used to his taking Blaze's place."

"Where is Blaze? Why isn't he here?"

"Imagine being able to do what you want to do and being able to do it forever," he said. "Blaze is in heaven, chasing squirrels."

So animals *did* have souls, I said to myself, satisfied to wipe out one very disagreeable strain in theological thought.

"And you play your violin," I said, sure that this was what he would want to do forever.

"No. After all these years, it just doesn't feel right without your mother next to me on second, smoking up a storm and criticizing my intonation. How is she?"

"She's okay," I said. "Demanding. You know how she is."

"She always kept us on our toes," he said.

"Yes."

"Don't let her make you feel too bad about the kid," he said. "She's a cute kid." (Like all parents, they sometimes quoted each other without knowing it. Or maybe he did know it—had been listening, invisible but not insensible, at the foot of my mother's bed when I displayed Tavy to her.)

All at once, I wanted to know what *he* thought about the fact that the mother of his children didn't like children, but I could hardly ask him this directly. It might disturb him, and I didn't want to make his restless spirit any more restless. "Do you really think Tavy's cute?" I said.

"Adopting her was the right thing to do. And I think you need her."

As he said this, his voice dropped to a spectral pitch, like an undertone, and I realized I could see the back of his chair through his body.

"You're fading!" I cried.

"I always did fade about this time of night. Good night, Nina," he said.

He was gone.

Oscar came tearing into the kitchen. He made a circle from the kitchen through the dining room and living room and foyer back to the kitchen—again and again.

"Oscar's gone crazy," I said to my mother, waking her up and helping her from the wing chair to her bed.

"Your father must have been here. He and Oscar never got along. They saw themselves as rivals for my time."

Oscar leapt onto the bed. He had a beard, a Confucian beard, and his eyes were clever. My little dog at home was not nearly so clever, but sweeter. And clever, just not so clever.

My mother wanted pills, a glass of water, a cup of cocoa, to make a list. Tavy was crying upstairs. "Mommy, Mommy, Mommy," she yelled. I ran upstairs, downstairs, upstairs. I felt as if I were running back and forth between my past and the future.

Tavy never saw my father. Apparently, since she had not known him in life, she was not supposed to know him in death. He took an interest in her, however.

"You'd better get her started on the violin right away," he said. "She's already almost too old."

He was resting his chin in his palms, elbows propped on the linoleum-top table.

"I don't know," I said. "I remember how painful it was when you gave me lessons. It felt like my arm was going to break off."

"That's ridiculous, Nina. Your arm couldn't have hurt. Nothing is more malleable than a young child's bones."

I remembered it hurting.

"She takes ballet lessons," I offered. In the Meadow Scene, she had been a bee, buzzing her way across the stage in a black leotard striped with yellow crepe paper.

When I said she took ballet, he started to fade. I knew he wouldn't consider ballet music real music, and I said, "You can't just fade whenever things don't go the way you want them to."

"I don't see why not," he said. "It's one of the advantages of being dead."

"Is that you, Arthur?" my mother called from the other room. "What are you two talking about?"

She pulled herself along in her walker, entering the kitchen by degrees. Finally she was in her chair across from him. They looked at each other over the table, a doll-size table for doll-size people in a doll-size house in a doll-size country.

"Well, Art," she said, "it's a hell of a note, isn't it. I'm just barely alive and you don't seem to be quite dead."

"Would anybody like some ice cream?" I asked.

They both nodded. I dished it up into three bowls; it was vanilla. They wanted chocolate syrup so I heated the open can in a pot of water on the stove. It was an aluminum pot and I wondered if it had been a contributing factor in my father's getting Alzheimer's. I drizzled the syrup over the ice cream. Tavy was asleep upstairs, snug in her dreams. Oscar sat on the floor at my mother's feet. Unlike Blaze, he liked peaches but not ice cream.

"What's it like over there?" I asked, perching on the tall stool at the sink counter. I felt like an overgrown child in a high chair. There wasn't room for a third chair at the table.

"I don't really know," he said. "I haven't had much of a chance to look around yet. The climate is better, I guess. Not so much rain. I suppose this is because heaven is not an island."

Was it a continent? Maybe heaven was the *ocean,* and our entire universe one small island in it. "Do you have to listen to a lot of harp music?" This had been nagging at me. The Mozart Flute and Harp Concerto was nice, but for an eternity?

"I don't think you understand. Being dead isn't at all like being alive. You don't *do* things over there, you just are them. I believe it's got something to do with everything's happening faster than the speed of light. Because everything happens faster than the speed of light, doing and being are the same thing. You don't listen to music, you *are* music," my father said.

"How lovely," said my mother, who had always had a running argument with the world as it was. She thought it would be desirable to shed both the body and the ego, emerging as a work of art rather than a worker of art. In this, she reminded me of van Gogh. Or Buddha or Einstein, for that matter, since she was in no way parochial about the forms of beauty.

"A poem does not mean but be," I said, slightly disgusted.

"Close," my father said. "But still not exactly right. There's still meaning—nobody wants to eliminate that. It's just that it now resides in what *is,* not in what *isn't.* If you think about it, you'll see that on earth it is always absence that is meaningful. And that is the source of all unhappiness."

I found all this very disturbing. Although it sounded like a fine premise—heaven as eternal being—I was not at all sure I would in fact want to give up either creation or contemplation, which is what the premise seemed to entail. There had to be a separation between maker or thinker and the thing made or the thing thought about, or else there wouldn't be any making or thinking. If unity was all, there was no relatedness—and I liked the idea of relation. I liked being in relation to the thing I was trying to bring into being and liked losing myself in that effort. I liked the idea that the idea of union was predicated on the idea of divorce. It wasn't just the paradox that appealed to me; it was the idea of desire, of longing for achievement. Throwing that out would throw out a number of other things, too—the concept of development would go, for example, as in the sustained developmental passage of a Beethoven string quartet, and that was the linchpin of my philosophy of art. That was the baby I didn't want tossed out the window with the bathwater. (I had seen Tavy not so much as an opportunity to revise the story of my own life as the chance to write a sequel. She was the extension of me; she was my self projecting itself into otherness, my self losing itself, ultimately to become herself—the way a novel, muscling its way through time, emerges on the last page as something that can suddenly be seen to be both inherent in and utterly different from the opening sentence.)

In brief, if there was no gap, no shortfall between start and finish, there was no possibility of becoming.

That is to say—if my father was to be believed, and though reticent, he had always been a man of truth—the continuous tense had, in heaven, epiphanically revealed itself to be a predicate.

"Let me get this straight," my mother said. "Blaze is not simply chasing squirrels, he somehow *is* chasing squirrels. He is the very idea of a dog chasing squirrels. Similarly, if I wanted to fly, I would just *be* flying."

I saw her with her arms outstretched—or at least the good arm outstretched, the other, flattened by stroke, tucked against the side—homing in on Heathrow.

"And if," she said, taunting him (she was ever the tease), "I wanted to make love, though God knows I never would, I would just *be* love."

"Lovemaking, actually," my father said, a glint in his eye.

"I'd rather be the idea of flight."

"Not the idea. The thing itself."

"I like the ideas," I said, feeling threatened, as if somebody were about to deprive me of them—as my father must have felt, as he sensed his illness encroaching on the private property of his brain. "I don't want to give them up. They're what make the things themselves interesting. A thing without an idea would be like a plane without an engine. It *wouldn't* fly."

"I should never have told you two about this," my father said, fading. "I should have known that if anybody would have criticism to make about heaven, it would be the two of you."

"You come back here, Arthur!" my mother called. "It's not fair of you to keep slipping away like this!"

But he was gone. I washed the dishes.

The house was in a close, a dead-end drive like a sclerotic artery to the heart of the development. Dogs and cats and children played on the front lawns and welcomed the paperboy, the milkman, the greengrocer, the butcher, the cleaning man, the window washer, the refuse collector, the television serviceman (in England, only the rich own television sets; everyone else rents), and the teenage boy who came to mow my mother's lawn.

To my mother's house also came the doctor, the district nurse who bathed her, the physical therapist who exercised her muscles, the hairdresser who washed and set her sparse white hair, the elderly female postal clerk who came out of her way to bring the stamps she allowed my mother to order over the telephone, and the neighbors—even when the part-time housekeeper and the part-time private nurses and the handyman who did her grocery shopping and the woman who stopped in to get her breakfast for her were not, as they now were not, there.

Among the neighbors was a retired constable who now donated his time to the local volunteer squad, taking sick people to hospital and collecting them when they were well, accompanying the elderly on their visits to the clinic at Mortimer, and serving as my mother's banker. The first of the World Wars had shattered his family's fortunes and diverted his own future from its expected course, through university, into the police academy, from which he had emerged as a staunchly conservative supporter of the class system. I never could fathom this peculiarly English tendency to applaud one's own oppression. He was like a tall, silver-haired, barrel-chested bird alighting from time to time in our living room, bearing not twigs in his beak for our nest but the cash my mother had asked him to withdraw from her account. He was both kindly and argumentative. Like many Englishmen, he could never really believe that any woman would seriously oppose any of his opinions, and of course my mother opposed them all. In her old age, my mother had become radicalized. She sat in front of the telly making wisecracks about Maggie Thatcher. She styled herself a Social Democrat, but recognizing that her party hadn't a prayer, was willing to throw in her lot with the labor unionists. Malcolm, the male bastion of suburban conservatism, thought these political sympathies adorably female and unbelievably ridiculous. My mother invariably responded by acting adorably female, right up to the point where *he'd* say something ridiculous, and then she'd spring the particular trap she had set on that occasion. They were devoted to each other and had great fun playing this cat-and-mouse game, each being convinced that the other was the mouse.

"The trouble with Reagan," my mother announced from the wing chair one day as Malcolm towered in front of her, his back against the bay window as if he were shielding us from the world, "is that he's so stupid it's impossible for anyone to communicate with him. Now you take Star Wars. Everyone's running around building satellites and laser guns because nobody has ever stopped to figure out that in Reagan's mind this was a reference to *Gunfight at the OK Corral.* We could all get killed because he thinks being president of the United States is no different from being president of the Screen Actors Guild."

My mother's eyes were guileless, even blank: In age, they had the peculiar quality a television screen has in the dark when it is turned off, that ability to glow without light. It was the expectant thrust of her jaw, the way her chin was tilted slightly up—as if she were somehow ready to take it on the chin—that gave her away. I wondered how long she had been waiting to say this to Malcolm.

Malcolm has a high color. His face turned as red as the light on the washing machine in my mother's kitchen; he looked like he'd entered a spin cycle. Tavy, who had materialized in the living room holding Teddy upside down by one leg, looked up at him. "Are you going to die too?" she asked.

"This child is a necrophiliac," my mother said.

"Now, now, Tavy," Malcolm said, bending down to confront her at eye level. When he said her name, it sounded like Tah-vy instead of Ta-vy. "You must not think that everybody's going to die just because your grandfather did."

We had not informed the neighborhood of the intricacies of Tavy's appearance on earth, so he didn't know that Tavy's grandfather was also her great-grandfather.

"If you die," she said, looking him in the eye and gnawing on Teddy's leg, "you can have some ice cream."

I looked out the bay window, both fascinated and embarrassed while she went on to explain her statement.

"That's what Grandpa does," she said. "He has ice cream every night in the kitchen."

"And do you say hello to him?" Malcolm asked, humoring her.

There were bluetits and coaltits crowded together on the evergreen, and a small brown wren in the sumac bush. The Woodbines' Burmese cat was watching the wren closely.

"No," she said. "I can't see him. But Mommy and Grandma do. I hear them talking to him when I'm in bed."

Malcolm stood up, knees cracking. He brushed Oscar's dog hairs from his trousers. "She certainly has an active imagination. I guess it's an artistic family, isn't it, Eleanor."

"More's the pity," she admitted.

"I should think that artists are well-nigh obliged to be a bit illogical," he continued smoothly. "They say there's only a fine line between genius and insanity." He glanced slyly at my mother, as if he'd scored a decisive point.

I excused myself and went out to the kitchen and sat down in my father's chair at the table and laid my cheek against the cool linoleum of the table top. Because my father had made this table, I felt like I was placing my cheek next to his.

Nobody in the other room, I was thinking, knew how close I had come to crossing that line, once upon a time.

I opened an eye and realized that Oscar had followed me and was looking up at me. It was the first time he had treated me like something other than a potential enemy. I picked him up and began to stroke him. My little dog at home had density, solidity, a firm, round stomach emphatically real, not to mention greedy. Oscar fell across my lap as lightly as silk; he seemed to be made of cloth, I was wearing a live, gold skirt.

From the other room I heard sounds of laughter. Malcolm called out, "I'm leaving now!" and I heard the door shut behind him. I shook Oscar off and went back into the living room. Tavy looked worried. "Mommy, do I imagine things?"

"Of course you do," I said. "Everyone does."

"But do you talk with Grandpa, or not?"

"Why not?" I said. "Why shouldn't people talk to the dead? Where are you going to find a better bunch of listeners?"

"Take it from me," my mother added. "Your grandfather makes a whole lot more sense than Ronald Reagan. Even dead."

Despite these brief (but for me, how shining!) moments of communion among my mother, my daughter, and myself, there was more often a tug of war going on, with me as the rope.

I was nervously aware of my mother's deep skepticism about me, her feeling that my having elected to live with and care for a child made it doubtful that I'd complete the work I had always insisted I would do. She looked at me with the corners of her mouth turned down in disgust and even fear, as if I'd betrayed her, as if my action had been a wanton assault on everything she'd tried to teach me. To myself, I thought, Beethoven had his nephew—why shouldn't I adopt my grand-niece? But I had more sense than to say that out loud.

When Tavy was being cute, I felt vindicated—but also guilty, for proving my mother wrong. And when Tavy was cranky or mean, banging a spoon against the floor just because she enjoyed the distress it caused us, or screaming until she seemed to have turned into a tiny human horn, all noise and out of tune, I avoided my mother's eyes, guiltily fearing a told-you-so look. All this guilt was getting me down, and I would no doubt have felt sorry for myself if there'd ever been any time to, but my days were cataracts of busyness, chores cascading from dawn to dusk, one long waterfall of obligation.

I had tried to do right by them both, and they both seemed to think I had failed them, I had abandoned them, each for the sake of the other.

What I would have liked was a stiff drink. What I got was ice cream.

In the kitchen that night, my mother and father and I discussed my brother. "It was our fault," my mother, in a breast-beating mood, said, referring to his spectacular decline and fall, which had ended in his death from alcoholism. My mother got into these self-blaming moods but perhaps they were more an expression of her perfectionism than of pity. "We had no money and couldn't give him any of the things he wanted. When he was a freshman in college, he had only one pair of pants. One day your father discovered he had nothing to wear under them."

This fact dazzled me. I had never understood exactly why we had always been so broke. According to my parents, my brother and I had made excessive demands on their finances, yet my brother had no *underwear.* Birthday presents were a Hershey bar. We seldom got books and never lessons or anything like that. Maybe the violins, the bows had consumed all the money. Maybe we were just poorer than I ever really understood.

"Alcoholism is a sickness," I said, "a disease. People know that now."

"He could have quit," my mother said. "People do."

"There's a problem here," my father interjected. "At what point does addiction override free will? If you quit drinking, are you still addicted?"

"Members of AA refer to themselves as recovering alcoholics," I explained, "no matter how long they've been dry."

"But then Mother is right, drinking *isn't* purely a disease. It's a disease you can choose to have or not to have, and what other disease do you know of like that? Believe me," he said, "I could have used a choice when it came to Alzheimer's."

We were all silent for a minute. To lose your mind, I was thinking, what a sorrow, what a shock.

In the hospital, I had thought I was losing mine: It used to disappear for hours on end, then slip back, like a teenager into the house, at the last minute.

I'd never told my parents about any of this because they had said that they did not want to hear any bad news; they had had crisis-ridden lives, burdened with debt, they said, and they wanted no more stories of trouble. We were a family with secrets—where the money went, who was crazy, who slept with whom, whose child was whose, how anyone felt.

"You'd better be careful that Tavy doesn't start drinking," my mother continued. "Your father had a sister who drank." My father clicked his tongue against the roof of his mouth at this mention of Aunt Millicent, a husky-voiced redhead who had died at age seventy surrounded by empty vodka bottles, but who, he thought, my mother should now be willing to let rest in peace. "And your brother—"

"Your son," I reminded her.

"And I suspect Babette drinks, wherever she is."

Babette was Tavy's biological mother, a teenage runaway last seen heading for California. No one knew what to think about her. Suppose she was a hooker. Suppose she had AIDS.

Suppose, I thought more happily, she was a starlet in scarlet, a bikini'd bathing beauty in oversized sunglasses, lounging on a rubber raft in a Beverly Hills pool, tiny American flags decaled on her insouciant toenails?

"You don't know that," I said. "Babette could be a teetotaler." Though this seemed unlikely, if she was hanging out around a pool in Beverly Hills. "And it's a little early to worry about Tavy's drinking habits."

My father said, "What a morbid conversation this is."

"You're dead, Arthur. What do you expect?"

A still moon shone in through the kitchen door, which had a key-lock, a latch, and top and bottom bolts because a couple of years ago my parents had gotten worried about the wave of granny-bashing that was rolling over England. I undid all the locks and let Oscar out. He trotted down the narrow walk that led from the patio, along the hedge, ten feet tall, on the right side of the lawn, to the second patio, under the oak tree, where rhododendrons and rose bushes bloomed.

In the moonlight, his gold coat gleamed like a pound coin. I wondered again why my family had always fretted so about money. (I knew that money was one of my major themes, waiting for a critic who could trace and analyze its appearance in my various works.)

Oscar sniffed at the bushes, then raised his head and looked at the hushed night sky, as if listening to some constellatory music only animals could hear. Out there, in that darkness, there might be answers to all our questions. Or there might be just more questions. I shivered, unsweatered in the cold, and called to Oscar to come in. He turned around to look at me, and though he was at the other end of the lawn, in the dark, I could have sworn he was right in front of me, bright as dawn, hypnotic as a gold watch. In the cool dampness of the English dark, he was like some strange changeling, a silky, sulky midsummer sprite.

I slept in my father's bed. Tavy was on the cot in the extremely small room that my mother had used as an office for keeping the household finances. No one used my mother's bedroom; the fiction was that when she was feeling better she would move back upstairs.

On the wall facing the headboard of my father's bed was a window, and next to it, a framed photograph of my father's violin. The violin had been auctioned at Sotheby's. The photograph was actually four small photographs: From a book featuring his violin, among others, he had cut out four plates and had taped them behind four "windows" razored into a piece of cardboard; then he labeled the mat in his flowing composer's hand, and put a frame around it. I now wondered why he'd never felt entitled to have a photograph professionally made and framed.

The window faced west, so night clung to it as long as it could. As light began to reach down from the upper storey of the sky, doves cooed under the eaves as if to welcome it. Magpies and hummingbirds sent out their own BBC signals—Better Bird Casting. Still half asleep, I listened to that dreamy music as if it were a score—*the* score, the one I had always been trying to find out.

I couldn't lie in bed for long because my mother wouldn't permit it. At five-thirty, there'd be a huge pounding noise coming from the ceiling below, and I'd wake in a rush of adrenaline, thinking alarm. She was beating on the ceiling with her broomstick.

"If I don't have to sleep," she said, "I don't see why anyone else should have to." She actually said that to me, as I stared at her, bleary-eyed, from the foot of her bed. I was wearing an old shirt over a cotton nightgown, and socks that had caused me to slip as I ran down the stairs, banging my hipbone bad enough so a stabbing pain would sometimes radiate up my back. I wanted to tell her that her "toughness" was no longer cute. That it may have been cute fifty years ago, but now it was indistinguishable from a lack of consideration for other people.

But I just stared at her, amazed she could say such a thing and too afraid of hurting her to confront her. I'd always been afraid of hurting her. The thing was, the older I got, the more I began to be angry about this. "We don't want to know about any problems," she'd said, but I wanted her to *know* me. This anger . . . it was as if part of me was regressing. At this rate, when I reached her age, I'd be a withered-up three-year-old, wanting everyone to make up for my mother's selfishness. It was figuring this out—that generalized anger, anybody's generalized anger, stemmed from a belated desire to have someone make up for early neglect and was a kind of regression—that saved my temper: I realized I was dealing with a three-year-old. And I already knew how to deal with a three-year-old.

Tavy, Oscar, and Teddy were taking tea in the living room. With each day that passed, Oscar had become a little less grudging toward Tavy, and now he was lying on his stomach on the green carpet, a thimble-sized teacup of painted wood just beyond his punched-in muzzle. Teddy was sitting up, leaning against the wing chair. Tavy was pouring.

When I saw the miniature dishes, bright golden wood painted with a delicate row of blue and green flowers, I felt myself being carried back in time, tugged out to sea by the strong undertow of memory, that current of images and sensations that has so much to do with the direction we take in life but which we are usually unaware of.

I fixed breakfast for my mother, Tavy, and Oscar. "You forgot Teddy's breakfast," Tavy said, looking at me accusingly. I gave him a dog biscuit, but then Oscar wanted one too. I unlocked the kitchen door and shooed the trio into the backyard.

On the brick patio under the oak tree, they played in the summer light. They were like creatures from another world, a world of timelessness whose dimensions had spread out by mistake and gotten ensnared with ours; otherwise, these small aliens would not be known to us even to the temporary extent that they were. I leaned against the doorjamb, letting my spine sag. I wanted to weep, thinking that one day Tavy would be my age. I would be a demanding old woman. One day Oscar would make a last trip to the vet. One day even Teddy would go to the vast grave of teddy bears, the stuffing knocked out of him, ears and eyes and button nose beyond repair.

"Come here," my mother yelled, snapping me out of my sad reverie.

I had helped her into the wing chair in front of the telly, but the screen was dark. She was reading a biography of Dickens. She lit a cigarette. I had to keep an eye on her because whenever she opened a new pack of cigarettes, she performed a ritual coda by touching the lighter to the cellophane wrapping, starting small fires in the ashtray.

"Yes?" I asked.

My mother the pyromaniac watched as the cellophane flared and died, the bitter odor of burning plastic a sudden, sharp note on the air. "What's going to happen to your work now that you've got Tavy to take care of?"

I knew that she had been waiting to ask me this just as she had waited for the right moment to taunt Malcolm with her remark about Reagan.

"It's going to deepen," I said. "It's going to widen."

I understood that she would feel compelled to argue the opposite case, since she had always believed that having children had hampered *her*. "It's not that we didn't want you," she rushed to assure me. "But you don't know what you're getting into. All I did for years was worry about you children."

This last statement was not true, but it must have seemed true to her. She wanted to believe it. It even occurred to me that maybe the reason it had not been true was that if she *had* paid any attention to us, it *would have been* true. Maybe she had turned away from us not out of indifference or selfishness but fear, feeling that, if she were to acknowledge our existence, the attendant responsibilities would suffocate her.

Thinking about her blighted life, she started to cry. More and more, she was doing this, swinging between moods. She'd be angry one minute, disconsolate the next. If you said something to cheer her up or comfort her, she'd look at you with those clouded eyes that didn't seem to see you and say, "Ha." Like that: "Ha."

I yanked a Kleenex from the box and handed it to her. She let it drop, slamming her fists into her chest as if some internal mechanism had suddenly gone haywire and pulled her arms up short. The same screwed-up guy wires had twisted her face into a look of agony. I thought, Oh God, oh God. I grabbed the buzzer for the Lifeline Unit. A voice came over the speaker: "Mrs. Bryant? Mrs. Bryant?"

"This is Nina Bryant," I shouted. "I think my mother is having a heart attack."

In no time, there was an ambulance in the driveway. Malcolm had come over and was standing in front of my mother, trying to persuade her to let them take her to the hospital, where they could run tests to see if she had indeed had a heart attack. The ambulance drivers waited at the door to the living room, caps in hand. Tavy and Oscar had come in from outside and wandered among the grownups as if among tall trees.

"I don't want to," my mother said. "The last time I was in hospital, I had to stay awake all night because a lesbian kept trying to pinch me."

The three tall Englishmen stared down at the carpet. I knew my mother sounded crazy to them: Scrunched-up old ladies weren't even supposed to know words like "lesbian."

"It's true," I said, as if my mother were on trial and I was her defense lawyer. "I was there once when it happened. The woman was ninety-three but she was horny. The nurses just laughed at her and took her back to her own bed, but from my mother's point of view, it wasn't funny at all."

Imagine what it would be like to be unable to get away, unable to get out of your own bed, lying there in the dark, feeling like prey.

"It's important to find out whether or not you've suffered a heart attack, Eleanor," Malcolm said again.

"Important to whom?" my mother said. "It's not important to me."

"It's important to me," I said, and she started to cry again.

She wanted to die, or at least she said she did. She made jokes about how, no matter how hard she tried, she couldn't seem to pull it off. She said if she could just die, she'd give God a piece of her mind. It was a hell of a way to run a universe, she'd tell Him: all this evil and illness, death and decay and bad art.

She said she wanted to die, but the truth was she was afraid to. She had so much invested in being herself. Dying meant giving all that up, and nothing scared her as much as giving up.

I attributed this fear of surrender to some early-developed sense of being easily overwhelmed, perhaps in response to having two sisters enough older than she was that it was like having three mothers. Or maybe the loss of an Edenic childhood, lived among cypresses and water moccasins and bright birds as flamboyant as flying graffiti, in a bayou in Louisiana, had translated itself into lifelong anxiety about further loss. Or maybe, as the youngest, the baby of the family, her father's favorite, she had felt forever cheated, after she discovered that no matter how good a daughter she was, she was not going to be allowed to remain his daughter forever.

I think she had been shocked to find herself an adult, and with more than her fair share of responsibility. She had done her best to recover, tossing out all childish things in a wholesale psychological housecleaning. In the battle to define herself against whatever it was she perceived as a threat, she had defeated the almost pathological shyness of her youth and gone on guard against all revelations of vulnerability. The result was—my mother, the seventy-eight-pound warrior on twenty-four-hour-a-day alert. She had not surrendered to herself; she wasn't about to surrender to anyone else; she could not bear the thought of surrendering to death—she kept thinking there had to be a way she could do this on her own terms.

It was because she hated the thought of surrendering that she disdained politicians. It was why she disliked sex, though she *said* the reason she didn't like sex was that it was about as interesting as having someone stick a pencil in your ear.

And yet, what a passionate romance she'd had with my father for fifty tumultuous years.

Now, in her old age, she was as small and brown-spotted as a mushroom, growing in the forest of her bed. Her skin, creased as leather, was as soft as suede. Her breasts had vanished, receding when they became no longer relevant. And this was a woman who had been five-six-and-a-half, with outstanding legs.

I made more of her beauty than she did. She hardly ever wore makeup; for her, her beauty was just a fact, like her height.

For me, her beauty was a standard. And it was a clue, as if, by deciphering it, I could understand why her youth had been so different from mine. It was interesting to me to imagine her at twenty, say, with her hair cut in a "windblown" style, and wearing a white coat bought specifically for walking along the shore on those lovely gray days in Gulfport when the breezes were cool and there was spray from the surf and a hint of storm in the air. She would look out over the Gulf in the direction of Mexico and South America, constructing the future as an exotic landscape just over the horizon. She danced the nights away with her boyfriends, who were plentiful, at a waterfront pavilion in Biloxi. Her mother had made her a white organdy evening dress, trimmed in red, for the Valentine dance, and a black-and-white striped dimity with a black velvet sash for afternoon parties. Sometimes she and her friends went to drive-in movies, or they organized torchlit expeditions to spear flounder in the shallow water at the base of the seawall. In the afternoons they sailed, or played putt-putt on the miniature golf course by the municipal pier, or drove up and down the beach road, stopping occasionally for Cokes and hot dogs.

When I was the age she had been then, I attended a banquet with my parents. During dessert, the man sitting next to me turned to me and said, as if this were a fact I had to be forced to face, "You'll never be as beautiful as your mother." I didn't realize he was in love with her, besotted as a boy. As soon as the coffee cups were cleared away and the dancing had started, I got the car keys from my father, excused myself and went out to the car, let myself in and curled up in the back seat and cried, long into the sycamore-scented night. I cried on the drive home. I cried all weekend, shut up in my room. My mother's response to all this unexplained self-pity was, as usual, disgust, but I was afraid that if I told her what the matter was, she would feel guilty. I didn't want her to feel she'd let me down genetically. My father came into my room and tried to get me to talk, but I couldn't tell him, either, because he would get worried that there was something going on between my mother and the man who had spoken to me, because he was always worried that he loved her more than she loved him and she might fall in love with someone else and have an affair and leave him. (He *could* be restless; he *could* be imagining that he had been wronged; he *was* always that jealous.) To make himself more attractive to her, he had recently spent nine hundred dollars on Arthur Murray dance lessons, in secret, so he would be able to dance with her at the banquet. I didn't know how to dance either, but girls weren't supposed to need lessons.

"Do you remember when Daddy went to Arthur Murray?" I asked her. Art imitating Art, I was thinking.

"Ha," she said.

"Ha?"

"Nobody's dancing now."

She had such a sad look on her face—her mouth dragged down and trembling, her eyes like one-way windows that she could see out of but you couldn't see in. She was wearing her favorite outfit, a pink "sweatsuit" with a pastel-blue bunny over the heart. She had high cheekbones and in profile still looked like the young Katharine Hepburn.

Though she read constantly, she also liked to be read to. I sat at the foot of the bed, squinting, under the pale light of the overhead fixture, at the microbe-sized print in her gilt-edged "fine" editions with ribbon bookmarks. Tavy would join us, her small face screwed up in tight concentration as if she were following every word of *Barchester Towers*. One afternoon my mother broke into my reading to ask, "How far back can you remember?" I started to answer her when she said, "Not you. I'm talking to Tavy. Do you remember lying in your crib?" my mother asked her. "Do you remember the curtains in your bedroom blowing in over your crib? I do."

Tavy stuck her thumb in her mouth.

"I remember tying and untying a gauze bandage on my big toe," my mother went on. "I remember the lavender kimono I was wearing when my parents took me to the hospital to have my tonsils out—and that was before I was two. It seems like the closer you are to these events, like Tavy, the better you'd remember them, but it's just the opposite, isn't it? They come back to you as you get older. Isn't that ironic!"

"Probably the older you get, the farther back you can remember," I said. "Probably one day you have a blinding recollection of being born, and in the same instant you die."

We looked at each other and started to laugh, a few collusive giggles at first and then we laughed harder and harder. Tavy just looked at us and continued to suck her thumb. I was afraid she thought we were laughing at her, but I couldn't seem to stop long enough to explain. I didn't know how to explain. Later, I wondered what she would remember of this.

I knew I was not paying enough attention to Tavy. Not that she was alone—Malcolm frequently looked after her, and she had become a great favorite in the neighborhood. She was also gifted at the art of amusing oneself. Lately she had taken to giving song recitals to Oscar and Teddy, who sat on the floor facing her. She revised the texts of these songs with abandon. "Where, oh where has my little dog gone?" became "Puppy gone. Where, oh where be?" "Oh come, let us adore him" was transformed into "Oh come little outside door him." There was one song she liked to sing that may even have been an original: "Oh Jeesy, Jeesy, Jeesy, they all play with toys, and they don't take up the nickels."

But I knew she felt I had deserted her. When I put her to bed at night, and she stared up at me without saying anything, or rolled over onto her pillow without throwing her arms around me to say good night first, I wanted to apologize. *I* wanted to apologize when she was *good,* because she was an active, risk-taking, free-spirited kid who was *supposed* to be misbehaving, who was *supposed* to be apologizing to me, and if she was being good, it was because she thought I had lost interest in her and believed that the only way for her to get my attention back or please me was by changing her ways.

I knew what it felt like to struggle to impress one's existence on a parent by impressing the parent.

But Tavy did have an existence, and my mother might not have hers for much longer, so it seemed to me my first duty was to her.

But I also acknowledged that I might have been seizing on that fact to excuse another, which was that I felt ashamed, in front of my mother, to have been found out as a human being, a female human being at that, one with a desire to be a mother herself that had been so uncontrollable that she had dared to adopt.

And I felt ashamed, before Tavy, to feel such shame.

It was a mess. I was trying to be—I *was*—both mother and *daughter.* And I didn't want to lose my mother.

Since we didn't know for sure whether or not she had had a heart attack, I thought I'd better go on the assumption that she had. From the local health service, I got pamphlets on how to do CPR. But I knew it would be an iffy matter, blowing air into lungs already rendered half-inoperative by emphysema.

She would not consider a nursing home; that would've meant giving up Oscar.

They were a pair. She and Oscar would sit up side by side in the single bed, the one smoking a cigarette and drinking cocoa, the other chewing on a rubber shoe.

Malcolm said that after she died, he would take Oscar.

Because my mother was always cold, the house was usually sealed tight, even though it was summer. I imagined we might live there forever. I imagined us whirling through space and time like Dr. Who in his telephone booth: There was no telling where we would end up, except that wherever it was, it would be in our little brick house.

And if we were in our little house, we were probably in the little kitchen, talking. Sometimes just talking, and sometimes talking things over.

My mother liked to talk about how she had met my father. He had been even shyer than she, so that she had had to propose to him. When he said yes and asked her to set the date, she said, "Two o'clock."

Their timing wasn't great. It was 1933. The Depression years burned away any vaguely romantic notions they may have had about life. And made them afraid—if they had not already been afraid. They lived in an unending expectation of catastrophe, to which my father's reaction, had he been free to have one on his own, would have been flight, and my mother's was fight.

It could sometimes be hard to get past her "tough talk." My father would simply let her go on. While she criticized whatever it was she was criticizing, he placed his fingers on the edge of the table, spreading them wide, the heels of his hands hanging over the edge, raising the knuckles so that the tips flattened out, then letting the heels of his hands fall again so that the fingers became as straight as clothespins. He had used to do this as if he were studying his hands, or even admiring them. They were strong hands, flexible until he developed arthritis, unexpectedly large. Suddenly I saw him as he had been in 1933, matinée-handsome, darkly intense, completely naive, and decked out in the wardrobe he'd acquired with his first paycheck—a white linen suit and yellow-and-white polka-dot bow tie with matching handkerchief protruding from the breast pocket.

As I stared at him, the green shirt and gray slacks reappeared and then re-metamorphosed into the white linen of yesteryear. It was confusing: His younger and older selves seemed to take turns appearing and disappearing like the images on the playing cards Tavy had at home, which were one thing when you held them at an angle and another when you held them straight up. I blinked my eyes to bring him into focus.

It occurred to me that this was more or less the way my father had always related to us: wavering in and out of focus.

I had a question I wanted to ask him. It seemed to me that it had to be a question that was on my parents' minds too—my mother's to ask, my father's to be asked—and yet no one had dared to bring it out into the open. I thought the time had come. "You know," I said, as a kind of prologue, "this was a family in which there were always a lot of secrets. Too many, if you ask me—"

"Ha," my mother said, interrupting triumphantly. "Nobody asked you."

"You've got ice cream on your top," my father said to her. He tore a paper towel off the roll and rubbed at the spot. (Paper towels had always been handy in this household, because my parents were always bringing up phlegm; stress and nicotine had undone their once-young bodies so!) "Pink becomes you, Ellie," he said.

"Ha."

She was going to start crying again, overcome by his compliment. I was determined not to be deflected. Into the space of that instant during which her mood was shifting, I rushed with my question. I asked my father if he had seen my brother "over there."

My father pushed his empty bowl away with a sudden show of revulsion, as if he wanted to disown the ice cream—or his love of it. He crossed his legs. He took off his glasses and squeezed and caressed his nose where they pinched and settled them back on his face. I remembered that on sunny days he used to wear tinted lenses that clicked onto these regular glasses, and when he didn't need them, he'd flick them up where they overhung his face like little dark-green awnings.

"No," he said.

We were silent, absorbing this news which wasn't really news since we'd half-known that if my father had seen him, he would already have said so, but which nevertheless seemed to increase in ontological stature by being spoken out loud. Then my mother said, "I was hoping that even if God had made the mistake of allowing evil on earth, He might have seen the error of his ways. But no, He had to go and create hell. What kind of God loves evil so much He can't get enough of it?"

"You're jumping to conclusions, El," my father said. "First of all, the fact that I haven't seen him does not necessarily mean that he's not there. Secondly, even if he's not there, it doesn't necessarily follow that there has to be a hell."

"Where else would he be?" I asked, taken aback by the brusque note in my own voice. I seemed to be saying that was where he belonged. Nina, I reminded myself, if you can't excuse even your own brother from hell, who's going to excuse you?

But then I thought, That's what we need a God for: to grant forgiveness where the rest of us can't quite manage it.

My father was saying to my mother, "Let's not beat around the bush here. The truth is, I never saw all that much of him when we were alive. I had to earn a living. I had to support us all. The result was, I never had time for him when he was little, and after he got bigger, he didn't want to have anything to do with me. He refused to believe that I had *wanted* to have more time with him. Well, if we didn't see each other on earth, there's really no reason for us to see each other now."

What he had just said was only partly true. My brother had had seven years of basking in the parental sunshine before I came along. But my attention had been arrested by something else he said. "Do you mean," I asked, finally registering what he'd said earlier about jumping to conclusions, "that you don't *know* whether there's a hell or not?"

"Of course I don't know. How could I know? Hell is about not-being, and as I've already explained, the whole idea of heaven is that it's about *being*. It's not about not-being. Being can't know nonbeing because it would entail a self-contradiction."

"Then let me ask you this," I said. "If being can't know nonbeing, how can goodness know sin, which is also a kind of absence since it means 'missing the mark'? And unless goodness can know sin, how can God know time?"

I was thinking that questions like these might have been why theologians had come up with notions like limbo and purgatory. Probably you went into that line of work out of a hunger for absolutes, an addiction to drawing dichotomies, but by the time you reached middle age, you felt surfeited, you were tired of your lifelong binge, and you began to develop a secret craving for what was relative, for the in-between, maybe even, at least on rare, indulgent occasions, for the indefensibly vague. Oh my God, maybe you became a closet Hegelian.

My father said, "You were always one for the questions, Nina."

"As long as we are on the subject of specific persons," my mother said, "I have a question." A kind of timidity invaded and softened her voice. "What about my mother?" she asked.

My father laughed. "How could Saint Peter turn away someone who was buried wearing her Presbyterian pin for perfect attendance?"

"Is she happy?" my mother asked—and I knew she was holding her breath for the answer, though she had very little breath in her lungs that she could hold.

"She's with your father," my father said. This time, when he reached for a paper towel, it was to dry the tears on my mother's wrinkled face.

These nightly conversations were telling on my mother. In the morning, she looked haggard, the skin on her face not just passively sagging with age but *tugging* at her, trying to pull her down into old age and death. There was a tug of war going on, between her fighting spirit, which could not bear the thought of surrender, and a deep desire for peace. She had so little use for the world, and yet here she was, syllogistically obligated, by her own sense of herself as someone whose essential nature it was to oppose, to side with the world, opposing death. She was a lover of abstraction now having to align herself with the world of physicality *against* abstraction. This battle was being fought daily, even while she was talking with my father. He drew her to him by his physical magnetism, but he himself—being a ghost—was an abstraction. These contrary vectors were exhausting her; they seemed almost to generate a friction that was wearing her down. Day by day, she seemed less *there*. Her bones were shrinking away from her skin, as if she were getting ready to molt. As for flesh, there was hardly any left. Just the dress of skin over the sewing form of her skeleton.

From lavender kimono to pink sweatsuit with a pale blue bunny: This was the haute couture of a life, the sartorial arc of her passage on earth.

It was high summer. The neighbors to our left had gone to Spain; the neighbors to our right, the Woodbines, were in Florida (which Mrs. Woodbine, who had traveled the world over, insisted was the place on earth she found most different from England, more "exotic," she said, than Turkey, or Egypt, or even Sri Lanka). Malcolm and his wife had sent us a postcard from Devon, where they were walking twenty miles a day. The neighborhood was like a ghost town, and would have been even without my father's nocturnal visitations. Even when the ice-cream man came in his truck, the bell as clear and cool as an ice cube in the sweet lemonade of daytime, only one or two children dashed out from their houses, ten pence in their palms.

Some mornings we sat out on the patio, my mother wrapped in blankets, her face turned toward the sun, Tavy digging in the stone-potted geraniums, Oscar snoozing, the extravagant curlicue of his tail a kind of cadenza to the theme of his body, bluebirds and swallows threading their song through the bright seam of day. Butterflies floated on currents of air so light they were imperceptible—a phenomenon we knew existed, from the evidence of the butterflies, but which was inaccessible to our senses. My mother slept. For a few minutes, I felt as if time had stopped. Then a shadow passed over the sundial of my mother's face as if to remind me what time it was—and what time was—but nothing else moved except the butterflies with their delicate, soundless bobbing, Tavy's busy little wrist and spoon, and Oscar's twitching tail. Far off, an airplane homed in on Heathrow, but from where I sat, it seemed more like a bee making for its hive. I had the sense that I was intimately familiar with this scene. Not that I had experienced it before in exactly this way, but that I had been somehow prepared for it, perhaps *had* experienced it before but from a slightly different perspective, perhaps my mother's or Tavy's or that of someone who wasn't with us now.

Maybe time, I thought, was like light and functioned sometimes as waves, sometimes as particles. Maybe some of the time it flowed from past to future (or, as Augustine thought, from future to past), but maybe at other times it bunched itself up into a lot of not-quite-infinitesimal quantum-like balls, bouncing around like crazy, some kind of pinball machine, the universe a penny arcade, somebody—who?—racking up one hell of a score.

It was so strange, living through these weeks during which my mother grew ever more contingent and delicate, almost, in a sense, younger, because her mind, while retaining its wizardly sharpness, was relinquishing its scope, narrowing the range of its interests to concentrate on the one central fact of existence, the self, while my daughter, my mother's great-granddaughter, blossomed like some sort of small, rustling bush, progressing from toddlerhood to little-girlhood.

Tavy was walking with assurance now. Instead of looking always as if she was just about to trip, or as if she thought the world was not merely round but about to spin out of control, she raced through the house as if she were training for the four-minute mile. "Who's got happy feet?" I'd say, and she'd break into a silly dance and collapse giggling. For a moment, I felt redeemed: I was a good mother and I had a happy child. So what if she had sneaked into Malcolm's kitchen when his back was turned—he had been baby-sitting her for the day, giving my mother a breather from the commotion Tavy couldn't help creating—and grabbed his jar of pickled walnuts, expensively sold at Harrod's, and carried them outside to feed to the squirrels, turning them all into baffled gourmets?

But it was hard on my mother, all this energy, this top wound up at birth and set to whirligig her way through a long, probably headlong, life. I suggested to her that we should leave, but she wouldn't have it. She knew what was coming and didn't want to face it alone. She had panic attacks that she wanted me to be there to see her through. When people have panic attacks, they feel as though they can't breathe, but I think it was *because* my mother couldn't breathe that she had panic attacks. When you have emphysema, there are times when no matter how hard you try to breathe, no matter how much air you manage to suck in, it seems to do no good because there aren't enough air sacs left in your lungs to hold the air. You try to breathe, you make the motions of breathing, but you still don't have any breath. Some stony gargoyle is squatting on your lungs. Some mysterious statue has been planted right in the center of your chest, and the intricately branched bronchioles beneath won't grow, the bellows won't blow. It's like being suffocated from the inside.

I fixed her a supper of peaches and cream. It was one of the few things she'd eat, though even with this, the bowl would be on the floor for Oscar before she'd finished half of it. I sat beside her, a human vending machine for Kleenex, paper towels, cortisone pills, blood-thinner pills, laxatives, cigarettes, matches, chocolate. We were deep into summer, having left a trail of shiny litter, but it was a trail which would never lead us out again. The leaves on the old oak tree were a restful, sleepy green, as if they'd manufactured all the chlorophyll they needed and could now relax for a while.

Under the high hedge, a hedgehog rolled itself into a prickly ball at Oscar's approach.

My mother asked me to plump up the pillows behind her back. Her legs, under the blanket, were so pathetically thin that they seemed to me to be, as she never was, apologetic. They seemed to want to apologize for being helpless, and I would have patted them in the reassuring way that you pat children or pets, except that the cortisone my mother took made her skin so thin that it tore like tissue paper, you could punch holes in it with your fingers.

Sometimes, at night, or in the early morning when the tree and sky and the chimney across the way that topped the tall fence at the end of

the lawn presented themselves in the frame of the window like a painting, lying in my father's bed I cried, not knowing what else to do. I
cried quietly so I wouldn't wake Tavy or get my mother's broom-
handle going. To cry in front of my mother would have been, somehow, to steal the limelight from her, since this was her tragedy, not
mine; and I didn't want Tavy to see me cry, because it might make her
feel insecure. So I kept my crying a secret from both of them, but I
couldn't keep it secret from Oscar.

Oscar came into my room, curious and wanting breakfast, and
jumped on the bed. He put his face next to mine as if to ascertain that
what I was doing was, in fact, crying, and then he sat down next to my
face and simply watched me until I stopped. I don't mean to hurt your
feelings, I whispered to him, but you're my mother's dog, and Blaze is
in heaven with my father, and I miss my dog, who is in America. I felt
such a wave of longing for my own little dog, who had been through so
much with me, and who would soon be the only creature left on earth
who knew who *I* was, who had experienced what I had experienced in
the past eventful decade. Not even Tavy knew me the way my dog did.
I was so tired of trying to understand what everyone else needed—I
wanted someone who understood me.

Oscar was unmoved. When I still didn't get out of bed, he sat on my
chest, his plumy tail feather-dusting my teary face, blocking my view. I
got up, crawling into a pair of jeans and one of my father's shirts. I had
always thought it would be creepy to wear a dead person's clothes, but
now I found it comforted me. It made me feel close to him.

On the way downstairs, I peeked into Tavy's room. She was still
asleep on the cot in the room that was my mother's office. The sun had
crossed the windowsill and highlighted the open book of her face. She
had her thumb in her mouth. She liked to pick a piece of fuzz from the
lightweight summer blanket, stick it on the knuckle of her index finger
and then suck her thumb. It was a kind of padding, I guess, designed to
prevent her knuckle from irritating the tip of her nose. I laughed at the
thought of such a sensitive little nose.

Through depths of dreams, she felt my presence. She stirred, kicking
at the sheets and blanket. She opened her eyes, in which I was afraid to
read how much she knew: I did not want to know if she knew that to the
extent to which I was my mother's daughter, I was not free to be my
daughter's mother. The sunlight shining on her face seemed, rather, to be

radiated by it, every strand of her hair gleaming, streaming into rays. She held open her arms and I reached toward her, leaned into her. I sat on the bed, squashing Teddy, and picked her up and held her, held her tight.

Oscar, his tail as erect and sweeping and haughty as the Arc de Triomphe, posed at the doorjamb, facing into the hallway, poised for the trip downstairs.

It began as an ordinary day, a day like any other: breakfast for all, the toothbrush tray and a sponge bath for my mother, the "News at One." In the afternoon, I read to my mother from *Wuthering Heights,* and Tavy listened while she colored in her coloring book. After supper, after the evening news, I took Tavy upstairs and put her to bed with Teddy, and my mother and I talked for a while in the living room. Then I put her to bed. She could no longer traverse the distance between the wing chair in the living room and the cot in the dining room even with the walker. I tucked her in, brought her a glass of water. "Is there anything else I can get you before I go up?" I asked.

"Do you think he'll come tonight?"

"If you want him to," I said.

"I don't want to die alone."

She had never come flat out and said that before. It gave me the willies. "Why are you talking about death?" I said. "Dinner wasn't that bad." I had fixed her a soft-boiled egg but burned the toast.

"Will you stay down here tonight?"

Oscar was curled up on the pillow, on top of her head like a golden crown. She looked so small, so vulnerable. Her cloudy eyes were like leaded windowpanes. She was a little house that everyone had moved away from. "I'll sleep on the couch in the living room," I offered.

"If you hear Daddy, please wake me up."

"I promise," I said.

In the living room, I lay down on the couch, still in my clothes. Then, like a victim of monoxide poisoning, I fell into a colorless, odorless sleep.

When I heard him in the kitchen, I rolled off the couch and went in through the foyer, trying not to wake my mother.

He was so handsome—he looked the way he had looked in his youth, dark and quiet and earnest and dedicated, a man who, though he was much too Protestantly reserved ever to talk about his beliefs, thought that there had to be a God and that it was clearly a God who loved him, the proof being that He had let him be born after Beethoven, which meant he could spend his life playing Beethoven string quartets. This was the greatest miracle of my father's life and he never ceased to be wholly thankful for it.

I simply could not understand how he could now be content merely to *be* a string quartet or even string-quartet-playing. Why, he had never even wanted to *be* Beethoven—that was a hubristic ambition his daughter might plead guilty to, but all he had ever wanted was to *play* Beethoven. "You *must* miss playing the violin," I said, desperately wanting him to be what, who, he was: himself—not an idea or a predicate, even an eternal one. *Himself.*

"It's like I told you, Nina," he said, patient with my impatience. "My intonation has just gone all to hell without your mother around to criticize me."

Then it was clear to me, what he was saying. "No," I said.

"Yes," he said.

I felt cold. I felt as if I'd just been pulled, dazed and trembling, from an icy pond into which I had stupidly, *stupidly* stumbled. I was shivering with realization. I wanted to un-realize what I had realized. Maybe if I didn't know what was going to happen, I thought, it wouldn't happen. It would be the reverse of predestination.

"There are solo sonatas," I said. "There are records with one part missing. When Mother was busy, you used to practice by yourself. I stayed in my room, listening. In the hallway, listening. For years. In the end, you said, every member of a string quartet is responsible for himself. Or herself. Nobody can play your part for you."

"That's right," he said. "That's the first thing you learn when you shut the door to the practice room and start to play scales, for the first time. It's like anything else that matters. Nobody else can do it for you."

"I don't know if I agree with that," I said. "When you played the violin, when Mother played, it was like my heart was playing its own chamber music. I mean, I have always applauded you both. I hope you know that."

"Thank you," he said. And I realized that I had stumbled into the same pond all over again and that, no matter how I tried to circumvent it, that pond would always be there, waiting for me to fall into it and surface shivering and forever changed. My father's formal thank-you had signaled the fact that we had come to the end of something, but I still didn't want it to be over. I was an audience clamoring for an encore, while the musicians backstage just wanted to put their instruments away and go home. "Will you wake her?" he asked.

I hesitated. "Do I have to?"

"I'm here because she didn't want to do this alone."

"But you just said everything that matters has to be done alone!" I was still the star pupil, aggressively blasting holes in everyone else's argument so no one could draw a bead on mine.

"Death *can't* matter," he rebutted me, "because it *isn't* matter. Life matters, but death doesn't. Please bring her in here."

He had become so commanding—a presence, in spite of his nonexistence. He was more real to me, at that moment, than he had been since I was a child, an infant even.

I remembered that I had seen him naked once, not so many years ago. He had talced himself after a tub bath and was drying himself off with a large towel. He had looked so pale, from the talc, almost snow-white, and yet so—*embodied.* That was how he looked now: pale as a ghost but embodied.

When I had seen him like that, naked, I'd ducked into the next room, not wanting him to know, not wanting to embarrass him. I ducked into the next room now.

"He's here?" She said the words as soon as I touched her shoulder. She raised herself off the pillows. Her hair, tousled from sleeping, was sticking out in wispy white corkscrews. It looked like smoke, as if her scalp were smouldering. Or like fog—the white, twisted columns of fog that drift silently through bayous.

"He wants to talk with you," I said.

"He's come for me."

"I don't know what you mean!" I cried.

"You know perfectly well what I mean, Nina. Don't be an ass about this."

"It's hard on her, Eleanor," my father said, as we pushed through the swinging Dutch gate into the kitchen.

"It's harder on me." She sank into her chair. "Nina, fix us some ice cream, if you don't mind."

I got the glass bowls from the cabinet and spoons and scooped up four dishes of ice cream, placing one on the floor for Oscar in case he decided he liked Rum Raisin, but he refused to come into the kitchen. He stayed by the gate, inscrutable as the Dalai Lama.

Because it was night, because my mother was old and cold, the furnace was on. We three were held in the kitchen as in an embrace.

I forced myself to eat the ice cream because my parents obviously wanted me to. They wanted to think I was happy, they wanted to be released from all guilt, freed of all anxiety. There was nothing new in that—but how could I be happy when they were leaving me? How was I supposed to feel good about what was happening? I didn't have my mother's ability to detach herself from sentiment. I didn't have my father's humility, which had allowed him to be grateful for even the smallest favor from God, such as being born after Beethoven.

Instead, I was angry. I felt they had played a dirty, rotten trick on me. They had let me think that my father had come back because he was lonely and missed my mother, but he had come back to take her away.

I felt a despair that was like amputation. I had thought I was helping her—talking with her, reading to her, looking after her wants and needs. But what she needed was to cut off life. She was gangrenous with the past—maybe that's how we all become. To get well, she needed to be freed from it. I was the amputated appendage.

Nothing I had done had been enough to keep her from being lonely and missing my father.

They handed me their empty bowls and I ran water over the dishes in the sink. When I turned around again, my father was helping my mother out of her chair.

"You're not going already!"

It came out like a scream, a sort of scream or controlled shriek. I was afraid I had waked up Tavy. We stopped and listened to the house, but she slept on.

"Remember," my father said. "Violin lessons as soon as you get back to Wisconsin."

I nodded. My eyes were filling.

"Don't cry," my mother said. "It disgusts me to see anyone cry. Besides, I'm happy to be with your father again."

And how happy she looked! She was as radiant as a bride, she was a bride. Before my eyes, she had become again the vibrant young beauty who had liked to stroll along the Gulf shore and dance late into the salt-scented, breeze-blown nights. She was again the clear-eyed, firm-profiled young woman who, to my father's amazement, shared his love of the Beethoven string quartets. Who would have thought that there could be a girl like this, or that she would be waiting for him? When he had finally accepted this as yet another miracle he had no choice but to believe in, he gathered up his courage and drove to Gulfport, in a Buick he'd bought for seventy-five bucks at a bankruptcy sale. It was, as I said, 1933.

But now my father had picked up my mother and carried her in his arms to the door to the backyard. "Open the door, Nina," he said.

I dried my hands on my shirt—his shirt—and went to the door. Outside, the leaves of the oak tree were like hands, all playing the sky as if the sky were a musical instrument, the wind an invisible bow. I unlatched the latch, unbolted the bolts, unlocked the key-lock.

"Stand over there, Nina," my father ordered, jerking his head in the direction of the little table he had made, the two chairs and the high stool.

I moved over to the table.

"Good-bye," said my mother. "I know you're determined to be a better mother than I was, but that may not be as easy as you think. In any case, you must not let Tavy keep you from your work. Make sure you get a decent price on the house. Vote Labour."

"Good-bye," said my father. "I'm sorry if you think I didn't love you enough, but I always had my hands full with your mother. So you see," he added, grasping her tightly, "nothing is any different from the way it's always been. Do you understand?"

My mother had her arms wrapped around my father's neck, and they were smiling into each other's young face.

She laughed.

And then my father carried my mother over the threshold of this world into the next.

Lunachick

In the bar at the Fess Hotel, where a young professional crowd hung out and met one another without quite being on the prowl—so that if you just wanted to sit and talk with someone without its going any farther, that was okay—she met an assistant D.A. named Manny Durkheim. She thought a man should be like a poem. He should have an interesting image and be musical in a way, and maybe he was easier to fall in love with if you didn't altogether understand him.

He asked her out for Saturday night but he couldn't believe he was going to go out with a woman with a purple streak in her hair. He hit his forehead with the heel of his palm and said, "I can't believe I'm doing this."

"Me, either," she said.

"What I mean is, I never met anybody like you before. You're so sophisticated."

If you wanted it to go farther, that was okay, too.

She had driven herself home through drifting snow, a white curtain blowing past her headlights as if the sky were sighing, the sky-god's breath clouding on the mirrory cold air. Her front-door key was like an icicle in her hand. She waited for the cat to come back in and then she went upstairs to undress in the bedroom for which she still needed to buy a real bed. This was *her* house! Her *house*! She climbed into flannel pajamas. Falling asleep on the futon, Zora Neale Cat in a crook of her arm like a small bundle she was toting on her journey into the elsewhere that dreams are, she thought about how Manny Durkheim had

such long lashes it had seemed as if they would get tangled up whenever he blinked—which he'd done a lot because he couldn't believe
what he was doing—but instead met in a swift fluttery kiss and parted
as his eyes opened wide again.

Then her own eyes closed, and she fell into sleep like falling into a
ravine.

In the morning, still in her pajamas, treating herself gently because
she was soft with sleep and unhardened against the day, she made real
coffee and drank a cup while she read the Midwest edition of the *New
York Times,* and then she poured herself a second cup and went back
upstairs, to her study. She set the blue cup down on the desktop and
pulled the application form toward her. The blue of the cup was cobalt,
a color that seemed to pulse like a heartbeat. It seemed to throb like
a headache. It seemed to give off a dangerous molecular shine, radio-
active rays. For a moment, she stared at the first question, feeling stupid with early-morning desire—for the money, for Manny.

She stared out at the Norwegian spruce in the backyard—the backyard was the real reason she had bought this particular house—and
waited, as if the answer might light on one of those evergreen
branches. As if it might already be there, cleverly camouflaged against
people like her who would hunt for it.

Q. Please describe your project briefly. It always struck her as rude,
this question that the application inevitably began with. It was the most
personal question she could think of. Do you have orgasms? How do
you feel about oral sex? What are you going to think about for the next
six months?

What concepts do you plan to be intimate with?

She liked to live with her ideas, get used to them the way you were
used to your own family, before she introduced them to other people.

There was a beginning period when she still felt shy around her own
idea. Or the idea still felt shy around her, and she had to be careful not
to intrude upon its sense of privacy. After you got to know it better,
after you'd had a few dates with it and maybe a makeout session or
two, then you could take it along with you to a party, see how your
friends reacted to it.

And she was attracted to such strange ideas. "Jasmine," her mother
had written, in the cramped arthritic penmanship that made Jazz wince
to read it, "I don't know where you get these ideas."

"I don't either, Mother," she'd written back, her disingenuousness a form of obstinacy that had been the only way she could figure out to live her own life. "I guess they're just attracted to *me*." She replied more or less the same way whenever her mother asked her why she wasn't married yet.

Jazz thought about her mother living alone back East in the small co-op decorated with too many spider plants, a kind of social security of photosynthesis on the Upper West Side, that she'd bought when she retired and moved out of Ithaca. "You can *have* affirmative action," her mother said when she retired, "but I'm ready for some negative action. Like snoozing past nine in the morning!" A former dean's-secretary with a streak of purple in her personality, a divorcée for so many years that, she liked to say, she often forgot *she* had ever been married. Whenever her mother said this, Jazz felt an obscure hurt, as if she'd been subtly attacked, but her mother accused her of being "overly sensitive."

"I guess it's what makes you an artist," her mother would say, something mildly sarcastic in her tone, "but you really shouldn't let it interfere with your *life*."

But her mother's life had come down to this: shuttling back and forth in a special bus between that small apartment and the hospital. Sometimes Jazz felt guilty about having moved so far away, and then she had to remind herself that it was better for both of them to be apart.

A. I plan to hire two students as backup doo-wop girls. Wearing a motorcycle chain around my neck and a discreetly large metal cross over my pubis, I plan to portray in my own person the bondage in which Western religion traditionally has held women. I will call my group Heavy Irony.

She thought about Manny Durkheim. She could add a couple of Stars of David to her costume, she thought.

Q. What preparation have you made?

"If you were smart," her mother had said, making it plain that she wasn't, "you'd take typing." In college, she kept changing her major. As an English major, she had written poetry and worn mock turtleneck sweaters. As a drama major, she had memorized poetry and made up her eyes. As an art major, she dripped paint onto canvas and went to bed, for the first time, with her boyfriend.

"You could move in with me," Hoyt had proposed, his voice pleading and accusatory at the same time, as if he were already angry with her for saying no although she had not said anything yet. "I mean, if you wanted to, I wouldn't mind."

She was at his place, the Sunday papers spread around her on the floor like a skirt of newsprint. He was a creative writing instructor, a fourth-year graduate student at Cornell. He was writing a novel, and every time he read about someone younger than he publishing a book, he became deeply depressed and went to the movies. He would go to the one o'clock show, he had admitted, and not come home till after eleven. This was how he experienced creative despair.

He wanted an answer. He expected an answer. He wrapped his hands around her ankles, like manacles. She felt her veins pulsating under his grip.

"You have a roommate," she pointed out, a little embarrassed that Raphael so clearly had been told to find somewhere else to spend the weekend. Jazz was sure that Raphael secretly hated her: He smiled at her too brightly.

Raphael had teeth as white as gesso, and he was so beautiful that Jazz always felt a bit abashed around him, humbled as if before a masterpiece in a museum.

"Rafie wouldn't mind."

She didn't know whether he meant that Raphael would move out or that he would make room for her. She was afraid to ask.

Q. Don't you think it's a bit strange that you've been living with a guy for four years?

A. If I were living with a woman, would you feel like moving in?

She had been completely unprepared for the telephone call that had come only a month after she had gotten her job here in the Midwest. (She never thought of it as Wisconsin, not yet. It was undifferentiated, a state by any other name, a huge farm in the middle of America, surrounded by malls. Or a huge mall in the middle of America, surrounded by farms—she was not sure which.) "You would like her," Hoyt said. "She's a lot like you in some ways."

"Really?" she asked the telephone, thinking that her heart was like a mall in the middle of her body, a place where people came to try things on without having to buy them. "Does she think about the same things? Does she feel the same way about oral sex?"

A. I have bought contraceptives. I have prepared myself for every emergency, every contingency. I have laid in supplies of drinking water and flashlight batteries. I have purchased a Radon Testing Kit, though I am afraid to use it because if the radon levels are high I can't afford to do anything about it. I have made a pilgrimage to Graceland. I have shaved my legs. If necessary, I will buy a gas mask.

Saturday night the temperature was subzero. She had bought a little heated house—a cathouse!—and put it on the front porch, and Zora Neale seemed content to curl up inside it, but suppose the house got *too* hot and her fur caught on fire? Suppose her tail got itself lit like a wick and the flame ran right up Zora Neale, turning cat into candle? Jazz reached inside the little house and pulled Zora Neale out, fluffy and warm, a purring mitten. So Jazz was standing there, holding her cat, realizing that she would never dare to leave Zora Neale in the little house unless she was there to keep an eye on her, which meant Jazz either had to sleep on the front porch in subzero weather, which was stupid, or bring the cathouse inside the real house, which was also stupid, or let Zora Neale sleep on the futon, which was where Zora Neale had been sleeping up till now anyway. If her department knew what her life was really like, she thought, she would never get tenure.

"Are we taking the cat with us?" Manny Durkheim asked, appearing on the step.

The movie was about a woman pretending to have an orgasm in a restaurant. It was a form of oral sex.

He reached for her hand and held it. The last man she'd gone to a movie with had leaned into her and said, "Do you want to hold hands?"

A. *If you have to ask, you don't know.*

"So," Manny said, later, walking her to the door. She felt as if she were being put back into her cathouse for the night.

"Thank you for the evening," she said, giving him her hand again, this time to shake.

"You're very welcome," he said, shaking it. His lashes were like little dancers, a *pas de deux* danced on the spotlighted stage of each eye. She felt as if she were being twirled around and around. "I can't believe I'm doing this," he said, and he kissed her.

What didn't he believe, she wondered, the handshake or the kiss?

She kissed him back.

She had bought this particular house, a white frame house with dark red trim on the front door and windows, because the backyard made her think of her childhood in Ithaca. There was no grass in the back-yard, because of the shade the tree cast and the needles it shed. Wild-flowers, with the secret glee of survivors, sprouted next to the garage and along the back fence, and in the summer, when she moved in, there had been shy violets and tiny assertive forget-me-nots creeping around the back of the house. Birds nested and sang in the tree, and she nested and sang in her house. The scent of evergreen and shadow, deep and stirring, carried her back to Cascadilla Gorge, where she had spent many hours alone or with the playmates of her imagination, who had more or less become the personae of her performance art.

Q. How many people will participate in your project?

One time, she had hired male students to be her backup, and then she'd called herself Susannah and the Elders. (Even though the elders were younger.) She thought she might do a piece called The Three Faces of Evil (Hussein, Gorbachev, Bush).

Q. Does your project require the use of animals?

Zora Neale leapt up on the desk and curled up next to Jazz's coffee cup. The cat and the cup made a study in black and blue, they were black and blue in the study, the portrait of a bruise, study of a bruise.

A brown study.

Jazz had a distant memory of her father hitting her mother, or it could have been her mother hitting her father. Maybe it wasn't hitting; maybe it was only yelling. Maybe it wasn't a memory but a dream.

She must have been very small, whether it happened or she only dreamed it happened. It was a memory that came from the time when she used to pick wildflowers in the gorge, violets and forget-me-nots and dandelions, and sell them to Cornell students for a nickel a bunch. She had been a scrawny child with eyes almost as black as Zora Neale, a flower child from the streets. "They probably think I starve you!" her mother said. "You're such a little con artist."

She could still feel her mother's fingers pressing into the soft under-side of her arms, pinching, making dents of paleness that she looked at later in the bathroom mirror, raising her hands as if somebody were robbing her. But her mother was glad to have the money from the flow-ers anyway.

Something moved in the tall tree, a wing, or a forked tail, like a whiskbroom sweeping dry needles to the ground.

Q. What is your timeline?

Her timeline! The very thought made her breathless. She sometimes woke up in the middle of the night—it was a sort of detour on the long journey each night forced her to make—her face slick with the sweat of anxiety, her heart repeating itself like a machine gun. When she woke up like this, she would be thinking, Not yet! I'm not ready to die yet! Please! She had never told anyone this.

But suppose she woke up in the middle of the night and Manny was beside her. Suppose he stroked her hair and told her she had nothing to worry about. Suppose he told her that he would protect her.

Would she believe him?

And her timeline, well, her timeline had wandered through months and years of cohabitation with no one but herself, her ideas. You could go a little crazy, living alone.

You could go a little crazier, living with someone.

A timeline was like a river cutting through a ravine, a gorge. Sooner or later the landscape would flatten, the river would spread itself out like milk in a saucer, it would slow and widen into dreamy circles of itself.

He surprised her by turning out to be shy in bed, or maybe he was just profoundly untheatrical. "You have to get used to the idea that you're the kind of man who could find himself in bed with a woman like me," she reminded him.

It was already morning. Cold light was breaking into the room, a burglar stealing the night away.

He grew angry, the back of his neck red as the University of Wisconsin. She thought it was so interesting the way white skin was like a palette, the color-wheel whirl of it. He sat up and reached for Zora Neale, and when he spoke he seemed to be talking more to her cat than to her. "I'm not the kind of man who anything," he said to the cat. "And you're a woman like yourself, nobody else. I'm the one man in the world in bed with the one woman in the world who is you." He turned, and set Zora Neale down on top of Jazz's head. And this seemed, to Jazz, actually to make a kind of sense, that she should have a hat that was a cat. "It makes you look Russian," Manny said.

She was sure, though, that he would break it off with her the first time he saw her do her act.

When he sat in an auditorium and viewed her 1950's bullet breasts, when he watched her do the Gaza Strip Tease.

When he listened to her one-woman rendition of "The Martin Luther Kingston Trio."

When he caught her impersonation of Ross Perot. "Government of you people, by you people, and for you people!"

When he watched her perform the piece called "Hack Writers!" in which, taking her title as a directive, she slashed a photograph of Bret Easton Ellis, chopped a copy of Ellis's latest book into bits. Ashes to ashes, pulp to pulp.

Observed her newest skit: "Cybersuck, or Vampires with Laptops."

And when he heard her recite her dramatic poem. It was titled "A Psychological Profile of Women in the Arts: *Lunachicks?*"

How was Manny Durkheim to be expected to deal with any of this?

"You have so many ironies in the fire. Do you know what an assistant D.A. *does?*" he asked her. She shook her head. Zora Neale had leapt away, sitting on the bookshelf like a figurine. "Well, of course part of the time what an assistant D.A. does is drag into court the deadbeats who refuse to pay child support. But look, a lot of the time I'm trying to help children who've been molested by their parents. We try to figure out what's the best living arrangement for them. We try to get rapists to agree to HIV testing."

"Have you been tested?" she asked, realizing she should have asked this the night before. This was the question you had to ask in these days of the decline and fall of the Roman Empire.

"Don't think I'm easily shocked," he said. "I'm not."

Snow sifted past her study window, white roses planting themselves on the evergreen branches, on the decaying wooden trellis a previous owner had left in the backyard, on the garage, the fence. She was thinking how easily shocked she was. She supposed it was the source of all her work—that sense of shock, that awful feeling, located somewhere in the pit of her stomach, or behind her eyes, a place behind the eyes where you *felt* what you saw, which was that things, everything, all things, were really, really shocking. She thought it was possible that she had spent her entire life in a state of shock and that that was why reviewers so often found her work shocking.

My whole backyard, she thought, *has blossomed into snow, one huge flower of frost.*

But no, the feeling was located in the pit of her stomach. It had been there ever since the year after her father left, when her mother tried to make her eat the bowl of cream of wheat. All that whiteness, blossoming on the table, that snowy cereal, it had blinded her, it made her feel sick and dizzy. "Hurry up and eat your breakfast," her mother had said, shrugging her arms into a thrift-shop wool coat.

Then, her mother did not have arthritis, or anything else. If she wanted to, her mother could dance her way through the apartment. Her young mother could do any dance anybody had ever thought up. She could slip a sock onto her chin and say, "Now who do I remind you of!" and Jasmine could shriek, "Daddy!" and her mother could say, "I think I'll shave this beard *off*" and yank the sock off and throw it in the hamper and Jazz would try to decide whether she was supposed to laugh or cry. It was not always easy to know which was expected of her.

"What's gotten into you?" her mother hissed. "If you're not going to eat your breakfast, you can have it for lunch," she said, snatching the bowl away.

At lunchtime, Jazz home from school and her mother home from work, the bowl was brought out from the refrigerator, but now the cream of wheat looked even uglier, looked left over. Jazz dipped a spoon into it but she just couldn't get the spoon past her lips. She tried, but her mouth seemed to have gotten locked, and her hand was on the outside of her mouth without a key to it, only the spoonful of blizzardy cream of wheat, like melting snow.

"I don't know what you think we're made of around here," her mother said, "but it's not money. You're not going to get another thing to eat until you eat that bowl of cream of wheat."

The bowl of cream of wheat at dinner.

At breakfast again.

At lunch again.

Dinner again.

Again, again, again! The third night, Jazz's stomach had stopped hurting from hunger. She felt like she didn't care if she never ate anything again in her life, but she didn't want to die and she thought maybe she would if she was never allowed to eat something else. She stayed awake as late as she could. When the apartment was dark and the only sound was the refrigerator humming, she sneaked out of bed and slipped down the hallway to the kitchen, sliding her hands along the wall in the dark. She kept feeling as if she was going to faint. She opened the refrigerator. The light from the tiny refrigerator bulb seemed as bright as the light of the first day, when God said, "Let there be light." Peering into the refrigerator, Jazz remembered that when she'd first learned to open the door she had opened it again and again, trying to catch the light being off. The bowl of cream of wheat was on the top shelf. She pulled a chair from the table over to the refrigerator and climbed up and got the bowl of cream of wheat, carrying it carefully with both hands over to the garbage can. She was about to tip the contents of the bowl into the paper bag lining the can when her mother flicked on the overhead light. *Please,* she thought, *don't let there be light.*

Her mother didn't say anything. Not a word. She took the bowl from Jazz's hands and set it on the table. In the bright overhead light, the cream of wheat looked yellowish, as if it were as sick as Jazz felt, as if it were jaundiced. Her mother moved the chair back to the table and placed a spoon beside the bowl of cream of wheat. Then her mother crossed her arms and stood there, waiting for Jazz to eat. And Jazz did. Jazz finished and said, "May I be excused?"

"You may think you're going to throw that up. Well, think again, young lady," her mother cautioned her.

She fell asleep as fast as she could so she wouldn't think about how much she wanted to gag. She dreamed about the *gorge*—didn't that make a Freudian kind of sense? She dreamed she was falling into it, falling and falling and falling. She always remembered this dream as vividly as if she had had it the night before. She was falling through forever, and the one good thing about that was she never hit bottom.

"Have you ever noticed," she asked Manny, "how you can tell how old someone is by who was starving while they weren't eating everything on their plates when they were kids?"

"The Cambodians," he said.

"My mother said her mother used to tell her it was the Armenians."

"So," he said, looking her squarely in the eye. "Who do you think we'll be telling our kids it is?"

"I can't believe you're doing this," she said.

"It could be anyone," he said. "My God, it could be so many."

Zora Neale had taken to sleeping in the heated cathouse, which Jazz had brought in and moved to the study. Zora Neale curled up inside it like an unraveled ball of yarn winding itself back up, and when Jazz, having done one more morning's work, pulled her out, the paws tucked under like miniature muffs and eyes like little suit pockets that had yet to be slit open, her fur was as warm as a welcome.

While Zora Neale slept, Jazz scoured the tree in back for answers to the application form. *Q. What steps do you plan to take to bring your work to the public?*

A. I will be videotaped by Public Access Television. She would make herself publicly accessible. Some might say she might as well be living in a cathouse.

A senator or two would certainly say that. What would an assistant D.A. say?

Q. How will this grant enable you to strengthen or develop your talents?

But what were they, her talents? An ability to localize theme in her own person, self-dramatization or, conversely, the ability to renounce her individual self for the sake of a political message. Her talent, when you got right down to it, was for propaganda. And what was propaganda if not the forfeiture of individuality in the name of something else—even, in this day and age, the name of individuality? Sometimes it made her want to tear her hair out, purple streak and all, this knowing that what she was doing was performance *life*. She had submerged herself in symbolism. She *was* her symbol. Her self she had left behind long ago, abandoning the child, that child hungry for love, in Ithaca, to the budding performer in New York City, to the tenure-track teacher—*Have curriculum vitae, will travel*—in Madison, Wisconsin. And Madison, cold as it was, had been like a housecat, warm as a welcome, responsively purring. Even the senior members of her department, who had been resistant to the idea of performance art—*Is it art? Is it even performance?*—had surrendered, because it would not have been politically correct not to. In short, this grant would help her to promote herself, in more ways than one.

No, there were no answers in the tree. There was a tiara of ice-diamonds glittering in the tree's hair, but there were no answers. She fixed herself a cup of coffee and read the *Times,* and she thought about calling Manny at work but she was afraid to—he might think she was dependent on him. And she thought about calling her mother but she was afraid to—her mother might think she was dependent on *her.*

It was like radon: You might be dependent on someone but you didn't want to know that you were, because the cost of doing something about it was too high.

When she got tenure, she thought her mother would be gratified, but her mother hardly seemed to notice. She had thought that her mother, the former dean's-secretary, would be pleased by her daughter's academic success, but it turned out that this meant nothing to her—at least, not now. What mattered to her mother now was that Jazz was living halfway across the country. Her mother would have liked for her to drop everything, quit her job, and come live with her. Jazz told herself she would fly to New York for her mother's birthday. She could do that, she told herself, thinking it was strange how what was important one day turned out to be not at all important a few days, or a lifetime, later. But she had wanted her mother to be impressed!

She went to a faculty meeting, which was held in a large, austere room with uncushioned stacking chairs, and when she got home, Manny called. "It still startles me to realize that we all look like grownups," she told him, about the meeting. She wanted him to think she was witty and observant. She wanted him to understand that she was a responsible, economically capable working woman, with or without a purple streak. In her mind, she was still five years old. "At least the others do. They were all wearing suits and high heels."

"The same people?" he asked.

He was right: The department was full of responsible, economically capable working women. The younger women had huge leather handbags, and prescription sunglasses that they wore even in the winter. The older women wore Phi Beta Kappa keys. The older women, Jazz thought, looking at them and comparing them with her mother, were not women with a purple streak in their personality. But then, unlike her mother, they had not grown up in a shack on the outskirts of town, the windowpanes taped, the front yard pure dirt in summer, mud in winter, a perennial eyesore. *My father kept a dog on a chain,* her mother had said to her. *The chain reached to the ditch in front of the house. The dog was always hungry, and mean-tempered in his hunger. Think of that dog when you don't want to eat your breakfast, why don't you.* They were also probably not women who came home from the dean's office one day and donated all the furniture in the apartment to Good Will, sudden as that, face splitting wide open in a smile as if her face were a log that someone had taken an ax to. That abyss of a smile had looked to Jazz like a ravine, a gorge. Her mother had hunkered on the floor of the empty living room, her arms clasped around her knees, rocking and laughing.

"Where's your spirit of fun?" her mother used to ask. "Where's your sense of adventure?"

Or she would sneer and say, "You little spoilsport. Why can't you *act* like you're happy?"

There were children in the neighborhood who invited Jazz to play with them: Marly, Juanita, a girl named Priscilla whom they called Popsicle. Her mother wanted to join in. "Don't be such a fuddy-duddy!" her mother chided Jazz, her eyes as round as money. Her mother was tall, and when she leaned down to talk to Jazz, Jazz was afraid the money would fall out and roll along the floor. "I swear, Jasmine, sometimes I think *you're* the old one and *I* am the one who knows how to enjoy life." Juanita explained to Jazz's mother that they were playing hide-and-seek. "You can be It," Juanita offered, generously. Jazz's mother pressed her forehead against the side of the cement building, her eyes squeezed shut and her hands blinkering the sides of her face, just like a little girl, and counted to one hundred. When she opened her eyes, the children were gone, hidden in a doorway, behind a parked car, behind a trash can in an alley. One by one she ferreted them out, Marly, Juanita, Popsicle, each little girl shrieking and squealing as she raced for "home."

Jazz watched them from the beauty salon next door to the apartment building. This was one of their favorite hiding places, and she was certain her mother would look there soon. She sat down in one of the waiting chairs, her feet not reaching the floor, and looked at pictures in the styling magazines. Permanent lotion and hair straightener made the salon smell like a laboratory, and Jazz began to scare herself, thinking maybe it *was* a laboratory, maybe her mother had let her stay there on purpose and soon someone would come out and take her into the back room and start to do experiments on her. It was getting dark outside, the cars had turned on their headlights, and she was getting even scareder, so she put the magazine down and went home. The trouble she had walking up the stairs! Her feet dragged, and when she'd get one foot on a step, the next one would refuse to follow until she sighed heavily, and then she could lift that foot but the other one didn't want to budge. Finally she got to the top, and sighing one more time and squaring her shoulders, she walked into the apartment. "Gotcha!" her mother said, springing at her from the kitchen. "You're It!"

Jazz wanted to cry but she seemed to have forgotten how. Crying was like long division, she thought, easy if you did it a lot but really hard if you didn't.

"I knew you'd have to come home sometime," her mother said. "I didn't need to go looking for *you*. Admit it now. Aren't I the clever one?"

A. *Mother, you are so clever that you knew from the beginning how to break my heart, how to make me love and hate you at the same time. Now you are old, even older than you should be at your age, as if you ran through all your energy—that enormous fortune or misfortune— too quickly, and your hands are curled up like little paws and your eyes are like empty pockets and your black skin is as wrinkled and worn as if it were moth-eaten fur or wool, and I wonder if the cobalt treatments will help, if anything will help. Yes, Mother, you are the smart one, you are the everything one, you are the only one, the only parent in the world.*

"I knew you'd have to come home sometime," her mother said, when Jazz had taken off her prescription sunglasses and put them away in her huge leather handbag, which she set down on the floor next to her small suitcase. She bent down to hug her mother. When had her mother shrunk so? Jazz felt like Alice grown miles taller than everything around her, a skyscraper casting her metropolitan shadow over this little tarpaper shack of a woman. She felt as if she had put her mother in the shade, but all she had ever meant to do was make her mother proud of her.

"Hi, Mom," she said. "Happy birthday."

Q. *How can you say that? Maybe this is the last birthday I'll ever see!*

A. *What else can I say? What could I ever say?*

This was a bad business, Jazz thought, answering questions with questions, even if it was in your own mind.

"I bought a cake," her mother said, and Jazz thought her mother's eyes were like candles, lighting up her dark face.

They made a sort of birthday party, the two of them, and the next day some of her mother's friends from in the building stopped by to meet Jazz. They told her mother what a pretty daughter she had, but they added, speaking about her in the third person, "Why does she wear that purple streak in her hair?"

"She's an artist," her mother answered. "Artists are different from you and me. More *au courant*."

When she heard her mother saying this, Jazz felt her heart beat faster, the way your heart speeds up when someone you have loved from a distance pays you a compliment. You think that the world will be changed, now. You think that this is just the beginning. She went into the bathroom and closed the door and did a quick little two-step, a short but snappy shuffle and slide. She was dancing to the bongo beat of her heart, that old rhythm-and-blues.

That evening, when all the friends had come and gone, her mother said, "I don't see why you have to wear that purple streak in your hair."

"I thought you liked it!" Jazz cried, and it was as if the words had fled from her throat, refugees from the prison camp where, for so long, they had been kept under lock and key. "I thought you—" *Liked me,* she wanted to say, but the last two words stayed behind, having grown so accustomed to the routine of prison life that they shied from freedom.

"Oh, well," her mother said, "what I like or don't like doesn't matter, does it? Not anymore."

"Of *course* it matters," Jazz said. And she chastised herself for forgetting that it was her mother's feelings that were what counted now.

"In that case," her mother said, "I wish you would get rid of it."

Jazz felt outwitted. All her life, she realized, she had felt outwitted.

It was a shock to find yourself outwitted, and that was why she had always been in a state of shock.

Shocked and outwitted.

"Being black is different enough," her mother explained. "There's no need to go being the color purple on top of being black."

After her mother had gone to bed, Jazz lay on the couch in the living room, which was where she was sleeping, and looked at the lights in the building across the street. There were so many plants in the apartment that it was like looking at the stars through treetops. She thought about how much she would miss her mother when she died—for she would miss her, her mother who had struggled so to see that her daughter got an education, her mother who knew that they were not made of money, her mother who was jealous of her daughter for being her daughter—but then she thought that her mother would simply be moving farther away, and the part of her that had been strong enough to rescue herself from her past reminded her that that would be *better for both of them.* Part of her wanted to cry, but she seemed to have forgotten how. *I've always been terrible at long division, too,* she thought. She tried to remember the time her father had hit her mother, or her mother had hit her father, or she had dreamed her father hitting her mother, or maybe it had only been somebody yelling, but no matter how hard she tried, the memory stayed out of sight, in some corner of her mind, playing hide-and-seek. She tried to remember whether her father had left because of the way her mother was or whether her mother had become the way she was after her father left. There was a timeline there, a river cutting through a ravine, but whenever she tried to follow it, it spread itself out like milk in a saucer, it slowed and widened into dreamy circles of itself, and she fell asleep. In her dream, the river was made of tears, and forget-me-nots grew along the banks.

The next day, heading downstairs to catch a cab to the airport, she said to her mother, "Do you remember the wildflowers?"

"I was so scared," her mother said. "I thought everyone would know how poor we were. I was afraid Welfare might take you away from me."

"I'll call you," Jazz said, holding her mother's hand but being careful not to squeeze it, because of the arthritis.

"You don't need to act," Manny whispered, after sex. "You don't need to pretend. Tell me what's really going on."

It made her want to cry, his telling her she didn't need to act. He was so generous!

Then she *was* crying, her tears, a river of them, matting the hair on his chest. "I don't know what's going on," she explained. "I've always been this way. I've been underground my whole life. It's like I'm frozen." But she had never before slept with a man who would touch his forehead to hers in a Vulcan mind-meld! He liked to touch her eyelashes with his. He called this an eyelash-kiss. "The truth is," she confessed, ashamed, "I wouldn't recognize an orgasm if it walked up to me. I think I don't even know what's real and what's not." And she cried some more, a higher mathematics of weeping.

"Sure you do," he said, patting her back as if he were burping her. "If you didn't, you wouldn't be such a good actress. You'd just be a realist, like me, and you'd never have dyed your hair purple." He sighed and said, "We're going to be fine, just as soon as you stop seeing things in black and white. But there's no rush. We're not on a schedule here. There's no timeline." Then he fell asleep. He always fell asleep after sex, as if sex were a sleeping pill, a Mickey Finn.

She slept in the crook of his arms, feeling like a small bundle being carried away somewhere.

She and Manny had bought a bed, a real bed. Zora Neale slept with them because Jazz had read that electromagnetic fields could be dangerous; the heated cathouse had been carried off by the trash collectors, who had needed an extra five dollars before they would take it. Now when Jazz woke up in the middle of the night, Manny never stroked her hair and said he would protect her, because he slept through everything. In the stagy light of the reading lamp, Jazz watched his long lashes tremble, as if they were wildflowers and a breeze had touched them, wondering what dream was passing through his sleeping head, what country he was passing through in his dream. He slept through Jazz's anxiety attacks—she had awakened from a dream, or nightmare, of an application form that had asked, *Where Do We Come From? What Are We? Where Are We Going?*—and also Zora Neale's obsessive relocations from the foot of the bed to the head of the bed to the middle of the bed. In the morning, Jazz made real coffee, and Manny drank a cup of it before he went to his office in the courthouse. One day, shortly after he had pulled out of the driveway and she had settled herself in the study to work on the script for Heavy Irony, with funding by the Arts Board, the telephone rang; it was her mother.

"You're still with Manny?" her mother asked, but Jazz knew that what her mother was really asking was, "Manny's still with you?" And there was no answer to this, either, at least not any answer she could make without reminding her mother that she, unlike her daughter, had been a deserted wife.

"Mom? How are you?"

Jazz looked out the window at the tree, which was as white as the ghost of everything past. There was more snow coming down. In Wisconsin, there would always be more snow coming down.

"I was just wondering if you're happy out there," her mother said, loneliness in her voice like an ache, like pain, like a disease no one had ever found a cure for. And Jazz, whose heart, though she may not have known it, was always like something unfunded and free, brave as *samizdat,* gave the performance of her life, *for* life.

"Oh, Mother!" Jazz said, lightly, and with only a modicum of irony. "I've got everything I want. I've got my work, Manny, a house, tenure. Even the grant. What a question!"

Your Chances of Getting Married

Sleep with a slice of wedding cake under your pillow, they say, *and you'll get married,* but there was that study to prove what I already knew, that I had a better chance of being killed by a terrorist, and besides, I had reached a point in my life where I was more worried about crumbs than husbands.

Actually, I sometimes thought they were the same thing.

So when my child and I got home from Rajan and Lucy's wedding, I put our share of the wedding cake in transparent bags in the freezer compartment. I didn't think to thaw it out until a year later, when I was rummaging around for something we could nibble on our way to the Merchants' Parade, an annual civic event involving floats and State Street sales. It kept just fine, because underneath the frosting, it was carrot cake. Almost all cake in Madison is carrot cake. I think there's a city ordinance that says it has to be this way. This would make sense, because our mayor, who was a hippie the first time he was mayor, years ago, this time around is retro hippie, and retro hippies all eat carrot cake. Carrot cake is brownies for the nineties.

There are no cars allowed on State Street, and the buses were on strike, so, as we made our way from the bookstore at the bottom of State to the Square at the top, Tavy and I were eating our respective slices of the wedding cake in the middle of the road, which is where the Beatles had once said they wanted to "do it."

Actually, the Beatles had apparently been willing to do it anywhere in the road. It was the Pretenders who, in a postmodern Reaganite reference, specified the middle of the road.

I was neither a hippie nor a retro hippie, being a single mother, but I knew about rock lyrics because every year my poetry students tried to persuade me that Bob Dylan was a Provençal poet. That Bruce Springsteen had heard America singing, and that Madonna was poetry in motion. (For the found-poem assignment, one student brought in a news item about Madonna with the heading "TAKES DIDDLE ACT ON THE ROAD.")

Actually—one of the more pedantically precise of my students told me—it had been Paul McCartney alone who sang that particular Beatles song. Paul sang, played the drums, everything, but he and John Lennon had an agreement that every song either of them did would be officially "by" both of them.

It was a traditional marriage.

All along State, and on the streets squaring the capitol, people were waiting for the parade to begin. Some of these people were my students, or my former students. They had written papers I had read, papers in which they achieved an accidental brilliance. They wrote notes that they slid under my door, to explain why their papers were late. *I guess I'm just going through a phrase,* one student had written, making my heart beat faster, a teacher's kind of love. *We live,* wrote another, in a paper about modernist poetry, or perhaps about life in Madison, *in a world of allusions.* The students like their life here so much that after they take their degrees they are inclined to become cab drivers, or waitpersons at local fern bars, instead of going out into the real world. But not all of the people were students. Some of them were bikers, because Madison is also the home of a national motorbike convention every summer. The bikers ride through the streets in wide, stampeding herds, like buffalo. But on State Street, even the bikers were pedestrians. They wore biking boots and leather wrist bands, as if ready to ride at a moment's notice. It occurred to me that it was a little odd that all these bikers would turn out for a Merchants' Parade, but then what did I know about bikers.

Finally, some of the people were taxpayers like myself.

Among this last group were Rajan and Lucy, whom I saw holding hands as they peered into the window of Tellus Mater, gazing romantically at Danish cookware. They had a new home to furnish, a house they'd bought on the east side, a typical east-side Victorian house with gingerbread trim that if you asked me looked like a breading baked on the griddle of the road.

Rajan is so handsome, even from the back. He doesn't even have a bald spot on the back of his head, and most men I know now have at least a bald spot in the back. I know men who are considering plug transplants. I know men who hold a magnifying mirror to the back of their head and reflect their bald spot into a magnifying mirror on the wall, hoping the Minoxidil has started to work. When the wind off the lake lifted Rajan's dark hair, it seemed a strangely intimate thing for wind to do, as if nature herself was making love to him. He has the kind of body that can get you to thinking elemental thoughts.

I focused my daughter's attention on something on the other side of the street. If I had been fond of Rajan, she was only now getting over losing him to another woman, and I didn't want her to be upset all over again. It's hard enough to deal with rejection at any age, but when you're only four—

We had made this journey, up State Street to the Square, before, she and I, but she never tired of it—though she frequently tired and demanded to be carried. I looked down to see how she was doing. She had white frosting all over her red lips as if she'd been foaming at the mouth, and her cheeks were like rosettes, and she looked, to tell the truth, a little like a wedding cake, standing there, all sugar and spice, in the middle of the road.

I wiped her face clean with the hem of my skirt and pulled her in the direction of the Puzzlebox. "I'll buy you something," I said, feeling guilty about not having succeeded in getting Rajan to fall in love with me and marry me so she would have him for her daddy. "What do you want?"

"A whistle."

"Why do you want a whistle?" I asked her. "It's one thing you don't need. I promise you, sweetie, one day boys will do the whistling for you." This is the way a single mother sometimes finds herself talking.

"A whistle."

Her scrubbed face looked a bit like a whistle, scrunched and clean as. I bought her a silver whistle on a chain and hung it on her neck. "I don't want you to blow this until we get home," I said.

Actually, I knew more about bikers than most people would suspect. I have a cousin who is five-two and female, but when she goes to a party she carries her party dress in her bike basket and dons her black leather suit with black leather jacket and crash helmet and gets behind the wheel of one big mother of a bike. When she arrives at the party, she changes clothes and puts on heels. You have to give her credit.

For something.

Once, she told me, she was going with a guy named Blake, and he came around to visit while she was doing her wash for the week. They made it on the floor of the laundry room. *It was really great,* she said, *bedding Blake in the middle of the load.*

Tavy stuck the whistle into her mouth but looked at me and when I gave her a hard look back she puffed up her cheeks but she didn't blow. She let the whistle fall onto her chest like a necklace. She was wearing green shorts—her favorite pair—a tube top that kept slipping down since there was nothing to hold it up, and sneakers. Children are so small—we forget how small they are. Jesus Christ, I thought, I used to be that small.

You'd think the world would be careful with its small things, but on the contrary, those are the very things it tends to misplace. Small things are so easily overlooked.

I felt so sad when I thought this, because, well, because. Because whose childhood is happy. And I wanted Tavy's childhood to be so happy that someday she'd look back on it and think, That wasn't so bad! That was even pretty good!

But she would've been happier with a father.

But it had been so long since I'd had a date. And the last date I had had had asked me if I liked to go walking. "Sure," I said, wanting to be outgoing and amicable at the beginning of a relationship. *I can do that,* I was thinking. *I can go for a walk.*

"I like to walk at the mall," he said, "early in the morning. A lot of us do."

I had a vision, then, of mall-walkers, many of them Minoxidil users. I was glad they had a place to walk but I was not yet ready to give up the outdoors, even if the only outdoors I got to these days was State Street. The whiff of dope as we passed Rose Records, the sinuous jangle of Middle Eastern music as we passed Zorba's, the Indian vendor politely peddling pita, the bright colors of sweaters from The Gap, the wind off the lake that smelled of clogged algae but lifted Rajan's hair so suggestively—I was not ready to give up all this for early morning walks at the mall. My date had been a man with plans, all of them free. "I want to take you to Happy Hour at the Bombay Bicycle Club," he

said, expansively. "They have the best free munchies." He had a cou-
pon that would let him get two meals for one at Harper's Club and
Restaurant, which offered free live entertainment and dancing. He said
he was working on an oil deal with some Arabs, and it broke my heart
to look at him as he said this, over the lunch he'd had to pay for, the lie
branching, blossoming there between us on the table like tall artificial
flowers that made it hard for us to see each other over or around, an ob-
fuscation that would cloud our vision of each other forever. Except that
I refused to see him again.

I had tried writing a poem about this experience, making art out of
life, but I had to give it up because I kept getting a headache in the middle of the ode.

My chances of finding a father for my daughter were about as good
as my chances of finding someone to collaborate with.

"Mommy," Tavy said, yanking at my skirt, "I don't want to walk
anymore."

I picked her up but she was getting to be a big girl. Luckily, we were
almost at the Square.

At the top of State Street, in the center of the Square, stands the Wisconsin state capitol building, a truly beautiful building, airy as confec-
tionery—with the qualification that underneath the frosting there is
carrot cake. It is a white wedding cake of a building, though solid and
with a granite dome and, on top, instead of a bride and groom, a statue
of a woman who is usually identified, wrongly, even by longtime residents as Miss Forward—*A very forward miss,* my third-grade teacher
had said to me, making me stay after school—robed Grecianly in gilt.
In fact, her name is Wisconsin, and Miss Forward is one of the other
statues that distinguish the grounds. Roads enter the Square at each of
the four corners and in the center of each of the four sides; the capitol
looks pretty much like a wedding cake in the middle of all these roads.
Marriage of the people, by the people, for the people, I always say, my
populist sentiments running deep, whenever my friends go off on a political tangent at dinner parties.

It had gotten to be noon, and the sun was hot. Wisconsin shone. A
gardener was raking up the grass clippings from the lawn in front of the
capitol. Tavy and I crossed to the inside of the Square and I set her
down on the sidewalk in front of the capitol and shifted my shoulder
bag to the other shoulder. "The floats will come soon," I said. "They'll

come up that street, and turn there, and then come all the way around the Square."

Tavy bolted onto the capitol lawn.

"Tavy! Come back here!" I yelled. She was running around in circles, making airplane wings with her arms, going *Zoom, zoom, zoom.*

I was prepared for almost everything about being a single mother. I was prepared for the way a single mother lives in a state of complete exhaustion all the way through kindergarten. I was prepared for the anxiety and the guilt. I was prepared for financial strain. What I was not prepared for was the embarrassment.

Being a single mother means that you will be embarrassed at least once a day.

I looked left and right from beneath lowered eyelashes, hoping none of my colleagues was nearby. I walked over to Tavy in a kind of casual stroll meant to indicate that no, my child was not deranged, and locking her in a hold that had probably been barred from wrestling matches but smiling and nodding at the gardener in a way that I hoped would mollify him, I dragged her back to the sidewalk. When I looked again at the gardener, I saw our treading raked in the middle of the lawn he had mowed.

I found us a good place to watch from, and we waited for the parade to begin.

Pretty soon, the first float appeared at the top of one of the streets and started to make its way around the Square. Then there was a high-school marching band, and then the mayor rode by in a convertible, waving to everyone. Tavy's eyes were big with amazement; they were like windows that'd been thrown open wide to greet the day. Would she remember this day, when she grew up? Would she remember the day she had seen all the merchants of Madison sail by, a circus of commerce? "Look," I said to her, "there's the bookstore float!" Which was a large, open book surrounded by characters that had stepped off its pages—Sleeping Beauty, and Huck Finn, and Mr. Toad in his wicker garden chair, and, this being a university town, Jay Gatsby in a white linen suit.

"Mommy's book," Tavy said.

"Well, no," I had to say, a bit sadly.

The next float was from the Ovens of Brittany, and it was a work of art. It was a wedding cake, and as it moved down the middle of the road toward us, we could see the tiers perched on white-ribboned posts, the buttercream icing, the delicate embroidery of tiny crystals, coconut flakes sprinkled on the sides, and the sugar champagne roses. It was an extravaganza of a wedding cake, a fantasia of a wedding cake, a completely unnecessary and wonderful thing. There was a golden bell at the top of the cake, and it sent out a tinkly sound as the float rolled by, as if even on a warm day the cake, frosted all over, was cold and shivering just a little.

Most fabulously, there was a waterfall, spilling continuously, in some magical recycling act, into a pool at the base of the cake. There must have been a hydraulic pump inside the middle of the cake. I grabbed Tavy and picked her up so she could get a good look as the cake floated by. There were pennies in the pool, as if they'd been tossed there by the imaginary wedding guests to bring good luck to the imaginary bride and groom.

It was the wedding cake from the middle of which all blessings flowed.

I put Tavy down again—I simply couldn't hold her for very long anymore, and even though there were more floats on the way, none of them was going to be able to match the one we'd just seen. And anyway, it had made me feel lonely, you know, watching that cake go by. I remembered Rajan marrying Lucy and even though I wasn't in love with him, it made me feel lonely.

I must have been drifting fairly far out on my thoughts, because when I looked down to see how Tavy was holding up, she was gone.

Someone has stolen my baby, I thought, *and she will grow up in a trailer on the outskirts of a strange city, the child of weird, lonely people who will make her eat canned spaghetti for dinner, and she won't even remember who she is because she's too young.*

Just then I heard, as if it were a telegram sent straight to me, a cable delivered directly to the address of my anxiously awaiting heart, a sound. The sound of a whistle. The sound of a small silver whistle. *A small thing, misplaced.*

She had somehow gotten to the other side of the street.

As I started to rush toward her, I heard a biker shout, "Someone blew the whistle on us!"

And all the bikers poured into the street, surrounding the float from the Ovens. Several of them linked leather-banded hands and made a kind of fence around the float, which had stopped rolling. Other bikers were pulling the driver out from the car that pulled the float, and when one of them had climbed in behind the wheel, the bikers around the float faded back into the crowd. It was all so fast I felt dizzy, and I worried that I wouldn't get to Tavy before she disappeared again.

"Oh my God, if they're not taking the cake!" someone yelled. "They're hijacking it!"

Tavy was so little that she could lose herself among people's legs. The next thing I knew, she had reemerged farther down the street, nearer the float. She blew the whistle again, and the biker in the car pressed down on the accelerator too hard, and the wedding cake fell off the float into the middle of the road.

There was a moment of hush while we all tried to comprehend this. Then one of the students shouted, his voice rising like a banner unfurled, "Let them eat cake!" and rushed toward the wedding cake in the middle of the road, storming the bakery if not the Bastille, and all the other students followed, but of course it turned out to be, underneath the icing, carrot cake.

The biker ran from the car.

The students, racing for the cake, had knocked over the Indian man's pita stand, and the Indian man was sort of weeping. He wasn't actually weeping, because that wouldn't have been quite polite, I guess, but it was like his whole face was one big tear.

And the biker in the car, going too fast, had hit the float in front of him, causing the book to tip over and close its pages, and the characters to say some words that the National Endowment for the Arts would have rescinded their grants for.

I had almost caught up with Tavy when the biker who'd been driving the car, coming from the opposite direction, ran smack into me. He gripped me in much the same manner as I had gripped Tavy earlier, wheeling around behind me so that I became his hostage, with his tattooed arm around my neck. It had MOTHER stamped on it, in big letters, with a scary red snake in the middle of the O.

This was what I had had a better chance of, I remembered.

"You're fond of your mother, I see," I babbled. "Well, I'm a mother too. I was just looking for my little girl when you appeared on the scene."

"A likely story," he snorted. "Hold still."

Then, just as I was preparing to die, an ex-writing student who had heard the words "a likely story" from too many editors—*Your story seems likely to find a home somewhere, but alas, not with us,* they scribbled on their rejection slips—tore the biker's arm from around me and I hollered a "Thanks!" over my shoulder and he called back, "No problem! Piece of cake!" and I remembered then that I had always had to chide him for his clichés, but thanks to him I was free, free to dart after my daughter, who was still racing ahead, in the direction of the Indian vendor. She was stopped in her tracks by a man of could-be-forty-five-could-be-fifty-it-depended-on-how-you-read-the-lines-in-his-face in a dark open-necked shirt and blue jeans, who held her kindly by both thin, bare shoulders. I was out of breath when I got to her. "Doesn't it just kill you," he said, thrusting his splendidly pedagogical chin—the kind of chin that is so nicely defined that it leads you to believe that its owner could define almost anything, even make sense of your own life—out at the road, "the way students are always so eager to decon-struct a text? Critics never understand that *art* is real and *meaning's* the dreaded fake, a riddle, a code."

"So true," I said, whispering, and looking at his eyes that were as dark as his shirt, and his chest that, whatever the back of his head looked like, needed no Minoxidil. I realized I was in a kind of adrena-line addle, my pituitary gland doing that sacred dance of the hormones, where your hormones more or less skip around in circles while singing "praise be to the god of eros," that it had not done for so long.

"You're breathing too hard," he said. "You should exercise more. Take walks."

"In the mall?"

"The mall? Lord, no," he said, "why would anyone go walking in a mall?"

I had pulled Tavy toward me and held her in front of me, and it was not totally clear to me whether I was shielding her or she was shielding me.

From what?

"You see what trouble you've caused, Tavy!" I scolded her. "I told you that toy was not to be played with until we got home."

"Mommy, for heaven's sake, it wasn't little me that blowed," she said, firmly.

But this man was listening to our family spat. I knelt down and asked Tavy, making my voice low and calm and mature and in control so he would not think I was, oh, for example, an hysteric, "If it wasn't you, *who* blew?"

She furrowed her brows, as if trying hard to remember who had blown the whistle. Finally she remembered. "Mr. Toad," she said, her face unwrinkling, the drawstring pouch of it opening up, generous with explanation.

"I don't think so," I said. "Look."

Mr. Toad, still in his goggles and cap and overcoat, was sitting on the curb, eating cake and mumbling to himself something very like, "O bliss! O poop-poop! O my! O my!"

Oh, dear, I thought, *the wedding cake is now in the middle of the toad.*

The road looked like a battlefield after the battle. I looked at the floats piled in a jumble, the cake in a crumble. The wind had picked up and was sweeping over the smashed confection, and the coconut sides were shedding flakes in the middle of the road.

The man who had rescued my daughter said, "Your daughter seemed to be headed for the Indian vendor. Does she know him?"

"I guess he reminds her of someone," I explained. "Someone she misses." I was still looking at the wreckage spread out in front of us like a dinner table everyone had gotten up from, leaving half-drunk cups of coffee, and leftovers on the dessert plates, and wine standing and souring in the bottoms of glasses. Some of the crystal teardrops, which had been meant to be seen as sort of splashes that the fountain made, I guess, had gotten scattered, and it was as if what was left of the iced cake was pale and weeping, a weeping cake amid all the food. The wind was shredding the cake, its stitchery of crystals coming unsewed. "Why do you think they did it?" I asked, still whispering. I couldn't seem to speak up any louder. It was as if his good looks had snatched my voice away from me.

The three of us stared out at the Square, searching for an answer. As we stared, the mayor hove into view. For sure, he was no longer a radical dreading to take the middle of the road. He had with him the biker who had been behind the wheel, the biker who had had me in his grip. "Hey, folks!" the mayor said. He is that kind of mayor.

We moved forward to hear what he had to tell us.

"This man tells me that his friends wanted the cake because a certain couple of bikers want to get married but they couldn't afford a cake. Should we forgive'm?"

"You bet!" we all cried. We are that kind of town.

With that, all the bikers reappeared, and then, before our eyes, one of them took off her black leather motorcycle suit, and underneath it she was wearing a wedding gown, though from the way the dress stuck up in front, you could see she was going to be one mother of a big biker.

"Do it!" someone said. "Do it in the middle of the road!"

So a minister was found, which was not hard to find because, as I have said, most of the city was there, and he said a few things, and the bikers said their vows, and then the minister pronounced them husband and wife.

We heard sniffling during the service, but afterward, when we looked around, there was no mother of the bride to be seen, only the Indian vendor.

"I am sorry," he said, "but I am a poor man, and I pity my pita."

The mayor went over to him and said, "Here, here, don't get all worked up like this. I feel sure the city will reimburse you for your loss. Just figure it up and tell me what it comes to."

The Indian man smiled, showing teeth like the pearls, anyhow, in the crown. (As well as a few gold crowns.) "Oh yes!" he exclaimed happily. "Oh yes, thank you very much! We will a vetting make of the little we are owed. Thank you very much, honorable mayor, sir!"

By now, it was later in the day, and though the floats that came after the wedding cake float were fine, no one was paying them much attention. The sky was running through its berry shades, raspberry, blueberry, gooseberry and checkerberry, an orchard of colors. A few blocks south, I knew, the sunset would be like strawberry jam a hungry God was spreading on the lake, a vittle to be rowed.

The day was in tatters, the way days are at their ends, frayed, and worn so thin you could see right through it into night. It was not a thing that could be recycled. *How many of these do I have left,* I wondered, hoping that it would still be a very long time before I ran out of them. But nobody had an endless supply, did they, and then, too, some of the people you loved had run out of days already, and each time someone dropped away, out of sight, you realized that your own days were becoming ever more threadbare and that what you were seeing through them, a little more clearly than before, was darkness.

"I guess we ought to be going home," I said to Tavy, knowing that this was a way of saying good-bye to the stranger beside us and not wanting to say good-bye but not knowing what else to say. "You've had a big day. Let's go home and I'll fix you some canned spaghetti for supper."

I turned her around, my backward miss, and we started to go, but I felt like I was leaving someplace important, someplace I'd been to that, if no one kept me there, I'd never get back to.

And I felt like my heart was a cake that had fallen off its float. Not a wedding cake. Just a little cupcake of a heart, the whipped cream of it gone mushy, and no one would ever be tempted by it again.

"Thanks for grabbing hold of my daughter," I said to the stranger as we left.

I ducked my head and started to walk away, hauling a tired Tavy after me. It was rather like towing a little biplane that had run out of gas and sputtered safely to a stop on the ground but now needed to be dragged to the hangar.

"Hey, wait!" he called, and he came running up behind us. "Do you really have to go now?"

"Well, I—" I said, because, plainly, I am often like that, at a loss for words. Not because there aren't enough of them, but because there are so many that sometimes it is difficult to know which ones to use.

"Aren't you Nina Bryant?" he asked.

"Yes," I admitted.

He shook my hand, the one that wasn't holding Tavy's. "I thought so. I recognized you from your picture on the jacket flap. I'm in the history department. It was one of my students who started the revolution this afternoon."

"Nice to meet you," I said.

"I've been wanting to meet you," he said, "because I have an idea I wanted to talk with you about. I thought maybe I could interest you in collaborating with me on something I have in mind."

"You're kidding," I said.

"Also," he said, his eyes looking into mine as if he could see in me something I'd forgotten was there, some small thing I'd overlooked, like marriage, like romance, like a belief in the likelihood of either, all those years when I'd been sternly clearing out the psychological clutter, "I *could* be in love with you."

He just said it, right outright, like that. As if he knew exactly what words he wanted to use.

"We have to go home now," I said, holding Tavy's hand a little tighter. I knew a crazy person when I saw one.

"I know it sounds crazy," he said, looking irrefutably sane.

And I thought of the fact that I had never even slept on my slice of cake but had just put it in the refrigerator freezer and forgotten about it for a year.

I thought, too, of the fact that if I was ever going to get over being scared of men it had better be now, because it really was getting late in the day. Would a man be any *worse* than a terrorist?

"There's no such thing as love at first sight," I said.

"Sure there is."

"Maybe rarely," I conceded. Of course, there were different kinds of love at first sight. I had fallen in love with my daughter at my first sight of her and that was going to last forever. I had fallen in love with my parents at my first sight of them, and that had lasted forever too, all through our lives in America and even after they moved to England for their retirement, taking only the things important to them, like the violin and the china, settling in a little village outside Reading. I had loved them even as I watched them grow old and fragile and cranky, watched their bodies collapse by slow degrees until they could no longer make the trip into London for concerts. They drew up wills; they had letters notarized that said they wanted to be cremated. My mother was somewhat claustrophobic, and she'd always been frightened by stories of clawmarks, fingernail scratches, found on the inside of coffin lids after an earthquake had brought the coffins to the surface. I had followed their instructions to the letter, and when they died, there was no Reading wake, and I'd auctioned off the fiddle and the Spode.

I had fallen in love with my parents at first sight and it had lasted even beyond forever.

So falling in love at first sight *was* possible, and if I could do it, probably anybody else could too, but it didn't happen every day. You had to admit it didn't happen every day. "I mean, come on," I said. I was so confused. He had an attractive rumpled look about him, as if he were a room and needed someone to straighten him up. He had this orderly academic disorder about him, like a house in which there are books and papers stacked on the coffee table and nightstands and spilling over onto the kitchen table and the dining-room table, and next to the dining-room table there is a floor lamp that casts a warm, cozy light to read student poems, student papers by, on into the night.

"Are you okay?" he asked, looking concerned.

"Don't worry about me," I said. "I'll be all right. I'm just going through a phrase." In a world of allusions, he looked like a comfortable place. He looked like a place I could live in for the rest of my life.

"But, I mean, come on! Do you know what your chances of going out for a walk one day and falling in love *are*?"

"Tell me," he said.

Maybe I was shouting, a little bit. Maybe I had recovered my voice. Maybe, you know, a writer's voice just insists on asserting itself no matter what. In the end, it finds the words it's been looking for and says what it has to say. "Well," I said, blurting it out, "your chances of going for a walk and meeting someone and having it be, really be, love at first sight must be just about as good as going out for a walk and—" I stopped.

He was so *sexy*. He was so *Socratic*. "And what?" he said, sexily, Socratically.

"Finding a wedding cake in the middle of the road," I finished, blushing quite like a bride.

How It Goes

At five-thirty I pick up my wife and she says Let's take home Thai. She parks her briefcase on the floor under the glove compartment, her toes on it like a footrest. She's wearing alligator shoes and her legs in stockings look both substantial and definite enough to squeeze and somehow hazy, cloud-hazy, kind of close and far off at the same time, like late afternoon through a screen door, like childhood, it makes me want to cry, but I know I'm just strung out it's been a bitch of a day. I'm just back from Chicago nine inches of rain in twelve hours the streets were like canals like irrigation ditches who am I kidding? like open sewers would be more accurate, the taxicabs like sickly yellow turds, the city suddenly less a city than an insane jumble of rocks at the base of a (what I need now is a long hot shower) waterfall and no sleep for three days while we wooed the boys from Kansas. Oatmeal. I say to her Well we made love to the oatmeal boys and now they're ours how about that and she says Fine that's good I'm glad the trip went well and I don't say a word about the rain but of course she saw it on the news and she says I was worried and I say You were?

She turns to look at me. Her face is like a cookie, cute and sweet, I guess I've got oatmeal on my mind but a child would go crazy with yearning looking up at that face, reach for her like a cookie jar but we don't have kids her career comes first. She's a lawyer. Everyone I know is married to a lawyer. Sometimes it's the husband sometimes the wife.

Of course I was worried she says I saw it on TV and it looked awful. There were people swept away. Whirlpools at intersections.

Tell me about it, I say.

And she closes up the jar of her face and turns to look out the window. This is how it goes.

At Bahn Thai we settle on one pork one chicken, there's beer in the refrigerator. She's still not talking. Neither am I.

The housekeeper has been here today and the place smells of Pine Sol. I keep saying we should get rid of a cat that pees on the couch but she won't hear of it she says the cat is like her child and I say The hell it is and she says I have no heart and I say she might be lacking an organ or two herself the way she carries on about that cat and I have her brain in mind but she thinks I mean she's not a complete woman because she'd rather raise a cat than a child and maybe there's something to that and she starts to cry and this is how it goes.

But tonight I don't say anything. I know we are walking a fine line here. I don't want to be the one to make us take an end-of-the-world, it feels like it would be that, misstep. I carry the food into the kitchen and serve it up on plates and bring the plates back out to the porch. It's still light outside and we can eat on the porch and watch the neighborhood. The cat follows us and takes up a position on the floor and sits there on her haunches gazing up at us like a reproof in person. She is old, that's her problem and I don't blame her for it I just don't like the smell of cat urine who does?

How did your day go? I ask, all ears but they're taking in the lawn-mower across the street, the Medflight helicopter overhead, the boombox making its way down the sidewalk next to the tufted tie-dyed gelatinous hair of what I would guess is a ninth-grader, the dog barking and the cars in their homebound rush.

How did my day go she says. She seems to be turning the question over, asking herself how her day went. Finally she says, Larry, I want a divorce.

My mouth is hot, Oriental. Snowpeas on my fork and what she says is she wants a divorce.

I ask you.

Look, I say, I know we've been having problems we got some big things we disagree on but a divorce? Do we need to zip right into a divorce? People aren't doing that so much anymore you know I say, they're taking time to work things out. AIDS, etcetera.

A divorce, Larry, she says.

I am so tired I'm just back from a twelve-hour flood in Chicago and kissing Kansan ass and countless hearty jokes about sowing wild ones and then driving the car home from the airport and picking her up and what she has to say is—well, you know what she said.

I look at her unhappily for a minute and wonder where we go from here when Sam comes around the side of the house and says You're back why don't you come over to our house we're planning to watch *My Brilliant Career* on the VCR tonight and I think great, that's just what my wife needs to see, frustrated ambition in the Australian outback, but we go anyway and Sam and Mary pop corn and we drink strawberry daiquiris and my wife is so fucking brilliant herself, so witty, You'd never know, she seems to be saying, how my heart is breaking I'm a great actress myself. Not until the movie's over do I start crying, and then the tears come, like rain in Chicago they fall and fall I'm out-Chicagoing Chicago and everyone's solicitous and embarrassed but no one really knows what to do about it least of all me.

They negotiate. They try to figure out do Sam and Mary leave the room so Lisa can comfort me, or since Lisa may be the cause of this do she and Mary go and leave Sam with me? This is a quandary. Meanwhile I am still crying and part of me is saying to myself Look, if the roles are reversed one of the things I get to do is cry so I just keep crying but the roles aren't reversed, not really, and this I know because Lisa throws me a look of deep disgust, which I catch before she changes it to one of concern and helplessness. There is such calculation here. She *is* a great actress.

Then it's just Sam and me and he says Hey, fellow, you go ahead, cry for all of us it's our turn. He's cheering me on. That makes me smile at least after a fashion and I say Lisa wants a divorce and he says Mary and I sort of thought that was coming sooner or later and I say I was hoping it would be later and he says Well if it's going to happen sooner is probably better don't you think and I say All things considered I'd prefer later if you don't mind and he says Maybe she'll agree to hold off and I say Maybe and he says Life's a bitch and I say Right and he says Hey and I say Hey and this is how it goes.

Look, I say to her in bed, we've made it this long, why don't we hold off a bit. We can divorce anytime, you know. We don't have to do it this minute.

She's asleep. You'd think she'd stay up and suffer some but she's sound asleep. I turn on the light just to make sure she's not faking but she's not I guess it's not like an orgasm, I think meanly and hate myself for it. But let's face facts, she's a lawyer not an actress.

When she sleeps her face softens, it kind of melts, the bones under her skin sink and blur and she looks about seven years old. Night is like a hole we drop into, a hole in time. You go to sleep and you fall down this hole and all night long you're seven years old. But I don't sleep.

In the morning she sits up and says she's thought it over though when she's done this beats me because all she's done all night is sleep. Larry, she says, I don't want to wait. I want to get divorced now. This is how she announced she wanted to get married. Larry, she said, I don't want to wait. I want to get married now. But I don't think this is a good time to remind her of that.

So I say Okay and we get dressed, moving around each other in little circles but never touching, little circles in the bedroom, the bathroom, the kitchen. When I'm in town I drive her to work. In the car we're stuck side by side. For the first time ever she props the briefcase on the left side of her seat so it's like a partition between us. When I shift gears my hand grazes the briefcase and I say Excuse me realizing as soon as I do that it's stupid nobody apologizes to a briefcase.

The sun is shining in my eyes and I turn the visor down. Unless a goddamned bird landed on the car hood an olive branch in its freaking beak you'd never know how it had been raining in Chicago. God, I think, impressed by this, it takes only a minute or two for the past to become past. It's like time is a kind of fast-drying glue that the present keeps getting stuck to and no matter how hard you tug at it you can't pry it loose again.

Listen I say I know I've been putting too much pressure on you. I guess we could wait where a child's concerned.

Children are not the issue here, Larry, she says. Children are a screen.

Then what's the issue?

Disappointment.

I could pursue this but I don't. Traffic is snarled on West Doty.

I drop her off and park under my building and go to my office. Billie is there ahead of me, flipping through files on her desk while the receiver's perched on her shoulder. She has one of those phone rests that lets her keep her hands free. Her red hair is pulled straight back in what ought to be a schoolmarm effect but what happens when she does this is that her flawless complexion, her high forehead look so brave, so touchingly exposed, so unself-conscious, that it breaks my heart and makes me want to weep I'm afraid I'll start crying again for some reason it seems lately I've got waterworks on the basis of which I should probably declare myself a public utility or should I say futility. Looking at Billie's forehead makes me feel hopelessly old so when she signals for me to get on my phone I just nod at her and throw myself in the chair and say Yo, of course I say Yo, who doesn't, I say Yo, Larry here, and it's Oatmeal on the line.

We've reconsidered, he says.

You've reconsidered, I repeat, parroting him.

And he says, it's just like racquetball the way this keeps coming back, they've reconsidered. They think maybe they don't want to sell after all.

This is my cue to dance but I'm so tired my verbal feet don't want to move. Well I'm sorry to hear it I say I think you're making a mistake, which is the worst thing I could say because what else can Oatmeal do but take offense nobody wants to be told he's making a mistake this is basic sales psychology don't you think I know that?

Billie is looking at me hard.

What's wrong? she asks when I get off.

Nothing's wrong I say, what makes you think something's wrong?

Jesus Larry she says, what kind of dunce do you think I am I can tell when something's wrong. Tell me.

Oatmeal just canceled.

What else.

Billie is a sharp little sister is what I'm thinking. Lisa wants a divorce.

Oh.

Oh is right I say.

It was inevitable.

I know it's inevitable it still feels like I've been kicked in the balls.

I don't know what that feels like, she says. Please use terms I can understand.

I am maybe ten years older than she is but she looks so young to me it's like she's light-years away on the edge of the universe, that clear face shining bright as a star a quasar, too far to even think about reaching. Billie, I say, I'm going home.

You just got here she says.
I need sleep.

You learn things in business that's for sure, I'm thinking as I head home. Take oatmeal. They store it in these silos like say the Quaker Oats silos in Akron, Ohio, and every so often some poor sucker falls in it's like drowning. The guy tries to climb out but it's like quicksand he just keeps sinking deeper and deeper. Oat dust up the nose down the throat. Now here is the goddamn paradox the fucking oats are so dry they suck up all the moisture in the vicinity. When the crew finally vacuums out the oats and find the body it's drowned and dehydrated both. Looks to me like they oughta be able to mix it with a little water and reconstitute the poor bastard. What would it feel like, I'm thinking, to be condensed. What would it feel like to be yourself but take up less room. You wouldn't have all that empty space that your molecules float around in now. You wouldn't be all watery and wavering. You couldn't cry.

It feels strange entering the house at ten in the morning. All along the street, houses are shut up, as if they sleep during the day while the people are awake and working. I sit down and take off my shoes but I'm too keyed up to get into bed right away so I wander from room to room, not exactly thinking about things but not not thinking about them either. When I get to the screen porch I stand there for a while looking out through the screen. The mesh makes the day look muzzy, gauzy, something with a z in it. It makes me think of childhood, those summer days of riding my bike back and forth on the sidewalk in front of my house there were elms then and riding through the patterns of sun and shadow, well it was a kind of lace-light, something like a curtain and billowing, and there was this feeling of having so much energy and power in you that if you could pedal hard enough you'd propel yourself into the future and I decide to call my father. I go back into the living room to do this and as I dial, the cat comes over to me and starts curling around my feet, purring. She must like the smell of my socks. I think about sticking a knife in her belly or chopping her head off and sneaking it into Lisa's briefcase something really vicious like that and then I hear my dad's voice on the phone god he sounds old, creaky. Hi, Dad, I say, like it's normal for me to call him at ten in the morning on a weekday but it's not normal and he is instantly alerted I can tell, there's this energy of expectancy shooting over the wires all the way from Florida.

Howzitgoin'? he says.

It goes, I say. You know how.

So what's up?

Nothing much, I say, I just felt like calling.

Something's up, he says.

How's your blood pressure? I say, speaking of what I hope is not up. He had this heart attack a couple of years ago after Mom died, and retired and moved to Florida but he has to watch his blood pressure no red meat lots of fish oil. I can't help it I see him rattling around in his dinky little apartment which even though it's only two rooms and a kitchenette is too big for him, because ever since Mom died, his whole life has been too big for him, there are empty spaces all around him.

Blood pressure's fine, he says.

How'd you like me to come for a visit, I say, knowing a visit would do nothing but make us both hurt more, but what are you going to say. You could say Yo. You could say What's up or Hey. You could take a flying leap into a silo of oats and turn your brain into food for a horse.

Lisa's left you.

Well, I say, not yet but she's planning to.

I'm sorry, son, he says.

One second I feel too old the next too young, because I think I'm going to cry when he says son, when he says son I feel so young I feel much too young for him to die which I know he'll probably do in the next year or two and I want to cry again but I can't not over the phone with this old man who would just feel bad not being able to do anything about it so instead I kick the cat.

It's such a shame he says, but fifty percent of marriages fail these days I read it in *Newsweek* so don't feel bad it's not your fault it's the times. Everyone is a victim of his times. For your mother and me, it was the war. For you it's divorce.

I know, I say.

Your mother and I he says, your mother and I, we had our rough spots too everyone does.

I know, I say, although actually I don't and I don't want to think about my parents having rough spots I want to think their marriage was as smooth as anything. As smooth as Billie's forehead. As smooth as time, which just goes on being what it is, the same thing always, behind you, ahead of you, smooth as anything, smooth as a lawyer, a smooth cookie.

Everything works out for the best in the long run, he says.

In the long run, I think, *you'll be dead.* In the long run everything just falls apart the house the lawn work love marriage whole impossible cities, even empires. Empires launch wars that are death rattles in their own throats. They think they are making history but history is just something they become. Life's such a swindle. You keep hoping if you play the angles right you can come out ahead but all the time you're losing more ground than you're gaining. There's this torrent of events that makes you feel like you're being swept along somewhere a tremendous force carrying you in its current like it matters but then it's all over and where you are is exactly nowhere, nowhere, time goes by and leaves you high and dry. Look at this cat I think, she's falling apart too her kidneys are going, her eyesight. She's whimpering in a corner, under a chair, gray-and-white fuzzball she looks like one of those furry slippers with whiskers on them that little girls wear. I'm such a shit. No wonder Lisa wants out.

I tell Dad I'm glad he's doing okay and I'll be okay and I'll be in touch and I hang up and crouch down on the floor trying to get the cat to come to me but she's having none of it smart cat. So I pick her up by the scruff of her neck and carry her into the bedroom with me. The blinds are down and the room is dark. I unmake the bed that Lisa and I made a couple of hours ago trying not to look at each other from our respective sides, tucking the sheets in as if a sheet is a sheet is a sheet and not just about everything else you can think of too. I put the cat on the bed and peel off my clothes down to my underpants and crawl in and pull the maroon top sheet up over me and from the bedroom, street sounds are muffled you could hear yourself think but I don't want to hear myself think, so I lean over to the cat and whisper in her ear her pearly pink ear, Hey, where are your pajamas, the cat's pajamas? and she just looks at me and blinks, and I say, Listen, I'm sorry, I'm not going to hurt you I don't want to hurt anyone if you want to pee on the bed you go right ahead it's a free country and I'm saying this to her in a low voice and I stroke her back and she pushes her nose into my face like she wants to kiss me I miss being kissed, Lisa, once upon a time we were students then, stepping into the circle of my arms and lifting up to me her beautiful complicated face pale and freely given as a communion wafer that sweetest sweetness and I wrap my arms around her and say I'm sorry I'm sorry I'm sorry I'm sorry this is how it's going going gone.

Love in the Middle Ages

O saeculum, O literae! juvat vivere!
—ULRICH VON HUTTEN

There had been in her life a time, now historical, that was dark with fear and superstition: her fear; the superstitions of psychiatrists and psychoanalysts. This was in a place where winters were long and hard, the streets a sibilant soup of slush, sand, and salt, or treacherous with drifting snow, drizzle of ice sugar-glazing the leafless lindens. People were always turning away from other people to cough or sneeze into cupped hands. They lingered in coffee shops, the hot liquid in their throats like a medicine. Outside, cars skidded sideways to a stop in a ditch. Drivers exchanged license-plate numbers and the names of insurance agents wearily, as if they had been through this before, as if they had been canceled years ago and were now in syndication.

Winter in the year of our Lord 735. Snow is sifting into the moat, a thousand swans doing swan dives; it featherbeds the inner stone wall that stands near Lindisfarne, known as Holy Island, in the north of Northumbria in Bernicia. A stockade surmounts the stone wall, for those who would attack and lay siege to the court are many, including the Picts, and also the Mercians to the south.

The wind quickens, hurling itself against the stones like a lunatic beating her head against a wall. The falling snow glitters above the windblown water, phosphorescing, a final, brave flare-up. Touching down in the moat, snowflakes are snuffed out like candles.

To Nina, in this impossible place, there now came the suggestion of a new personal happiness.

Except that she refused to believe it.

Except that she was afraid to believe it.

Except that she was used to the way things were, her routine of child-minding, teaching, writing, and walking the dog.

But especially, except that she was afraid to believe it.

Though Nina loved some things wholly, things such as art and life, always ready to put either before herself, men were another matter. She had been unconnected to any man for so long, now, that she did not believe connection was possible. And who would ask her out?

"Single mothers are the romantically challenged of the world," she liked to joke.

The first time he kissed her, he touched his mouth to hers and then stayed there, mouth on mouth, as if resting, perhaps taking a short nap. Perhaps practicing CPR. For a brief moment of alarm she thought he might have forgotten what he was going to do. It had slipped his mind that he was going to kiss her! He had planned to kiss her, but then he thought of something more important! Breathing, for instance! And then, given that pause during which her fear walked past itself and out the door, she felt her heart bloom, felt the rose of it warmed and open, and he kissed her and kissed her until she forgot everything she knew: her past, her phone number, her name, why she never slept with men anymore.

The king and queen sit side by side on the high seat at the top of the table. Their dinner companions raise bronze cups of spiced red wine, cheering and toasting from places on cushioned benches. Platters of cold meats and smoked fish and flat wheatcakes glimmer blood-red or gold in firelight flung on the table by torches ranged along the wall and logs crackling in the hearth. Through thin slits in the wall, all in the hall can see the snow fall, fall, fall, the sky strangely lightening as the day grows darker.

The night before, a new moon's horns had lain downward, frowning, and forecasting a month of storms and bitter weather.

Present at the table, but made to sit far down along the side, is the
princess, who watches her distant parents—so kingly! so queenly!—as
if they were in another room. (It seems to her that they have always
been in another room.) Not present is the princess's brother—firstborn
and heir and, it is rumored, a follower of Merlin—who is doubtless
joyriding in a stolen car or drinking or in bed with one of the princess's
friends from college.

She had met him on the Square in summer, during the Merchants'
Parade. He taught in the history department. Like most academics, he
was deracinated, a man for all locales. Pittsburgh, Charlottesville, Palo
Alto had been some of the points on his trajectory, but weren't they all
the same, intellectually homogeneous no matter how ethnically di-
verse, one big reading list? He had the pampered academic's exuberant
desire to see the world benefit from his thinking. He was generous and
ignorant, a middle-aged male in a preserve for middle-aged males, a
place where middle-aged males grazed on grants or snoozed the afternoon away in endowed chairs, a place where they had a kind of mental
sex in institutes (Esalens for the mind, these "Institutes for Research")
and grew fat on footnotes—perpetrated by friends in other preserves—
that cited the few articles they'd written. He was a wild beast who had
never actually had to survive in the wild and therefore knew nothing of
the world Nina had come from nor anything of his own capacity for destruction; he had confused destruction with deconstruction—he had
confused death with anagrams!—and Nina was afraid of him. Yet when
she tried to imply something of this to him, tried to sketch (but gaily,
optimistically, as if she was, after all, talking about a very *slight* apoca-
lypse) the disaster and despair she feared might be the result of any further meeting (there was history and then there was her personal history,
which she was not about to repeat), he said, "You're very imaginative.
I guess that's what makes you a writer. Do you want to go to a movie?"

In the ninety-nine-cent dark in Middleton he put his arms around
her. Popcorn spilled down into the neck of her cotton men's shirt, but if
she reached after it she'd look as if she was trying to cop a feel from
herself. It was a movie from the eighties, about murder among monks.
The screen was thick with symbology. Nina felt she already knew
everything there was to know about sexual abstinence.

She shook his hand before unlocking her front door. Under the porch
light his eyes were hazel, a nutmeat brown.

Inside the hot house—it could be suffocating in summer—she paid the baby-sitter, went up and untwisted her daughter from the tangled top sheet, and let the dog run out in back and then back in, and then went to bed, letting her skirt drop in a sighing heap on the floor, taking the blue shirt off, her young-looking breasts bare. And buttery.

Torchlight dances over the woven tapestries and embroidered wall curtains and causes the swords and armor hung on pegs to gleam, a metal-plate and chain-metal mirroriness. The king has been inspecting the strength of his hold against invaders. It is late in November, "the month of blood": In November, people kill their animals, knowing the animals cannot survive anyway because there will not be enough fodder to last the winter.

Gleemen play pipes and fiddle and harp for the pleasure of the king and his queen. And beneath the music run these whispered words, making their way from guest to guest: Winds had swept a monk out to sea on his penitential raft, and only the priest's prayers had drawn him back, as if by the rosary's rope, to safety. Cain's gigantic progeny had risen from the whirling water, seas sliding from their shoulders, drowning sailors. People had reported seeing dragons on the heath, fires starting up first over here, then over there as if blown about by the devil's breath. Demons had been observed having intercourse at midnight. Infant demons grew to full size in a single day and played evil tricks on unsuspecting monks, loosing the mooring of rafts on the Tyne.

He took her to dinner at l'Etoile, an expensive second-storey restaurant she did not often get to eat in. It was still summer. The lights from the capitol, which the window looked out on, were as soft as candlelight in the aquamarine of early evening.

They talked about their jobs and former marriages. A waiter whisked glasses and plates away, returned with others. Nina listened as Palmer described his ex-wife: She had been beautiful, accomplished, lesbian. He had doubted himself. He had slept with women—he would hang his head to say how many—confirming his manhood, reassuring himself, but he was past that now. He was HIV-negative. What about her?

"What?"

"Have you been tested?"

"This is so mortifying," she murmured, wiping her mouth with a linen handkerchief the size of her daughter's nightgown.

"You shouldn't be ashamed. There's nothing mortifying about a disease. Although, etymologically speaking—"

"No," she said. "It's not that. I'm mortified to admit I haven't slept with anyone in a decade. I don't think I need to go for a test."

"In a *decade?*"

She didn't look at him. "Yeah," she said. "Is that a surprise, or what. I was surprised!"

"A *decade?*" Oil from the dressed mushrooms had gotten on his chin, giving him a glow like makeup. "*Why!?*"

"I was too busy?" she asked.

His fork had stalled in midair. "But you're so pretty!"

She looked up at him and then away and then back again, flattered and confused, gratitude making her simultaneously bold and shy. "I think I took a vow of poverty, too. I mean, the University certainly seems to think I did, because otherwise they'd have to pay me a living wage. But don't expect me to be obedient."

You can be a princess and still be forgotten during the festivities in the Great Hall. You can be there, among the company, and still know that on another level you have been banished—were banished before you were born.

Yet, looking down the long table at them, the princess is proud of her kingly father and queenly mother, of the way the whole realm pays tribute to her parents. Her face is rouged with the warmth of the fire, the wine, her own royal blood. She bends her head to take another sip, trying to hold the cup so as not to acquire, as has happened on other occasions, a red-wine moustache, and manages instead to dunk a strand of her hair in the cup. She already had broken ends, and now they are wet and clumped like seaweed and smell of booze. She adjusts her royal crown to hide the fact that she is having a really bad hair day— her parents hate for her to be anything less than a perfect princess! Of course, she thinks sadly, her mouth still fuzzed and grainy with the taste of hair and setting gel, she has to be careful not to forget she's not supposed to be anything more than a princess, either. God forbid she should outshine her brother, get grandiose notions about the throne, displace her mother the queen.

"I always wanted to write a comic strip," she said to him, *gaily, optimistically.* This was part of her strategy for letting him know that she was not so easily snowed, she was not a romantic—she was going to let him know this by telling him about her comic strip. "Not as a way of life. Just this one strip. In the first panel, there are two hilltops, and on each hilltop is a snail. On one hilltop there's a boy snail, and on the other hilltop is a girl snail. They spot each other and it's love at first sight.

"So they race down their respective hills, only they're *snails*. And the seasons pass: It's summer, autumn, winter. And they keep racing and racing to each other's arms. And it's spring again, and summer, and autumn. And they keep racing. At a snail's pace! And finally, one day, they really do meet, down in the valley, and their love has lasted all this time. He's got a cane now, and glaucoma, and she has a dowager's hump, but they get married. The last panel is headed: *Happily Ever After,* and it shows two tiny tombstones side by side."

"Writers," he said. "You don't get out enough, do you? You should join my volleyball team. We play the poli-sci department on Tuesdays."

Also absent, absent forevermore, are many friends, taken by plague. The princess has seen how they die: the skin blackening as if there is an eclipse of the blood, the painful, grotesque swelling, all the body's estuaries filling with sluggish fluids. Lymph nodes in the armpits and groin blown up like pig bladders.

And then that blackening, as if the skin were charred by burning fever. People with plague cried out, tossing on straw pallets all through the night, falling silent by morning. But the worst thing, thinks the princess, is the babies. She can't understand why babies should have to suffer like that. Babies, she thinks, all babies everywhere, should wear teensy crowns and romper suits, and when they get a little older they should be given velveteen dresses, and seersucker play-outfits and OshKosh B'gosh snap-on overalls, and be hugged and cooed to and get their chins chucked a lot and have the run of the court. And if they fall down, their mother the queen and their father the king should be there to put a Band-Aid over the sore spot and kiss the hurt away.

The reason the crowns have to be teensy is so they won't make the babies' heads lie uneasy.

Palmer wore her down. He wouldn't be put off. Nothing scared him—not her being a single parent, not her being in the public eye (of

Madison, anyway), not her incredibly complicated past, lived in several countries (and a few psych wards, too). She thought sure the snails
would do it, but he just smiled at her, a smile that squeezed his eyes
into the canoe shape of Brazil nuts. There were lines in his face like
snowmobile tracks, coming or going, depending on how he felt.

The more good-natured he was, the less she trusted him. What man
ever pledged himself to a woman on the spot? In the Middle Ages, all
right, but this was some fin-de-siècle folly. He might be a historian, but
she could see what was in store for the future—the female graduate
students; the return of that old sorrow of discovering she was not, after
all, first in anybody's thoughts. She saw the emotional distance that
would gradually develop, as if the house itself were expanding, the
bedroom miles from his study, her study, how he would come home
one day—in a year, five years, twenty—and ask for a divorce, his voice
breaking a little as if he were going through puberty. Which would be
pretty much what he would be doing. In a year, five years, twenty, he
would take back his books and exercycle and say he really hoped they
would still be friends. After he left, everything would go back to being
exactly the way it was now, except that her heart would have stopped,
when he said he was leaving her, just long enough for a little more
brain damage to take place. She was already concussive with rejection!
That's why she would be bursting into tears for no good reason—she'd
have lost control over certain bodily functions. She'd have trouble
breathing, the work of it almost more than she could bear. Give this
woman an oxygen tent! She should go home and make out a Living
Will, right now. For a time, she would be irrational and in pain, the
bones of her body bright and cold and snapping off like icicles, and at
night she would crawl around in the cave of her own cranium, that unknown, dank, cobwebbed place. All this, while her daughter needed
her—needed her to praise a scribbled drawing or button the top button
on the back of her jumper or arbitrate a dispute between Teddy the
Bear and a mob of plastic dinosaurs. No, Nina could not have this. She
refused to sleep with him.

"I can wait," Palmer said. He looked at her thoughtfully. "Maybe not
a decade. I don't think I can wait a decade."

*Monks on rafts may be frightened by whales or evil spirits rising
from the sea floor; a son of Cain can raise a full-blown gale merely by
seizing a monk by the hair and twirling him like a top.*

Cormorants, shags, gannets, and guillemots are birds of the shore. Monks of the time carry gospel books. Living in large groups, monks are in constant danger of infection transmitted by communal cups. Infectious diseases include smallpox, tuberculosis, and bubonic plague.

Stained-glass windows shatter light from church lamps, splintering it into stripes that paint the cornfields and countryside, sheep fells and cow byres. An angel approaches the boy Cuthbert, who later becomes a monk, and advises him to treat his swollen knee with a poultice. "You must cook wheat flour with milk," says the angel, "and anoint your knee with it while the poultice is hot." On another occasion, Cuthbert sees an angel whisk a soul off to heaven, and the soul appears to be in the center of a fiery orb, like a small wax figure in a paperweight.

The princess, a studious sort, has made herself a kind of home office behind a folding screen. She convinced herself that if she hid behind a folding screen her brother would not know she was there, or would forget to pay attention to her. Her brother the prince, who has absorbed all the Continental ideas of existential absurdity and artistic freedom from psychological and social convention and keeps telling her she is the only person in the realm who has ever understood him. Which confuses her greatly, because she doesn't understand anything, especially him. Most of all, she does not understand why her brother said it is a tragedy that they can't get married. And she does not understand why, on one hand, he said this and, on the other hand, he sleeps with her girlfriends from college.

At two o'clock every afternoon during the summer Nina walked over to Mrs. Kendall's house on Kendall Street—though, as Mrs. Kendall was fond of pointing out, she was a Kendall by marriage and her ex-husband's family had been from South Dakota anyway so God only knew where the Kendalls were that Kendall Street had been named after—and helped her daughter gather up her day's output of drawings and collages and cardboard cutouts and brought her home. Today Tavy was baking Play-Doh in the pretend oven. "What kind of pies are these?" Nina asked her, saying "yum yum" and poking a finger in one.

"They're not pies," Tavy said.

At this age, Tavy had long, straight, brown hair with bangs; eyes that sometimes seemed like cameras registering everything on a film not yet developed; and the cheekbones of her mother Babette, her great-aunt and adoptive mother Nina, and her late great-grandmother Eleanor—cheekbones already celebrated by three generations of men. She had on a pale yellow blouse that was like a slice of lemon and a skirt the smoky color of Darjeeling. My little tempest in a teapot! thought Nina. "What are they, then?" asked Nina. "Cookies?"

"Turd tortes," said Tavy.

After dinner—meat loaf, not turd tortes—Nina sat on the front stoop of her house with Tavy and their little dog. Tavy held Teddy the Bear in her lap. It was a beautiful, clear night, just late enough in the summer to grow dark before Tavy went to bed. The sky was cobblestoned with stars. Headlights hurried by in pairs, as if they were on their way to an ark somewhere. "Tavy," said Nina, "do you want to tell me what's bothering you?" She smoothed Tavy's hair back behind her ears. "You seem angry about something."

Tavy tried to smooth the little dog's hair back behind *his* ears. "Mommy's being silly," she told him.

Nina said to Teddy, "Well, Teddy, if Tavy won't tell me what's wrong, how am I ever going to make it right?"

"Teddy can't hear you," Tavy said.

"He can't?"

"He's just a *bear,*" she said.

"Can he think?"

"I didn't say he was stupid!"

"Then what is Teddy thinking?"

"He thinks you should marry Rajan. He doesn't think you should marry Palmer."

"Don't you like Palmer?"

"He's okay. But Teddy likes Rajan better."

"Honey, Rajan *is* married, to Lucy, remember?"

"She might die. She could do like Grandma and go to a foreign place and get old and die. Then you could marry Rajan."

"I'm sorry, sweetie," Nina said. "It doesn't work that way."

"I don't see why not," said Tavy, leaning heavily over Teddy, her chin in her hands, her elbows on her knees, her feet in their brown wide-strap sandals planted firmly on the chipped and cracking concrete steps that cost too much to replace.

In her home office in the castle keep she keeps her personal library. Donatus on the grammar of Latin; De Arte Metrica, *with its study of poetic scansion; Isidore of Seville's* Etymologiae, *Pliny's* Natural History, *the poets Sedulius, Juvencus, and Paulinus of Nola. (Perhaps she borrowed some of these books from the local monastery and has never gotten around to returning them.) During the winter, scribes' scrivening slows down; their fingers freeze up like the pistons of old cars and stall on the page.*

The monks smear resin from cedars on the books; otherwise, worms make holes in the vellum and binding boards and swallow words, and to no purpose for who ever heard of a wise worm? Precious and semiprecious stones stud gilt bookcovers worked in intricate designs. The princess glances out the window—moonshine makes a glow of frost, the whorled crystals a wavy pattern on the pane: frost-stars and frost-mountains. She hears wolves howling in the distance. There were travelers who walked a hundred miles to find books for their libraries; they carried the books in satchels, these backpacking librarians. They were sometimes eaten by the wolves.

Everyone has gone, settled down in some secret corner on a straw pallet or featherbed or sprawled on a cellar floor. The princess pores over her books.

This is what the princess has always done. She has always pored over her books.

A chill wind wickedly wriggles its way in around the edges of the frosted pane. Wax pools at the base of the candle and hardens; she chips at it with her nails. As she reads and writes, she stays alert to any sound, any shift in shadow—whatever might tell her that he is near and waiting. If her brother the prince is going to rape her, she doesn't want to be taken—taken!—off guard. She tells herself she is nothing if not regal. Even raped.

Nina and Shelley and Jazz stopped to have coffee and cranberry muffins at the bookstore. Palmer and three of his volleyball cronies were already there in a corner, a guitar trio with concertina accompaniment, knocking out "Whiskey Before Breakfast" and drinking Blue Nun white wine.

Maybe some of the customers were playing *taefel,* rolling the dice on the table, the cubes spilling out of a pewter cup. Once, rosaries were made from dried roses, were bracelets or necklaces of rose petals, were a rose garden of prayer. Hence: the name of the rosary.

Nina, Shelley, and Jazz took a table up front by the high churchlike windows. Jazz was saying, about someone in her department, "I think he lives on some other planet."

"Yes," agreed Shelley, who knew Jazz's colleague outside the University, "but I always found it an easy flight to that particular planet."

"Well, he's moved on into deep space," said Jazz.

Nina was listening to her two girlfriends, one older and one younger, and watching their expressive faces, one white and one black, and feeling the secret warmth of her involvement with Palmer. How astonishing it was to feel, after being so long alone, this sense of an invisible but ideal geometry, as if he and she were dots that knew their destiny was to be connected in a picture that would come clear. ("But when?" he had asked her again that weekend, the snowmobile in his face returning, crisscrossing the skin around his eyes. "Connected when?" And she said, "It's this chastity belt. I seem to have lost the key.") Even with her back turned to him, she saw him with one leg outstretched and the other propped on a footrest. She could almost feel the consoling softness of his sweater—the raveled sleeve of care knitted up in a cable stitch by Bill Blass—and his chest like something strong that she could lean against, a wall. She had thought this affection for manliness, for a man's way of being in the world, had died out in her, was a thing that had been catalogued and stored in the museum of herself, an artifact of feeling. But here it was, pulsing with contemporaneity. She thought he was beautiful, and she thought this very much in the same way she had once thought Bobby Kennedy and Dirk Bogarde were beautiful.

Jazz said, "Excuse me a bit, ladies, while I jive and jam," and went to sing with the guys.

With only the two of them left at the table, Shelley—who sometimes ran into Cliff, a geneticist, at the hospital where she worked—said to Nina, "He sure beats Cliff."

Cliff, not Rajan, was who Nina had been going with before she stopped going with anyone, ever. "Cliff doesn't even seem real to me now," Nina said. "And it's not just because it was so long ago. My ex-husband, for example, was longer ago, and he still seems real. But not Cliff."

"Some men really are unreal," Shelley said. "Oh! But, anyway, I mean, you know what I mean."

"You mean that some men don't leave a mark on the world. They don't go down in history."

Jazz's voice climbed over the music like a bird that flies in through an open window and out another, a bird like a famous metaphor for life.

"They can be all the rage for a time, though," said Shelley.

"Oh my God, tell me about it. A miniseries. Foreign rights sold to eleven countries. Paperback tie-in." Nina frowned, remembering Cliff's brief appearance on her bestseller list, the rave reviews she had so uncritically given him at the beginning, his Avedon-should-photograph-it profile, elegant and arrogant.

"What I think," said Shelley, "is that it's time you went back to the classics. Palmer looks to me like literature that lasts."

At high tide the horizon is a silvered blue; at low tide it is gold, as if an angel had tipped his wings toward the earth. Cuthbert, on the verge of starvation, was saved by two freshly cut and washed wedges of dolphin flesh that appeared before him as on a plate of air. A pair of dolphins frisked in the distant sea, each lovely and whole except for a missing triangle into which one of the wedges would fit. They seemed to have delivered themselves to him, willingly, unnetted with tuna, a dolphin-pizza delivery service.

Boats are wrecked on whales, nosed into disaster and salvage, or sunk by small forms of marine life that pierce the sterns' covering of tanned ox hide. Survivors often enter monasteries, devoting the rest of their lives to worship. Monks on rafts, affrighted by whales, may paddle and pole furiously, churning the sea into a beerlike froth. Everyone has something to do—the wheelwright, the mason, the blacksmith, the baker, the brewer, the cook, the beekeeper, the weaver. Prostitutes advertise their calling with handworked linen and luxurious brocade on their beds. Soldiers are armed with swords, spears, and axes; some turn the skulls of their slain enemies into drinking cups.

Every age has its customs: When a dead rat is discovered in the cook's flour, the cook pitches out the carcass and brushes away a bit of the surrounding flour but uses the rest without a qualm. Frequently, women who have been wives leave the secular life for the monastic when they become widows. These are some of the customs of the age.

Meanwhile, strewn among the princess's books are her personal effects: combs and needles, buckles and pins and brooches of bronze and bone. She wears a bracelet of blue glass beads.

She writes on goatskin, using a goose quill pen dipped in black ink that smells as sweet as perfume. Riddles, puns, and codes are much admired by the people of the time.

When her brother the prince comes into the room, he is laughing but in a way that seems, to her, mocking. He has sucked in his cheeks and raised his eyebrows and pursed his mouth in a skeptical moue and he looks like James Dean but a brighter, harder version, a movie star who reads books. A movie star who reads books by Nietzsche. He shoves the screen aside and lies down on her bed, his hands clasped beneath his head. She remains seated at her desk; perhaps she hopes that if she does nothing, nothing will happen. He is talking about their parents, the king and queen—their parents' failures and the contempt he is forced to feel. Again, a wolf howls. The candle has burnt almost to the end, its nub swimming in a hardening sea. The princess feels as though she has forgotten how to breathe. She feels clumsy, stupid, inanimate. She can't move. He rolls on his side and reaches out a hand, grasping her by the wrist. "Come over here," he says, "so we won't have to talk so loudly. We don't want to wake anyone." The world (which, she knows, everyone knows, is round, though everyone also knows that no one lives on the underside) has shrunk. It has gotten ever smaller, and now the princess sees that she is trapped in the middle of it, a world the size of an egg, a burning egg. A burning egg that scorches her ovaries, that turns her womb to ash. Her cauterized, useless womb. He doesn't kiss her. He just makes another quarter-turn until he lies on top of her. Her crown slips off and falls behind the pillow. He undoes the brooches of bone, of bronze. Her blue-bead bracelet slips from her arm, a sly little animal escaping like a salamander beneath a rock. It lies on the bed, a kaleidoscope on the tapestry and scallop-edged linens.

When she had been a very young princess, say, five, her parents had told her that if she could kiss her elbow she would turn into a boy. She had tried and tried, all the while being terrified she might succeed. She liked being a girl, she really did! She wanted to grow up and have lots of royal babies. But already she knew that it was better to be a prince. It was safer. Princes had things easier. They earned bigger salaries for less work. This, too, was a custom of the age.

With all these conflicting opinions swirling around her, Nina often felt as though she could not see where she was going. Was she, that is, going to go to bed with Palmer?

She still didn't trust him. Why *her*? she wanted to know. And why was he so set on marriage, which, even if it made a new sense in parlous times, remained a radical step?

"You've heard of the end of history," he began. They were in her living room, dog and daughter sleeping overhead. An ambulance raced past the house to the hospital, its air-raid siren like a blitzkrieg. A semi rumbled past, shaking the house on its foundation.

"I have," she admitted. Academics loved these catch phrases, the undangerous electric shocks of them, the semiotic therapy of them, administered to lift the black cloud of scholarly depression, give a drained brain a charge. The death of God, the authorless text, the end of history—you made a conjunction of a contradiction and the Guggenheim Foundation prostrated itself in admiration. But this had nothing to do with ideas; it was all grammar, as Donatus had known.

"I saw it," Palmer said.

Nina was wearing jeans and an oversized dark brown sweater and a Hillary headband, also brown, and white socks. She was sitting on the rug. She stretched out her legs so the bottoms of her feet could feel the fire Palmer had built in the hearth. She could make a joke now, or she could be serious. She decided to be serious. "What do you mean, you saw it?" she asked, hoping she was not about to find out that Palmer was, after all, weird. But if he was, after all, weird, that would explain, wouldn't it, why he'd said that he loved her!

He got up from the floor, sighed heavily, and threw himself into the Green Bay Packers chair, which was worn thin where her dog had, day after day for thirteen years, pawed in a furious flurry and then wound himself up like a clock before settling down to nap.

"I was walking home from school along the lake. It was a typically brilliant October day, the sky buffed to a high sheen, the leaves golden and flashing and the lake silver and sapphirine, everything lit, as with drugs, and shining. I was looking, you know, truly looking, thinking about what I was seeing and finding the words for it. And then it just stopped." He rubbed a hand over his forehead. "It just stopped," he said. "It didn't get dark, it was all still glowing, glints in the lake like fish, but these fish of light weren't moving. They weren't even bobbing. Nothing was moving, because everything was just repeating itself. The wind blowing and the waves breaking on the shore and the people jogging and the airplane, I remember there was an airplane, getting smaller, and all the other stuff—everything that was happening had finally happened too many times and now it didn't count anymore. It was pure repetition, and repetition is the opposite of history."

Nina, who had recently been experiencing flashbacks in which she remembered not just that her brother had come into her bedroom (she had never forgotten that) but how she had felt when he did, looked into the fire for a reply. The woodsmoke smelled cedary and dry, like a shelter for birds in the snow. She imagined her heart glowing like a little fire, the way she warmed to Palmer. Maybe even the way she was getting hot for Palmer! But her daughter was upstairs.

"History is over," he said. "Done with, used up, finished. Don't you see?" he begged, and there was, she saw, in him a kind of contagion no matter what the test had said. It could be a sickness unto death, but she knew a cure for it. "On the tomb of Bruni in Santa Croce are inscribed the words *History is in mourning.* All we have now is fiction," he finished. "On the other hand," he added, "maybe I'm just having a midlife crisis. I believe it would be my third."

"From a parent's point of view," Nina whispered, knowing that tenured professors had seldom heard a parent's point of view, "repetition is not the end of history. It's the beginning of history. Every child is the dawn of time."

The blue-bead bracelet slips from her arm, as if fleeing . . .

Nina went on: "What you saw was the world in *imitatio,* the photocopied world, the world that is merely a shadow cast by a larger reality. But what you *didn't* see is the *smaller* reality, which can be mistaken, at first, for a duplication but then reveals itself as essentially and eternally itself. You certainly don't have to be a parent to see this smaller reality, but being a parent may make spotting it easier. It's what children are— smaller realities. It's too bad you and your ex-wife didn't have any children."

"Thank you," Palmer said. "I knew you would save me."

"Who *are* you?" Nina asked, feeling as if she were remembering the words to an old, old song.

She held her breath; she could not imagine what she might have to offer him that he couldn't find more of, and better, elsewhere.

His thighs pulled against the cloth of his pants as he sat, legs athletically apart, in the Green Bay Packers chair. A sunburst of creases radiated out from the upper inseam of each pantleg. She looked away. "I had a vasectomy," he said.

"You and who else?! Every man I've ever known in this city has had a vasectomy. This is a city of vasectomies! I wonder why?"

"My wife didn't want kids. Look," he said, "if you don't marry me, it's the same as if we'd never met. Or it's the same as if we both had Alzheimer's." He placed his hands on his legs, cupping his knees in his palms as if hanging on but all he had to hang on to was himself. Or maybe he'd gotten mixed up and thought he really was a Green Bay Packer and was crouched to block and tackle. He looked so defensive, Nina thought, and so vulnerable, too. "I don't want to be forgotten," he explained. "Not again. I need to live with someone who is not going to forget who I have been to her." He let go of his knees, turned his palms up. "I can't keep doing this over."

"Tavy's the one you have to persuade." She was still whispering, as if not saying it louder would keep it from being too true. "I can't marry you if Tavy won't let me."

The bracelet is sliding from her arm, pale-blue beads spilling like ampules over the coverlet and onto the floor . . .

After the fire burned down, he left and she went upstairs to undress for bed, but first, as she always did, she glanced in on Tavy. Tavy looked like a pinwheel in sleep, arms and legs flung in four directions, her soft blue nonflammable flannel nightgown in a windmill splay. The little dog was sleeping beside her, on his back, all four legs in the air.

It was well into winter now, the medicine cabinet in the bathroom cluttered with half-used bottles of cough syrup, cards of twelve-hour time-release Contac punched out except for one or two remaining tablets, the basement laundry sink plugged with lint from months of washing Tavy's thermal undervests, the maple floor scarred with salt near the front door. Municipal snowplows packed the snow in at the entrances to driveways so citizens couldn't get out without shoveling all over again. Four-wheel-drive vehicles splashed mud and grimy snowmelt on passing pedestrians, who, in down parkas, looked bulked up, as if they were on steroids. This was life in an unfriendly clime. It hardened you, toughened your character, caused you to blow your nose and fix yourself a cup of hot cocoa to take to bed with you, where you lay propped up against a pillow, dreaming, a little bit feverishly, of a wedding even at this late date, with this late date, this date late in the millennium.

The bracelet drops from the bed to the floor, glass beads shattering bluely, a waterfall of pale beads . . .

Nina talked to Tavy. Tavy listened. Then Tavy wept. She wept from somewhere deep inside herself, her small back bent and heaving, the flexible spine outlined under her pullover, shoulder blades trembling as if something were pushing against them to get out—something like wings. When Nina put a hand under Tavy's chin and turned that fierce face toward her, it was a whole small area of turbulence, a storm, a tornado watch. Tears blurred Tavy's eyes and dripped down her cheeks, her nose ran, she swallowed tears and hiccupped, she used the back of her fist to wipe the tears from her face but more kept coming.

Already Nina could see the beautiful young woman her daughter would grow into, and she worried, knowing that beauty is often perceived as a form of power and that people seek, therefore, to prove their own superiority by subjugating it. (How many times, Nina remembered sadly, had men—in the days before she began to live like a nun—slept with her merely to establish for themselves the fact that they could. And each time, of course, she remembered ruefully, she had thought they loved her, and she had waited for them to ask her to marry them but they never did.) "Sweetheart," she said, beginning. But what she wanted to say was, *Get thee to a nunnery.* "Sweetheart," she said again, "do you really miss Rajan so much? We hardly ever see him anymore. Palmer is the one who does things with us now. And Palmer likes to do things with us. He cares about you very much."

"Is he going to live here?"

"I don't know. Maybe. Or maybe we'll all move to a bigger house. Would you like that?"

"Do you love Palmer?" Tavy asked.

"Well, I—"

"Do you love him more than you love Teddy?"

"Well, I—"

"Do you love him more than you love me?"

"Oh, no! Never never never!" Nina cried, amazed to realize what grownup fears a child can harbor. Or maybe she meant, What childish fears a grownup can harbor.

She is falling, too, slipping out of time and shattering into all her selves, so blue, so blue . . .

Nina had noted that the older she got the faster time went. She had a metabolic explanation for this: When you were a kid, you had so much energy that your internal mechanism was going faster than real time, so real time went by slowly. But as you got older, you slowed down inside, your brain, your nervous reflexes, even your heart—which became cautious and invalid, an old lady holding on to the wrought-iron railing for fear of falling on ice and breaking a hip: that was your heart—and now time sped by you, you couldn't keep up with it. Eventually it outstripped you and was far up ahead somewhere, out of sight.

You had been left behind forever.

But that wasn't the whole story. There was a Darwinian advantage to the way time worked. If time didn't go by faster and faster as you got older, you would always be in mourning for those you had lost— your parents, your alcoholic brother, your ex-husband who died too soon, before you both had a chance to turn ninety and meet again and get married all over again and get it right this time, the way it was meant to be. As you got older, the movie stars started to die, the politicians who had shaped your world, the writers who, even if you'd never met them, had been a part of your literary landscape. And the friends, too, including the girlfriend you'd been twenty-two and on lunch break with, and including the handsome male friend you'd gone to Luchow's with and laughed with all one afternoon while the band played polkas. They were gone too. If time were still as slow as it had once been, you couldn't endure it, feeling that pain for a thousand years every day. But time wasn't that slow anymore; it had gathered up enormous speed. It was only yesterday you broke for lunch, only yesterday your family were alive and problematic, only yesterday that you had been a new wife, shy and scared and deeply in love with a man who would break

your heart before he died. Time had changed so that the past was almost present. It was the only way the fittest were able to stand surviv-
ing. Nina called this her Theory of Evolution.

*Inside the fiery orb that was the size of a drop of blood the princess
lived in a miniature village, where the huts had thatched roofs and
there was a well in the town center, and there were neighbors and live-
stock. And then soldiers bore down, out of the hills, setting fire to huts
and lopping off heads and arms and legs, and burning the cows and
horses locked in barns. She felt her wine-dark hair burst into flame, the
seed pearls sewn into her gown glowing red hot, like miniature coals.
She felt herself gutted, nothing left to her but bricks and roof beams, a
smudge of ash, a last smoulder of smoke. This was what it was like to
be raped and pillaged, the Bosnian minority of yourself driven out and
made a symbol. A symbol of something.*

A grammar of contradiction.

History deconstructing itself.

*She felt despair and recognized it as destiny, a sad song she was
born knowing the words to. It rang in her body like a death knell, or the
theme music for the nightly news. Wars and death, wars and death—
they had happened before. By the time her brother thrust himself into
her, she felt cynical and exhausted, as if this was old news, something
that had already happened. That was the nature of doom—to be a
rerun, repetition, the end, the forever-fated end. History? What history? There had never been any history, only a screen with moving pictures.*

*But there had been a time—she remembered now, weeping from
deep inside herself, her back bent and heaving as he rolled off and she
turned on her side away, shoulder blades trembling as if something
were pushing against them to get out, something like wings—a time before history. It was so long ago; it was when she was younger, even,
than Tavy was now, when everything still remained to be discovered for
the first time. Tears burned her eyes. The betrayal at the center of her
life was like a trap into which she kept falling, over and over. She had
become a prisoner of expectation.*

*As if her brother had cared. As if anyone had cared. Her mother the
queen and her father the king—they had had their minds on matters of
state. She knew better than to bother them. She knew that as long as*

you still had your arms and legs you had nothing legitimate to complain about.

As if her brother had ever cared. He had confused her with anagrams, a game.

The students stuck such sweet suck-up notes into their end-of-semester folders. *Professor Bryant, I really liked your class.* Or, *Dear Professor Bryant, I feel I have learned a lot.* Nina tried to harden her heart against these not very subtle pleas for attention, but her heart grew soft anyway, the cheese spread of it, the cream cheese and crackers of it. Perhaps she was a woman with a deep need to be entertaining, to bring out food and drink and serve her friends.

Palmer was at the same table, reading blue books from his Honors section. After a while he capped his pen, put it down on the table, leaned across to her, and said, "Let's make history." And after he said that, he rose from his chair and held out a hand to help her out of hers, and he led her, chivalrously, upstairs to her own bedroom, and she followed.

But she was afraid!

But she was afraid not to follow.

But especially, she was afraid, and she mumbled, "Tavy—"

But he said, "Tavy is sound asleep. Kids can sleep through anything. And she might as well get used to my staying here."

"The dog—"

"That's an old little dog, believe me. He'd rather sleep than watch us have sex."

"He's never had sex."

"Wake him up!" Palmer said. "Let that old dog turn a new trick!"

Nina looked at Tavy's closed door, and part of her wanted to open it and look in on her daughter: *'Night, princess,* she would say almost aloud, brushing Tavy's hair off her forehead. But another part of Nina reminded herself that her daughter had gotten over her cold, and also over her hurt, and would be okay.

As they entered her own room and shut the door behind them, she looked out the window and saw that fresh snow had fallen, arborvitae wearing long white gloves on their limbs, like women at the opera. Frost-mountains sloped down the windowpanes into the valley of the sill. He lay down on her bed and, still holding her by the hand, pulled her down next to him. She was too embarrassed to look at him and ducked her head against his chest. He gripped her head with a hand on either side and lifted her away from him and looked her in the eye. It was like alchemy, the way the base metals of her brain became as bright as gold. She felt, suddenly, rich, as if she were the most fortunate woman in the world, and she wanted to give everything to him.

He undid the buttons of her shirt, the zipper of her jeans, the hook of her bra, the catch of her bracelet. Pale-blue glass beads sprawled like a rosary on the quilted comforter. Monks lost at sea could be tugged back to shore by people praying, if they prayed well enough.

There was always that fine print.

The wickedly cold air—despite the rope caulking! and Madison Gas and Electric made heating seem like something only a king could afford!—made her tingle, or maybe that was his hand. He got up for a moment and, in what seemed like a single swift movement, divested himself of sweater, shirt, slacks, socks, shorts. His naked body, white from months of winter living, was like a statue in Florence, hard-smooth and cool-warm as marble, a masterpiece, the human form in all its democratic beauty, freed from preconception and dogma. "You must work out a lot," she said weakly.

"Not really," he said, lying beside her again. "I just try to ride the ex-ercycle every day." He kissed the dainty wrists and ankles that proved she was a real princess, the vein in the underside of her wrist where blue blood ran (she knew from a grim night long ago) ruby-red. She smelled his disinfectant smells of drycleaning and deodorant, tooth-paste and soap, a slap of shaving lotion, a flourish of cologne, going down, down, down through all the layers of discovery to the Trojan base.

"You have an exercycle?"

She felt surrounded by him as by a Parthenon, a Colosseum. She put her hands on his shoulders, the rounded bones of them like amphorae, or well-wrought urns. A decade! she thought, disbelieving. Almost! As if she were encountering, in a way that would compel her to rethink everything she had been taught, an idea of antiquity, a belief in the dig-nity and excellence of Man, she caressed his neck and arms and calves. Touching him was like relearning some knowledge she had had and lost, knowledge of the world as a place that made sense. A place that could be studied, a place in which she could study without fear of inter-ruption. A place like a science, rational and with laws. She felt his back under her hands like a revival of classical literature. She felt him in her like a kind of wisdom, humane, not dictated by the powerful God of superstition.

The next morning she woke late, Palmer already downstairs in the kitchen, with Tavy, pouring dry dogfood and cereal into bowls. She got up and threw on jeans and a T-shirt. She stopped to look out the window, before she left the room, and saw that spring was on them, or almost on them, like a new age. The snow was melting, and the sun shining like the Renaissance.

Chapters from *A Dog's Life*

... one animal alone, among all that breathes upon the earth, has succeeded in breaking through the prophetic circle, in escaping from itself to come bounding towards us ...

—MAETERLINCK, "ON THE DEATH OF A LITTLE DOG"

CHAPTER ONE: ON BEING IN JEOPARDY

When my little dog was still a puppy, I was Visiting Professor at Western Washington University; the student literary journal there is called *Jeopardy.*

I worked in my office on nights and weekends, writing a novel. The secretaries kindly gave me a key to the faculty lounge so I could boil water for coffee whenever I wanted, and while the water was boiling, I'd sit in the lounge, my dog at my feet, and read old issues of *Jeopardy.*

I had to keep my dog with me at all times. My first week at Western, I'd left him in my office while I went off to teach a class; when I returned, he'd eaten the carpet—the *nailed-down* carpet. I hid from the chairman. I was sure my dog and I were both going to be sent packing. Finally, I confessed, and Maintenance ingeniously grafted a section of carpet onto the large area my dog had eaten. If my successor in that office ever has occasion to move his filing cabinet, he'll discover where the graft was obtained.

So my little dog and I would sit in the faculty lounge, waiting for the

water to boil, and while he gazed longingly at the carpet, I paged
through back issues of *Jeopardy,* and one day I came across a short
prose piece by my predecessor. She, too, had liked to work at peculiar
times, and she, too, had had a key to the lounge. One night she'd forgotten the water was heating, and the kettle burned. After that, she
wrote, she would set the kettle on the single-burner stove, remove the
clothespin that someone had stuck in the spout, clip the clothespin to
her little finger, and return to her office. She wrote with the clothespin
still on her finger. The pain of the clothespin kept her from forgetting
about the water, and she never again burned the kettle.

By the time I got to Western, the clothespin was long gone, and, as I
say, I couldn't leave my dog alone, so I always took him to the lounge
and waited until the water was ready. But I thought about her solution.
That clothespin had fastened her to the world; it was a way of making
sure she didn't think herself right *off* the world. "A footing in the mate-
rial world," she'd called it.

I'd call it a handhold, and a tenuous one at that. Whose grasp is se-
cure? I felt great sympathy for her plight. Writers love life; they are
like children who say aloud to themselves the names of objects not
only to learn the language but to reassure themselves that the objects
are *there.* We want a world we can talk about, as if the talk itself is a
proof of the world's existence.

Why do writers write? Because they love life and the world, and it is
all vanishing, vanishing more quickly than anyone can say. The people,
the trees, the favorite objects, the created art, the puppies, we ourselves
are all slipping away; we are falling out of our lives. No clothespin on
earth will hold any of us in place, and yet a writer will do anything she
can think of to hang on. Even write.

CHAPTER TWO: WHERE LOVE IS

I was packing to return to Wisconsin. Clothes spilled over every
chair, like a weird new trend in interior decorating—the Laura Trashly
look!—and books and papers occupied every surface inch of table.

That left the floor for me and my suitcases, and for my earrings,
which were in a small white cardboard box, a box that one of the larger,
danglier pairs had originally come in.

A friend stopped by to see me. I had not even heard from this friend
in many years, and as I sat on the floor, groggy from a whole string of

late nights of packing, I became mesmerized by the story of his recent life. He believed, actually believed, in something he called survivalism. He planned to hide out in the hills and when the rest of the world had destroyed itself he would reemerge, strong and healthy from living on fruits and vegetables—and skinned possum and potato roots—to take control of what was left.

I imagined that the hills were alive not with the sound of music but with hundreds of frightened men, men who had persuaded themselves that success would, still, come to them, if only they could wait till everyone else had come a cropper and failed. I saw hordes of wild men in store-bought army fatigues. They were roaming the hills, foraging for food, occasionally raiding a nearby farm, perhaps reading Robert Bly. When the sun went down, they slept in separate caves, each man alone and dreaming.

While my visitor was talking and I was listening, my little dog chewed through the white cardboard box and ate all my earrings.

I didn't realize what my dog had done until almost midnight, long after my visitor had left. Worried about my little dog—*could he get food poisoning from an earring? puncture his little insides on an earring post?*—I called the vet. "Take him for a walk in the morning," said the vet, "and see what comes out."

The sun gleamed like a gold hoop earring as we set out. In a few minutes, my dog had stopped to commune with a patch of earth. Sure enough, there was one of the rhinestone earrings, and here were both of the heart-shaped green ones, and here was an intricately wrought East Indian earring purchased in the East Village and there was its mate. Perhaps the earrings were a bit worse for the wear and tear, but my little dog was fine.

So we walked along, with me using a twig to fish around and a Baggie to stow my catch. By the time we finished our walk nearly all the earrings had put in an appearance.

I washed them, and later that summer my father, amused by the incident and delighted to be of help, volunteered to sterilize them. He transferred the sterilized earrings to a new container, which he labeled, in handwriting, "Nina's Earrings," as if next time my dog might read the label and be deterred from eating them. But I never wore them again.

All the same, I never could throw them out. They had traveled through my dog's body, and my father's hands, and that made them more than just mine. The label should have read "Nina's and Her Dog's and Her Father's Earrings." They were no longer mine to throw away.

I think, sometimes, about the survivalist. I think we survive, if we survive, not by taking to the hills and feeding on what's there, un-processed, but by being processed. Something swallows us and we make a long, dark journey at the end—the end!—of which we are still here, shiny and scintillating, bright as treasure, diamonds in the roughage.

I don't know what has become of the survivalist, but my father has died—that generous, self-denying man—and my little dog is no longer a puppy.

Yeats wrote,

> Love has pitched his mansion in
> The place of excrement.

And this is very true.

CHAPTER THREE: A FRIEND CAME TO THE HOUSE

A friend who is a writer and a lover of cats but not dogs came to the house for a glass of wine. She chose the couch to sit on. She still has that Easter morning, lilac and green-fern, freshness that we all have until somewhere around the age of forty, after which, even if you iron the sheets, they feel rumpled. *You* feel rumpled. And no matter how often you wash, the circles under your eyes stay dark. And your finger-nails turn brittle and break in layers, like sheetrock, your heels and el-bows look and feel like they've been hanging out after hours in a rough neighborhood, and then your eyebrows, discovering themselves to be completely exhausted, lie down almost on the tops of your eyelids for a long snooze through the next thirty years.

Let's face it. Once, your underwear was spanking clean. You could legitimately call it lingerie—satin tap pants, knickers from a London boutique, bikini briefs. Now you tell yourself that God would never let you get in an accident wearing what you've got on.

What you've got on is already an accident.

That's how it is after forty. Not terrible—just a little worn and torn, and maybe needing a nap in the afternoon.

I gave her her glass of wine and sat down to enjoy my own. My daughter was at school, reading with the Robins. (There were Blue Birds, Red Birds, and Robins, and they perched on straightback chairs in circles, reading aloud. Three rings, as in a circus.)

Just then my dog began to drag his bottom across the rug. Veterinarians call this "scooting." It is, they explain, a dog's attempt to "express its anal sacs." There is an itch so private that most people will discuss it only with their doctor.

My friend who is a writer drew back on the couch. Her features, usually rather pretty, had been stirred up by the sight and seemed to be swarming around her face in a frantic, local flight; then they returned, like bees to a hive. "How very doglike of him," she finally said, in a drawl like honey.

After she left I found myself wondering what she thinks writers do. Seems to me we're all expressing our anal sacs, too.

CHAPTER FOUR: THE DOG AND THE WATER-LILY

The poet Cowper's spaniel brought him a lily, causing him to vow that he, likewise, would "show a love as prompt as thine / To Him who gives me all."

My dog's doggier. He has never brought me flowers, but he once brought me a newborn bunny, the unfurred and ratlike body bleeding where my canine's canines had broken through the skin.

This happened before my daughter, a sort of water lily herself, entered our lives.

I didn't recognize it as a bunny; I thought it must be, as it looked to be, a mouse or a rat, and when my dog dropped it on the living room rug, nuzzling it with his muzzle and snapping his jaws at it as it squirmed desperately and flung drops of blood on the furniture, I grabbed a broom out of the closet and tried to sweep it away without actually hurting it, but also without touching it.

And so it lay, helplessly, under the bridal wreath bushes by the front stoop. The bushes were not yet in bloom, but buds had begun to stick out green tongues on the trees, getting ready for spring's sassy conversations.

I didn't dare look closer to see whether my dog's version of a water lily was alive or not, but I was pretty sure it was dead. I sprinkled the blood spots with Old Dutch cleanser and scrubbed like Lady Macbeth, with the same bad conscience.

My dog was barking and wagging his tail, waiting to be congratulated and thanked.

In the back, in the dog pen where he has his morning run, I discovered a rabbit nest—a small shallow-saucer of a hole where four bunnies slept peacefully, oblivious to their sibling's fate. They tended to pile on top of each other, a bunny paw resting on a bunny ear, a bunny nose quivering gently in a dream against a bunny tail quivering gently in another dream, a dream that no doubt bore a family resemblance to the first.

We let them stay there, my dog and I, until they were ready to take off on their own. I once caught a glimpse of their mother, and I wanted to apologize to her for being a murderer. I felt slightly less bad when I learned how many rabbits are born each year.

So my dog brought me something less like a water lily and more like roadkill. And yet he brought me a reminder, as well, of the nature of instinct. He *is* doglike, my little dog. And who would want to love only people? How parochial is a love that does not extend to other species. And I think he is somewhat godlike, too, giving me all he has.

CHAPTER FIVE: SOME OF HIS FAVORITE THINGS

He has his preferred ways of doing things. He prefers not to be in the kitchen, because I used to have to leave him there, behind the baby gate, when he was still a puppy and inclined to pee in the living room whenever annoyed. He likes his water cold, fresh from the tap. He likes his Milk-Bones arrayed in a row, a dessert tray, on the edge of the Green Bay Packers chair: I hold out each in turn and he butts his nose at it to say no thanks. Then, when we've gone through the entire row, he'll sniff at them all again and carefully select the flavor he prefers. He likes being tossed onto the bed in a swoop; this is more exciting than mere jumping. He likes getting up in the middle of the night and jumping down from the bed to race around on the floor, growling at a Chew-eez, shaking it in his teeth, hurling it across the room. He may roll over on his back, a tennis ball under his neck, and twist and turn (this is some kind of dance, perhaps, that he's invented—the Chubby Checkers of cairn terriers). He'll have these half-hour playtimes at two or three A.M. and then return to bed. As you might guess, he likes sleeping in, head on a pillow, tail curled around his legs, while I make breakfast downstairs. He especially likes low-fat milk to drink in the morning, and the Filaribits he takes most of the year to prevent heartworm. He likes popcorn. With a treat like a jerky strip, he'll prance out to the next room to savor it in private, but when it comes to meals he much prefers having someone stay with him while he eats. He would usually rather be with someone, and will lie down on an old quilt on the floor in my study, but he walks out the minute I turn the printer on, finding it too noisy.

He does not have preferences among people, loving everyone equally. When Tavy came, he fell in love with her immediately. When Palmer joined us, he fell in love with Palmer. He loves the meter reader, the mailman, the cleaning lady (who loves him). He even loves people who love cats but not dogs. He loves cats.

Few things in the world are not among his favorite things.

CHAPTER SIX: BIOGRAPHIA LITERARIA

He's the very Tototype of a little dog. He's my movable beast. He's full of sound, and furry. As on a barking plain, he turns and turns around the widening spirea, remembering things repast. We took a walk on the tame side. To the doghouse! L'amour the terrier—this ode on a Scottish cairn, this enchanting hairy tail, this doggerel (of course), these Great Barks of the Western World, this shaggy dog's story.

CHAPTER SEVEN: A NOTE ON THE HISTORY OF DRAMA

It was one thing to study the role of dogs in literature but another to know the stories dogs told themselves—their fictionalizing of a Milk-Bone into a mouse or rabbit, how small dogs can ask to be carried like a child with their front legs wrapped around one's neck, how, if they are boy-dogs, they will sporadically declare their independence by ducking one's hand when one tries to pet them. This is all drama; it is the great play that dogs enact, Sophoclean, Shakespearean, Chekhovian theater that tells them who they are. And when you, Palmer, grasp the back of my head and bend your face over mine, your thumb, tracing a line, as light on my jaw as a teardrop, your fingers on, in, my mouth like the words I have looked for all my life, something to say, something I wanted to say to you, you saying it to me saying it to me now, and again and again, tell me, is this literature, is this art, is this life? How real are you?

CHAPTER EIGHT: MORE BEES

There was another episode with bees. He was still a puppy. We were in my bedroom. I had opened the windows to spring. (It is winter here so much of the time that the opening of windows to spring stays in one's memory.) Bees had built a hive on the underside of the eaves trough, above my bedroom window. I guess they were not ready to be awakened. They had been wintering and wanted to sleep a little longer.

Suddenly the room was a mass of bees, a loudness in the air like a waterfall. I shouted, and waved my hands, and sure enough some flew out, but not all so I couldn't close the window, and they came in again. I called an exterminator. A man wearing a huge black hood with a veil in the front entered my bedroom. He had on thick black gloves. He knocked the hive down from the gutter and got the bees out and shut the window.

After he left I found my dog in a tight little ball under the bed—he looked like a little dustball, my cairn-bairn. I hauled him out. His nose was swollen where a bee had stung him. In his eyes was a look of bewilderment. A person would have laughed if that hadn't been mean to do. He pushed himself deeper into my arms. I wanted to describe for him what had happened, so he would understand and not fret, but our language of pats and wags, meaningful snorts and significant sneezes (which told me when he wanted to be let out), was not up to this task. There was nothing I could do except hold him till the hurting stopped.

CHAPTER NINE: ON KINDNESS (CHARITY)

He will stop and stand in front of the Milk-Bone box before we go upstairs, signifying that I'm to bring a Milk-Bone up for him. If there's already one on the floor or the chair, he'll carry that one in his mouth, so that when we get upstairs he has two, one to munch on for dessert, one to bury under a table—a snack in waiting. He's at least as smart as a survivalist.

In the early days, pre-Tavy and Palmer, whenever I had to go away, leaving him in the care of a dog-sitter, he'd start to tremble all over. It was an anxiety attack. When the taxi came to take me to the airport I'd have to set him down behind the baby gate, and he'd sit patiently, sadly, still trembling slightly. I would have hired Peruvians to baby-sit, if I could have afforded them; I would have paid Social Security.

He wasn't even deductible, but it was what he taught me about being responsible for someone I loved that made me know I could raise a child on my own. I love Tavy better because I loved him first.

He will actually go up to a cat and try to touch noses. Once or twice a cat has actually let him do this. It's as if they understand: He's a kind dog. He has a power to bite that he would never use (except that one time, with the newborn bunny, but maybe he was fictionalizing the bunny into a Milk-Bone). Imagine a man this kind. Imagine a person this kind, someone this willing to defeat the self's own instincts for the sake of someone else. Imagine a man this civilized, this humane. I don't know yet if Palmer is this kind. *Kindness kindness kindness.* This is a word that could change the world.

CHAPTER TEN: ONE DOG'S DAYS (*OR,* LIFE, AND TIMES)

He sleeps a lot now. He likes to catch a patch of sun on the floor and sleep in it, as if in a bright net, and sometimes, when the brightness has moved elsewhere, he is still asleep, though it's dark and cold all around him, and the cars speed by outside in an endless rush like a river.

Does he remember the things he did? Does he remember a day at Ian and Shelley's farm when he disappeared into the tall Scotch broom, chasing groundhogs and butterflies he never caught?

Does he remember the time two unchained dogs the size of ponies charged at us on the sidewalk near West High, saliva dripping from their bared fangs, and I picked him up and stood still while the dogs circled and snarled, and I was sure we were going to be attacked but a carload of teenagers saw us and stopped and the boys got out and ran the big dogs off?

Does he remember the quiet times of sitting side by side, reading, and exchanging an occasional pat on the head, lick on the arm?

He used to be a pup, a tiny thing with more energy than could be contained in him, or by him. He was always salt-and-pepper (with cinnamon whiskers), but now he's gotten grayer. When he was a pup, he played as a pup. He understood as a pup, he thought as a pup: but when he became a grown dog, he put away the squeak toys, the rubber balls with bells in them, and acted like a grown dog. Time speeds by in an endless rush like traffic. Sometimes I gather my little dog in my arms and move him from the place on the floor that has gotten dark to where the sun is now and set him down again, in brightness and warmth, for a while longer, and he sleeps on. These are the days, now numbered, on earth of a small dog who brought joy to the world.

Block Party

When we pulled out into the winter night and the real snow, our snow, began to stretch out beside us and twinkle against the windows, and the dim lights of small Wisconsin stations moved by, a sharp wild brace came suddenly into the air. We drew in deep breaths of it as we walked back from dinner through the cold vestibules, unutterably aware of our identity with this country for one strange hour, before we melted indistinguishably into it again.

That's my Middle West. . . .

—FITZGERALD, *THE GREAT GATSBY*

It was the year that no one dared to drink the water. Over in Milwaukee, people had clutched their stomachs and died cursing a rogue protozoan. Then there was the national problem of lead. All across the country, cities tested their reservoirs for lead levels. Stores sold out of distilled water, mineral water, seltzer.

When it rained, people looked out their windows and remembered how, when they were young, they had ridden their bikes through puddles, their yellow slickers shining in the gray gloom of rain light. They remembered lifting their incredibly smooth and, if they were girls, unmade-up faces to the sky, letting the rubber hoods fall back, letting the rain sprinkle their skin as if, as children, they were spring flowers, which, in a way, they were.

Now they shielded their heads with umbrellas. They wanted their water purified, modified, fluoridated, carbonated. This is why, when they decided to throw a block party, they brought bottles and cans that had been hoarded on kitchen shelves. Or else they drank gin.

But this was in the Midwest, and mostly they drank mineral water.

Perhaps you yourself live in, or have visited, the Midwest. Perhaps you yourself live in, or have visited, a small midwestern town that has burst out of its skin, wandered aimlessly off the beaten track, and fetched up—out of breath, slightly hysterical—in a mall. This modern Middle America is more medieval than it knows; it is Bosch in a base-ball cap, Dante in denim. Here there are long summer afternoons when daylight saving seems a sort of forgiveness, seems something that really does save us—for a little while, at least—from death. For, toward evening, the traffic, noisy beyond belief, slows. Speed bicyclists, avenging furies who see their job in life as one of menacing both dri-vers and pedestrians, go home to strip off spandex shorts from buns of steel before standing under energy-saver showerheads, being careful, however, not to open their mouths. The fire engines, ambulances, jet planes, hospital helicopter, buses, RVs, and trucks (tree-trimming, garbage, recycling, utility, interstate), all quiet down for an hour or two, although each year they quiet down less, and for a shorter period of time. The sky, pale as a scar, deepens to true blue. Reds rush in—pink, peach, cherry, scarlet, and magenta. As if the wound has been re-opened! Then it heals itself, as the stars appear, like stitches, and finally the dark blue of silence enters and erases an entire history of pain.

Perhaps this dark blue silence is like codeine or morphine. Perhaps eternity is a drug, an anesthetic. A numbness that lasts forever.

A tranquilizer that makes you really, really tranquil.

In this town, there will be events to mark births and marriages and deaths. There will be graduation parties and retirement parties. People will enter your life, but some of them will stay in it and others will merely visit for a longer or shorter weekend. Sometimes when you wake on summer mornings, you will remember those who have left and wonder where they are now—returned to cosmic dust, some of them, or drinking cappuccino with a new wife in another state.

There will be block parties.

A sawhorse and orange cones at each end of Joss Court blocked it off, and a picnic table had been set up in the middle of the street, between Sophie Amundsen's house and the Wallaces'. A cooler kept bottles and cans cold on top the table; it was Sam and Mary Clementi's picnic table, nicked by knives, ringed by glasses, even charred, from the days when people had smoked cigarettes and set them down on the table edge, remembering to pick them up again and puff on them only when the lengthy ash crumbled and fell and the cigarette had burned a black cradle.

Sarah was tossing a salad in a plastic bowl, and frowning, because she had chipped her nail polish getting the see-through lid off.

Nina, arranging deviled eggs on a plate, kept an eye on her daughter, Tavy, playing leapfrog with Suki and Ondine, fellow recent graduates from first grade, and on her small dog, who stayed close to Nina's feet, only occasionally getting up to check out someone else's shoes. The little dog navigated, these days, by nose, because cataracts clouded his once-bright eyes as if he lived in his own twilight zone. Nina had lately read that dogs could, contrary to what scientists had previously thought, perceive color but that the canine color-spectrum veered toward the pastel. She hoped the scientists had gotten it right this time: It made her happy to think that her little dog had seen the world, when he could see it, through rose-colored lenses.

And yet, as Nina finished with the eggs and set out pickles and black olives and selected an orange-flavored bottle of La Croix, she was not happy at this moment. She wasn't unhappy, either; it was just that she felt something was wrong, and not only with the drinking fountains and the tap water.

But she couldn't decide what was wrong. What could be wrong on such a lovely day?

But something was, if not actually wrong, not right.

And it was possible that something was actually wrong.

Nina's husband, Palmer, gently stabbed metal picks into bratwurst sausages, which he lined up on another plate. Guests would grill their own. He wore a baseball cap backwards on his beginning-to-thin but blow-dried hair, and a chef's apron over his jeans and T-shirt, and as he spilled lighter fluid over the charcoals he thought of the library at Alexandria, founded by Ptolemy himself, and how it had been rather like an Institute for Research, with its scholars supported by patronage. Timon of Phlius had called them "fattened-up pedants, constantly squabbling and pecking at one another in the chicken coops of the Muses."

Palmer thought of how it may have burned, if it had burned—catching fire from the warships Julius Caesar set ablaze in the dockyard in 47 B.C., ashes of papyrus fleeing on the nightwind, word parted from word like brother from brother, entire legions of lyrics lost, strophe turned away from antistrophe. This was the kind of thing Palmer thought about. Indeed, it seemed to him that he could almost hear the dark water swallowing fire, that lap and hiss against sinking hulls, the Hellenistic hexameters sizzling on their scrolls.

Sophie Amundsen wandered, cheerful and bespectacled, from neighbor to neighbor, a mobile radio station—thought Rich, an engineer—giving off signals now faint, now stronger, keeping up a patter that required no response.

Ian Wallace leaned back in his lawn chair and combed his fingers through his newly achieved beard, which was the color of Scotch broom and which Shelley hoped he would soon tire of and shave off. His brother, a sales manager in South Dakota, had died unexpectedly in March—a heart attack on the floor, in the middle of an inventory sale; a hundred television screens multiplying the same image of a frantic Phil Donahue wielding a microphone—leaving Ian the next in line who now—it seemed to Shelley—felt called upon to assume a patriarchal role he'd never, in fact, played. Hence, the beard, with its suggestion of wisdom. Hence, too, the occasional flash of fear, golden and darting, in the smallish pools of his eyes. He had flown to Sioux Falls to deliver the eulogy and came back with old photographs of himself and Robbie as boys, which he labeled and stuck into albums, seated at the dining room table while Shelley stirfried vegetables from the Farmers' Market.

Jazz Piano, her stomach out to here with what her husband insisted on referring to as her "baby grand," arrived, Manny Durkheim schlepping a ladder-back chair for his wife.

Nina introduced herself to the remarkable-looking fellow who'd bought Guy and Jordan's house, which had sat on the market for an unusually long time because of receivership or mortgage transfer or something. Just what the problem was had never been exactly clear to Nina, but she knew that it was never a good idea to let banks get involved with money.

"What do you do?" Nina asked, though what she really wanted to know was why he was living alone. Was he gay, divorced, bereaved? In other words, was he a possibility for Sarah? His name was Hugo

Gutsmer. He was short and broad, and his face, with deep-set eyes and sharply planed cheekbones and steep chin, was like a topographical map of difficult terrain.

"I'm an ethicist," he said.

"Do you teach in the med school?" She was thinking that he would already have gotten to know Shelley Wallace, maybe Conrad. But maybe he was in the philosophy department, not the med school. "I know you're not in the English department," she added. "We don't have any ethicists. Just moralists."

Many, many moralists.

"I freelance," he said, and for the briefest moment she felt an attack of vertigo, as if she were poised on the edge of a precipice. She looked down at him, into his eyes—eyes like volcanic pits, something molten and churning at the base.

Nina wanted to be sure she had understood him. "You're a sort of consultant? To whom?"

"Churches. Corporations. Anybody who needs help deciding what's right and what's wrong. The medical school generally relies on its own ethicists, but sometimes they call me in."

Nina gripped her bottle of mineral water tightly, as a thing that, unlike so much else, could be grasped, and said, trying not to laugh, "How does someone become a freelance ethicist? Do you have to have a license?"

"Oh no," he said, wrinkling a forehead wide as a mesa. He really was remarkable-looking. "Anyone can hang out a shingle and call himself an ethicist. It just takes guts." He smiled. "And a working knowledge of good and evil."

Nina thought of things she would like to ask him. Could you solicit advice from an ethicist at a party, the way you might want a few free words from your neighbor the doctor? Or your neighbor the private eye? Where would you start, she wondered.

As in a famous novel, your children—seven, and they might as well be your own and not your sister's (the sister who was like a mother to you), because you are like a father to them—are starving. You could steal a loaf of bread—that loaf there, on the display counter in the shop on the Place de l'Eglise. (The inner city, the ghetto.) What do you do? Do you break the law, for the sake of seven starving children?

Suppose it's not, after all, your children who are starving but your much-older aunt.

Suppose it's not even your aunt but a lifelong enemy, whom circumstance has brought to your door.

Suppose it's no one you know. Suppose it's a third-world country.

Aria, Isabel, and Judy had borrowed Tavy's jump rope and were taking turns in the middle. Aria's arms, toned, and bare under a flak vest, were like a rippling landscape—the gentle hills of her biceps, the smooth sloping run of her forearms. Isabel and Judy, turning the rope faster and faster, obliged her to skip till she was out of breath and plonked herself down on the pavement, drawing her long, chiffony skirt over her knees, her Nike high-tops pink and black like an old Cadillac. Aria wished she lived in Wyoming or Utah, someplace roomy. She wished that she were famous, with lovers.

Or say it's not only not your children—biological or adopted—it's not even you confronting this dilemma. It's someone else, someone else's starving children, but it's the law you voted for. What is the right thing not for you but for someone else to do?

Conrad, who had a round mouth with a moustache perched atop it like a little man riding a unicycle, ate a brat.

Or—a different ethical problem—your young son, after a car wreck—the Subaru!—the snow!—the guard rail looming large and hopeless as a fatal mistake—lies comatose in intensive care. The doctors have already uttered the words "irreparable brain damage." He is on life support—the same doctors have showed you, with careful casualness, the outlet, the plug. They have left you alone in the room. What is the right thing to do?

Conrad's great grief had, over time, worked its way out of his memory into his muscles. He no longer thought about what had happened, but his muscles were weak with unexamined sadness, as with an autoimmune deficiency, so that he seemed constantly on the verge of toppling, as if there was nothing to hold him up. When he did let himself think about the family he had had, he remembered not the end but the beginning—Siobhan, her smile that was like a handwritten letter,

old-fashioned, sweet . . . lilac-like . . . lightly fragrant with the perfume
of her. . . .

Mailed to him. To read over and over.

He had thought.

*There was an accident. (A woman and her son, say.) The hospital
asked your permission to remove organs for transplant. Funny, but
when you were renting videos for the weekend, planning your annual
trip to her parents, buying shoes for your kid, you never discussed the
possibility of dual death. You didn't know what your wife's feelings
about the transplantation of her, her son's, organs might have been.
What was the right thing to do?*

*Or—because time passes, even after it has been stopped forever—
say you are a still-young or on-the-young-side-of-middle-aged man
whose girlfriend has just told him that she is pregnant. You propose
marriage, but she says she is going to have an abortion. Do you say
anything? How do you feel? Do you think she has a right to do this?
What do you have a right to, if anything?*

Ingrid set a box on the bench and then took out from it, one by one, little
brown ceramic pots of yogurt and pineapple. Each pot had a small brown lid, a
hat. Ingrid's cheeks were pink with good humor, her hair, falling forward as she
bent over her brown pots, was bobbed and stylish.

Aria had inherited her stylishness.

*You are married, you have children. One at home, one in college.
Then you meet the person you thought you would never meet—the per-
son whose soul, body, mind are like synonyms for your own name.
What do you do?*

*You have a duty to your children, your husband, your lover, even
yourself. What do you do?*

*You have a duty to the concept of duty. You have a duty to love. Or
maybe there is no such thing as duty. Maybe there is only love. What do
you do?*

Was it the right thing to do?

The little dog stood up, nosing for crumbs, and brushed his nose
against Nina's bare ankle. She was startled by how hot his nose was.
From being in the sunshine, she said to herself. *From lying on the street.*

"But what a responsibility! It's so Kantian, isn't it," Nina cried, "deciding what's right and wrong, good and bad." Though she talked about the responsibility, it was the categorical-ness of it that actually bothered her. She never liked anyone to make up her mind for her.

"It's more like being a psychiatrist," Hugo Gutsmer explained. "I just sit there and let the client figure out what he thinks. I'm not in the business of short-circuiting free will."

Mary said, "But look at all the people who get it wrong. They embezzle from their bosses or cheat on their spouses, and then, you know, Sam has to track them down and find where they're living under aliases so the wrong can be put right. I frankly don't see what good ethical theory is when the practice is so screwed up."

Rich said, "I don't know. We live in a world where there are so many conflicts of interest, maybe arbitration is the way to go."

Ingrid raised her head from her brown pots and smiled at him. "Arbitration," she said softly, shaking her head, and her hair swung back and forth. "Arbitration!" Rich was lanky, but when he got caught up in a debate his vertebrae seemed to fuse and he became all backbone. It was one of the many things she liked about her lover—his intensity, his eagerness to see a thing through, even an argument.

For the sake of argument, say there are two candidates desperate for an adult heart, a heart that knows its way around the block even if it didn't get there this time. One candidate is younger, one older. One is a machinist, one a mathematician. One has a family, one hopes to have a family. The younger candidate, the machinist who has a family, has been on the waiting list longer than the older candidate. And has AIDS. Who has the right to the heart?

"Have a heart," you could say, but you would be able to say it only once.

Or say, not for argument at all, say for the sake of your sense of self, nothing theoretical about it, that you've learned that a coworker has been taking kickbacks on contracts, quietly releasing estimates so so-and-so can submit lower bids. If you blow the whistle, you'll be out of a job. Blacklisted. You have seven children, and they could starve. It's none of your business. What is the right thing to do?

Rich has to reach a decision soon.

❦

By this time, there were clusters of people, dyads and triads—Rich and Larry and Sam, Mary and Jazz and Sarah, Palmer and Manny, Shelley and Sophie, Ingrid, Ian, Nina, and the older children, and the little children. Conrad introduced the woman he had begun dating. (Jazz looked at Quinn closely. The high energy, glowing skin—Jazz recognized these as signs. She had experienced them herself, not long ago or was it a century ago, when she could still get up from a couch without help.) Mary refired the coals for corn on the cob. Jason, who would be twelve in November, moved to the Chestnut end of the street to hit a few bunts to Judy's throws. Shadows lengthened, stretching out slowly, silently—a yoga of sunset—from the picnic table and lawn chairs. The talk became a kind of ball game, too, ideas lobbed and caught, some with spin. The ice in the cooler melted. Jazz shivered, though the sun was still shining on her shoulders as if striking sparks from her black skin, and Manny produced a sweater from somewhere and helped her into it. Sarah was moved; it seemed to her that there had never been a man that thoughtful—none that she knew, anyway. She wondered how it was that she was single and childless. She looked far into the sky, as if someone might be waving to her from another planet, but when she brought her glance down to earth and turned back to the party, she felt that her life was based on a different premise from other people's and that, after all, she preferred her own logic. She had been in love with someone she would have married, but he had chosen to live the life of a bachelor-scholar, rising early to chase down footnotes in his home library. She thought of him sometimes when she was zipping around her condo, hurrying to close her lightweight luggage with retractable wheels, grabbing a cup of coffee before the airport limo came—thought how they could be the only two people in Madison already up and about and how they never saw each other. She listened to Hugo Gutsmer explaining his line of work to Nina and she said, "In Paris there was a sign in the hotel lobby that said *Please leave your values at the front desk.*"

Ingrid said, "Doesn't all ethics come down to the Golden Rule?"

"The Great Rule," said Manny. "That's what Jews call it. And we have a slightly different take on it. Hillel said, *Do not unto others what you would not have them do unto you.*"

"Who the hell was Hillel," Larry mumbled.

"*Nasi* of the *Grand Sanhedrin.*" Manny himself was amazed that he had remembered this from Sunday school in the synagogue. But—he remembered—he had been a dedicated, if pint-sized, student, raising his hand every time the teacher asked a question, wanting always to be first with the answer. He saw himself half-rising from his seat, trying to make himself more visible to the teacher. He was ten, with a yarmulke pinned to his dark, curly hair, a boy like a book—with his own opening sentence but also, between the lines, the literary tradition without which the book could not have been written, that source he would have to acknowledge. And suddenly Manny realized that if he and Jazz had a son he was going to insist on circumcision. "The Grand Sanhedrin was a sort of Supreme Court and Senate rolled into one."

"You mean like Wisconsin's state legislature," Rich suggested.

A heathen had come to Hillel and said he would convert if, while he stood on one foot, the rabbi could teach him the whole of the Law. *What you would not wish done to you, do not to another: That is the whole of the Law; all the rest is commentary and understanding. Go, now, and learn!*

The soft thud of ball against bat reverberated from Chestnut. Sophie fluttered, in a staticky sort of way, around the table, collecting empty bottles, crushed cans, paper plates seeded with leftover bits of potato chips. She dropped the trash into two different plastic bags, one for garbage, one for recycling.

"Do the right thing," Jazz said, giggling a little. "That's what Spike Lee and I say."

"Write the done thing," Nina volunteered. "That's what Emily Post says."

"Is it so hard to know what's right?" asked Sam. "Isn't there something inside us that knows, if we'd shut out the world long enough to listen to ourselves. . . ." He was a man who believed in an inner harmony, who found discordance a clue like a smoking gun.

"How can you, a private eye, think that—"

"I think people do know. I think people who screw up know they're screwing up but they're in the grip of a compulsion. The compulsion to screw up."

"History," Palmer offered, "would seem to say that plenty of people choose to do the wrong thing and don't see it as screwing up."

Gutsmer twisted in his chair. He had, some there thought, a face that was like the side of a cliff, a face a person could fall to death from. "If we could refer the choices to some instinct in ourselves, even if we didn't always choose to act on that instinct, there would be no need for ethicists. But there are dilemmas—instances where the choice seems to be between two wrongs, or two rights."

You have an opportunity to murder Hitler. Perhaps you don't know for sure yet that Hitler is going to be Hitler, but you can guess. On the other hand, you surely know murder is murder. What is the right thing to do?

And how do you live with yourself after you do whatever you do? Or after you fail to do it. . . .

"You're asking too much," Shelley said. "All any of us can do is the best we can do. You can't ask for more."

"Everybody makes mistakes," said Palmer, a statement that seemed to nearly everyone uncomfortably like a memento mori.

An arrow with a rubber tip flew past Sam's ear and pinged the street. Feathers jutted stiffly from the wooden shaft. Tavy reached over her shoulder into her quiver for another arrow, fitting it to the bow, taking aim, stretching the string taut. Suki and Ondine stood by, quietly intent, as if judging an Olympic competition.

Nina got to Tavy just as she was about to let go of the string a second time. Tavy twanged the bowstring while Nina scolded her. She stuck the arrow in her mouth to see what the feathers would taste like.

Hugo Gutsmer sighed. "If only we could just order people to stop shooting each other."

"If only we could order them to use rubber arrows," Jazz said.

"We do start out as savages," Gutsmer said.

"Do we?" Jazz argued. "I thought we started out as children who play with rubber arrows. It's only when we're older and ostensibly civilized that we bring out the heavy armament."

Palmer said, " 'Savages' is definitely not a good word in this context."

Mary begged to differ. " 'Savage' impresses me as exactly the right word to describe the behavior of the people who start wars. These people," she continued, "being mostly males of a certain age."

A small nation with a bitter history is tearing itself apart. Murder, torture, rape, and forced removal are the order of the day. (The disorder.) If American soldiers don't join the conflict, thousands more will die, perhaps even a complete culture. If American soldiers do go in, some of them, who had been charged only with defending their own country, will lose their lives or be maimed. Think of how their parents, wives, husbands will feel when they receive the news. Think, too, of how the orphaned children, the raped women, the tortured POWs feel as they are ethnically cleansed.

You are Congress. You are the President. What is the right thing to do?

Gutsmer ate several deviled eggs, one after another. "Of course," he said, "no one would ever give ethics a thought if we didn't worry about others' feelings. And none of us can ever actually feel another's feelings. So the ethical edifice, any ethical edifice, is an act of the imagination, which is pretty astonishing when you think about it."

"Nina would agree with you in that," Palmer said, covering Nina's hand with his own. "Nina believes in making everything up."

"Palmer thinks there's something that can't be made up," Nina countered. "History."

Palmer admitted it. "For all the talk about perspective and how history is written by the ruling class and so on, history seems, to me, to be, first of all, a record of death. And I don't think it's useful to deny the reality of death."

Isabel had joined them, finding a place on the bench. She had come into her own in the past two or three years, doing archaeological research for the State Historical Society. Her gestures, her way of moving had a bright, attractive definitiveness to them, as if everything she did was outlined in crayon. A blonde, blue-eyed crayon. Her mother put an arm around her and said, "I don't know. I work around a lot of death, you know, and I find it sometimes very useful to deny that any of it is very real."

"I think Shelley has a point," Ian said, and his voice seemed loud, because he had been quiet for so long. "What's to be gained by stating the obvious? One day there will be a block party on Joss Court and none of us will be here. We know that. But imagine what such a party would be like if we *were* here."

For a few moments, they all imagined that.

Except Larry, who was thinking of moving to Chicago. He had an offer. He could spend some time at the Art Institute Museum, maybe start collecting, go to openings.

❧

You have twenty-five dollars. (Or a hundred, or a million.) You want to buy a book, a CD, a bottle of Chivas, something. A painting, maybe. You've bought yourself nothing in so, so long (a period during which you felt your emotional life was an estate sale, something left over and up for auction). But you could send this money to Oxfam, Amnesty International, CARE. What do you do? When is it ever right to spend money on yourself?

So what if you are a commodities broker.

Children are starving.

"I'm not convinced ethics is erected on imagination," Mary, ever practical, said. "It doesn't take much imagination to recognize that if people aren't ethical, sooner or later you're going to pay for it. All you have to imagine is how you yourself feel when someone takes advantage of you."

"And then you extrapolate from that. You imagine how someone else would feel if you behaved unethically toward him." Gutsmer passed the ketchup to Larry.

"Or you just imagine how you would feel if you were in jail," Mary persisted.

"Psychopaths have no ethics," said Manny, agreeing with Gutsmer.

"What about artists?" Jazz asked. "What about the not absolutely disreputable idea of art being beyond good and evil?"

Nina remembered her own brother, who had subscribed to Nietzschean notions of art. "When was the last time you met a bohemian? Artists are all academics, now."

You have been friends since college with someone who has—you know that in this case the accusation is warranted—betrayed your country. A man in a suit thrusts a subpoena into your hands.

What do you do?

But maybe that scenario seems to belong to an earlier era. If so, transpose it to a modern-day university: Your close friend and colleague is undergoing review for tenure. Without tenure, she'll be out of a job, probably out of academia. Even with tenure, she's single, and this is a double-income decade. But her work does not meet stated departmental standards. What is the right way for you to vote?

Is your first loyalty to your colleague or to an idea of scholarship?

❧

"I met a Bohemian," Conrad said. "From Czechoslovakia."

"Ah, well," said Palmer. "Nothing stays the same, not even Czechoslovakia. If Kafka were around today, he'd be applying for a Guggenheim."

"He wouldn't get it," Nina said.

Tavy Bryant-Wright, resting her head in her mother's lap, had fallen asleep, and the last of the afternoon sun seemed to seek her out, landing full on her face. Nina smoothed her daughter's brown bangs from her forehead, her "shining brow."

You brought your newborn baby home from the hospital, raised her until she turned twelve, when she died of a congenital deformation of the heart. Then you learned that the hospital sent you home with the wrong baby. Your biological child is with the biological parents of the dead daughter, and she is tall, strong, her heart beats like a marching band—the live entertainment of it. You want your real daughter, the one you should have had! The one who is alive and pinning posters of Marky Mark on her bedroom wall. A bedroom that should have been in your house.

What do you do?

Is there any right thing to do here?

But this may not be, after all, a dilemma. This may simply be a tragedy.

Or suppose the biological parent of your adopted child returns after years to say she wants her baby back. But this is not a dilemma, either. It is merely Nina's worst nightmare.

Hugo Gutsmer said, "Okay, Nina, tell us. Do you think Faulkner was right when he said that a good writer is ruthless? *If a writer has to rob his mother, he will not hesitate; the 'Ode on a Grecian Urn' is worth any number of old ladies.*"

"No," Nina said. "But I think it may be worth any number of old men."

"You don't really think that," Sarah said. "You're making a point."

"Am I?"

"Maybe she thinks that," Palmer said.

"I think that," Shelley said.

"You?" Ian was working his hands rapidly through his beard, as if scrounging for something he'd lost in there. His car keys, maybe. "You think that?"

"Yes, I do. I think art is a way of denying death and acknowledging it at the same time. I think that's worth a lot."

Ingrid said, "Death doesn't need us to acknowledge it."

"But we need to acknowledge it," Shelley said. Her face was flushed, even though the light had gone. The street lamp had come on, white and round, an opening act for the moon.

"You said we had to deny it," Ian said, almost, for a moment, angry, as if his wife had fooled him.

"Both," she said, glancing down at her hands in her lap. "Both."

Sarah said, "I met an *academic.*"

You were in love with someone who didn't love you. You knew it, knew about the emotional withholding, the reserve. Did you wash your hair, put on a new nightdress, something that flattered you, wait for him to come to you at night? Did you sleep with him, thinking love should be free, shouldn't demand a return?

Was that the right thing to do?

If you didn't . . .was that the right thing to do?

Then Jason connected straight-on with one of Judy's pitches, hitting a ball that was no bunt, that rose in the air—a high fly ball—as if it were pulling the earth up behind it like a tablecloth. The ball seemed to stop for a moment at the apex of its arc and hang there like the first star of the night, star light, star bright. Their craned necks made the tired friends feel tilted and slipping, as if all the things on the earth were like dishes and sliding off. The softball seemed to pulse as if alive, as if catching its breath before the long journey down. And again, all the things and even the people on the earth were turned over and sliding off.

As if reminded of something they had to do—*Go, now, and learn!*—everyone began to pack up. Larry, Rich, and Sam hauled the table back to Sam and Mary's driveway. Sophie piled the white plastic garbage bag, and the clear plastic recycling bag clanking with empty mineral-water bottles, on her curb, near the fence. "Watergate," Mary called it, letting herself lean backward into Sam. Rich and Ingrid were going to drop Suki and Ondine at the children's respective houses on the way home. Judy and Isabel were going to a movie. Judy and Isabel asked Aria if she'd like to join them, but she said she had somewhere else she had to go, even though the place she was really talking about was the future, which still seemed to her, at fifteen, a place that would be big enough. Manny helped his wife out of her chair. Conrad and his new girlfriend asked Jazz when the baby was due, and Manny said the baby was still tuning up. Jazz groaned. "And not just because of my aching back," she said. Sam and Mary turned the sawhorse over and set the cones over the sawhorse's legs, the more easily to cart the stuff to their garage. Ian and Shelley fixed themselves a doggie bag of brownies, and Ian said, "I never deny death by chocolate." Larry kept feeling as though he was forgetting something, and then he realized it was because he was used to going home with Lisa. He asked Sarah if she had bought any interesting paintings recently, and she said he should call her sometime and she'd show him some prints she had found in Thessaloníki. Gutsmer, who had gone across the street to find the softball, returned with it. He stood under the street lamp, and the way the light fell on his face, it was as if he were an image of himself projected on a screen. It was a face of highs and lows. He tossed the ball to Jason, who caught it with one hand. Everyone said good night—it had been a lovely day— really lovely—they should do this more frequently—and went home.

Palmer, the bill of his baseball cap having moved around to the side as if it were an hour hand on a clock, carried Tavy, her head riding on his shoulder, her quiver of arrows slung over her neck, her bow clutched in her fist. Nina carried their little dog, his nose burning against the skin of her throat, where he had lodged it.

Palmer turned the light on in the kitchen. On the counter, the filtration machine hummed softly, as if singing to itself while it worked. Visible through the transparent upper half of the machine, the water's surface was shirred, like silk.

Nina and Palmer put things away in the kitchen—the barbecue picks, serving plates, leftover condiments. They cleaned up the kitchen, went upstairs, put their daughter and dog to bed, then went to bed themselves.

The curtains were open, and the moon was full and low. It seemed to be looking for someone—peering into windows, casting its beams like a searchlight.

Later—but it was still dark—Nina heard her little dog throwing up. She found him hunched on the floor in Tavy's room, heaving his insides out.

In the past, he had thrown up when he had eaten too many Milk-Bones, or when, as dogs will, he had licked too much gunk—dirt, his own shed hairs—from the carpet. Nina had grabbed paper towels. She had brushed his teeth with malt-flavored dog toothpaste—to make him feel better, to give him breath fresh as a young boy's. She had rolled over and gone back to sleep.

"Go back to sleep," she whispered to Tavy. "He's going to be fine."

Carrying him as she'd done earlier that day, she went downstairs to dial the emergency clinic. She wrapped him in a blanket and bundled him into the car, drove under the curious moon. The lights of the clinic were like stars, or surgical stapling. Parking the car, she carried the little dog inside. He was a baby in bunting, the coal of his nose sticking out. The top of his head was under her chin. He pressed against her as if wanting to stay as close as possible.

The veterinarian unwrapped him to give him a shot, then handed her a paper packet of pills and advised her to take him to the University clinic when it opened.

They went home—Nina and her small dog who, after all, had been with her longer than either her daughter or her husband. And had they waited at her side long days and nights until she could leave her desk to go for a walk?

He had stopped trembling and was breathing evenly, and his nose had cooled. Nina decided they would spend the rest of the night downstairs, in the sunroom, which was filled with mysteriously quiet moonlight.

In the morning Palmer shook her shoulder. "Nina," he said, "I'll take Tavy out for a while. Sleep."

After they left she talked to her little dog, telling him, or herself, he was much better now and was going to be fine. She took him into the kitchen and tried to get him to drink some water, but he refused to drink it. She could have sworn he shook his head no. It was filtered water, but he still wouldn't drink it. Then she gathered him up again and drove to the clinic at the University hospital. At the intersection, a speed bicyclist whipped by like a whippet.

A decade ago she had come to this hospital to see a shrink who told her to take control of her life and then became furious with her when, taking control of her life, she opted not to see him anymore. She had sat for an hour at a time in his office, shaded from the fluorescent light

fixtures by large ficus leaves. Today, Nina never thought about this—
that part of the past had dwindled to myth; all that mattered was what
had survived as feeling. *This feeling that her heart was like a kennel in*
which a little dog lived, curled up with his nose on his paws and
dreaming dog-stuff. There were doors here in the animal hospital
marked just like doors in the human hospital: Cardiology, Neurology,
Gastroenterology. Someone came and took her little dog away for
X rays. When they brought him back, he seemed exhausted, as if he'd
been interrogated.

At home, he crawled into his carrying case, which had been his
house when he was a puppy and which still sat on the kitchen floor, and
he stayed there for most of the week. Nina moved her work to the
kitchen table. Whatever she wrote seemed to turn to ashes. One by one,
her sentences split in two, subject and predicate scattering on the
nightwind. All that was left on the paper was wet splotches, the dark
water of her tears drowning her own words. Her husband and daughter
talked in low voices, walked on tiptoe, as if the kitchen were a sick bay.
They ate TV dinners on trays in other rooms. On Monday the clinic
telephoned and asked her to bring her dog to Oncology.

He had tumors—two. He was in pain and— Considering the situation, they thought— They strongly suggested! It was her decision
but—

She cried out (it *was* a kind of cry, not loud but wrenched, something pulled out of her), "No! Not yet!" The doctor, a tall woman in her
thirties with aplomb, looked at the nurse, another tall woman in her
thirties, also with aplomb. Nina realized that aplomb was something
that had not been granted to any of the women of her generation. They
had had to be passionate; they had had to crash through barriers head-
first, opening a way for the women with aplomb. She was passionate,
and her head hurt.

She scooped her dog up from the examining table and ran out of the
room.

Now she stops for the light at the intersection. In the rearview mirror
she sees a woman with flyaway hair, eyes owlish with weeping. It's the
middle of a Monday: Where can she go? If she goes home, she will
have to explain her behavior to Palmer, who is there doing background
reading for his Honors seminar in the fall. She has no explanation for
her behavior. Tavy will take one look at her mother, see that her mother

has flyaway hair and owlish eyes and is without aplomb, and burst into sympathetic, or possibly frightened, tears.

She goes to the park.

They sit down under a maple tree, she and the little dog, who is still wearing his blanket like a robe. His nose has heated up again, a tiny black furnace.

Overhead, leaves lattice the sky, a green trellis. Nina finds she is sitting next to an anthill and moves over, her hip next to her dog's hip, though his is blanketed. She strokes his muzzle, scratches him behind his ears. Through the gaps in the latticework—chinks that seem placed by design—she has seen a blue sky, shreds of a few white clouds drifting heedlessly by. "You've gotten pretty dogeared all right," she says, and he looks at her as if waiting to hear what she has to say next. "When we met," she says, "you were no bigger than a paragraph. Why, you were just a topic sentence. I'm so proud of the way you turned out. Sweet and funny and smart, lovable and loving."

He doesn't bark or move. He sighs a bit, flops down on his stomach. Nina checks to make sure nobody's listening. She has been locked up for less, and this is a city that hates dogs. Down South, she thinks, people love their pets more than politics, value friendship more than a careerist version of scholarship. Not up here. "When I first came here," she says, trying to cheer him up, "I wondered why everyone in the English department kept talking about the literary canine."

A finger of wind touches her on the cheek and she reaches up, feeling her own hand on her face. She has the sense that— No, she has no sense, no sense at all. Why else would she be here in the park with a little dog who is dying and in pain and needs to be going to sleep, not doing his obedient best to carry on a conversation with a crazy woman?

"They talked a lot about purging the literary canine. I worried about this sick dog of theirs." She hugs him.

They have left you alone in the room. What is the right thing to do?
What is the right thing to do?
What is the right thing to do?

She picks him up and scrambles to her feet, and perhaps the sky turns over as she does this, or it could be her stomach. His inoculation tag and red ID clink against each other. He wears a Scotch plaid collar.

When they get back to the hospital, she says she wants to be with him when they put him to sleep. They say that is not a good idea—her distress will communicate itself to him. It's been doing that for years, she thinks, and he's still been a happy little dog. She says she won't let them do it if she can't stay with him. She says this with aplomb she didn't know she had. They put him on the table again for the injection. Then she picks him up, holds him, cradles him, and nobody stops her. He gazes up at her with longing, a kind of desire, as if he wants only one thing now—her to stay with him. She holds him next to her heart, which is where he belongs, in this kennel that has always been his. His breathing slows. He seems to become heavier. His eyes are closed, as if he really is simply sleeping. When she brushes his hair, it moves, as if still alive. His tail droops over her arm, not wagging. *Oh god, not wagging!* His nose is a furnace that has gone out.

Snoozling, she used to call it when they shared a cross between a cuddle and a short nap, as they often would right after they had awakened in the morning, seizing a few more minutes before they had to separate for the day, she to be a writer, he to be a dog.

They take him from her. The nurse holds him while the doctor unbuckles the collar and hands it to her. Then the nurse leaves the room with him, with the small salt-and-pepper corpse of him.

Nina stumbles through a haze of tears to the parking lot, the plaid collar with its jangling tags dangling like a tambourine from her hand.

She drives home through rush-hour traffic. Palmer and Tavy are standing just inside the front door.

Tavy looks at her mother, takes in the flyaway hair, the owlish eyes, the complete lack of aplomb, and bursts into tears.

Palmer opens his arms and Nina walks into them as into a room. He puts his arms around her and she feels his embrace like being in a room. Tavy, wanting to be furniture, squeezes herself between their legs. Nina bends down and tells her it's okay, that the little dog has gone to be with Grandma and Grandpa.

Tavy doesn't buy it. She kicks Nina on the shin—an old habit, which Nina had thought Tavy had outgrown.

"It's true," Nina insists, envisioning a place where essence survives, not as an *object,* not even as *thought,* but as the linguistic construction of itself.

Take the proposition "It is raining." (For it *has* begun to rain, a summer shower over almost immediately, brief as anything pure, and practically nonacidic, a rain to make a person remember what it was like to lift her face, open-mouthed, to the heavens.) The "it" is semantically devoid, having poured itself out into the predicate; the proposition's meaning resides, then, one hundred percent in its predicate, although to assess its full truth value one would need to take account of the locative and temporal dimensions in which the proposition is embedded: Everything happens somewhere and sometime. (Or seems to.) And therefore the assertion "Her dog is alive and well and living in paradise" may be true for eternity, even if its full truth value can be assessed only *sub specie aeternitatis,* a place and time to which we all must come sooner or later. But how? It seems to Nina that this has become the question she must answer.

As in a story not yet known, she meets a man with a face like a map, a face that asks what direction you want to go in. Will you turn left, or right? Will you take the high road, or the low? But suppose, she thinks, everywhere you turn there is a fork in the road, and not a signpost in sight.

Then all the language of herself collapses into a despair of meaninglessness, as she remembers her little dog's earthly substance, the stomach that reveled in being rubbed, the ears that delighted in being scratched, the all of him that had been so there and was now so gone. "Do you recall the song you used to sing?" she entreats her daughter.

Tavy sings, "Puppy gone. Where, oh where be?" Her childish voice is flooded with tears but perhaps, even if it were not, it is a voice that is unlikely to debut at the Met.

"We should have started you on the violin," Nina says.

The sun is drawing shadows over the rain-rinsed scilla. Hyacinths inscribe capital flourishes on the air. As night falls, the hedge becomes a block of black on black.

After Tavy is in bed—Teddy, who has already lived forever, at her side—Nina makes Palmer promise to remarry if she dies before him. "I can't promise anyone will *want* to marry me," he protests. "Not too many women want to marry three-hundred-year-old professors. I'll smell. I'll have this truly disgusting archival smell of dried book paste and cracked leather. I'll *be* cracked, and leathery."

"Three hundred?"

"You weren't planning to die before then, were you? Now come to bed. You're exhausted."

"I don't want to go to sleep. I have to stay awake in case anything happens that I need to warn you and Tavy about." She wants to be on permanent guard duty.

She lets him help her out of her jeans, into the white silk nightgown that flatters her. She has always believed that love should be free, shouldn't demand a return. In bed, she fits herself alongside him, using his arm as a bolster. She thinks she is humoring him—she can't fall asleep, not yet, perhaps not ever. But soon enough, she is asleep. When Tavy appears at the side of the bed, holding Teddy by the arm, Nina only half-wakes to let her daughter in. "I'm thirsty," Tavy says, the way children do, but Nina is sunk deep in dream.

With no answer to her complaint, Tavy climbs over her mother and wedges herself between her parents. She lies straight and still, on her back, pretending to be a corpse, but her eyes insist on popping open. She hugs Teddy to her chest and stares up where she knows the ceiling has to be, but she's not really sure it's there. Maybe the only thing that's up there is the dark.

She feels the weight of her father on one side of her and the weight of her mother on the other side of her, and the warmth of both of them, and she thinks they need her. They need her to stay here between them, holding them together, keeping watch over them. There was no telling who might enter a house when it was so dark you couldn't even be sure the walls and ceiling were there. A monster. A robber.

Tavy feels the fearful burden of her task. She blinks, but the room is as black with her eyes open as it is when her eyes are closed. She's not even sure that her eyes are open when she thinks they're open—how can she be, when she can't even see Teddy's nose, or his pink felt tongue?

She squeezes Teddy tightly.

But the screen windows are open, she knows that even with her eyes shut, because she can smell the flowerful, end-of-summer night and hear tires turning on the damp road. Cars fly by, and the traffic noise almost drowns out the distant cry of a calliope.

Tavy knows what a calliope sounds like. She remembers the day on the Square when all the calliopes came from miles around. She knows that a calliope can be heard as far as twelve miles away. She knows that the word *calliope* means *beautiful voice*. Someday she will learn that Calliope was the muse of epic poetry. These are facts. It is also a fact that at this time of night just about everyone in the neighborhood is asleep, and so, though it could have been heard, the calliope is not heard except by Tavy.

Tavy finds it funny to think that she is probably the only person in the neighborhood who hears the calliope. She bets her father can't hear it over the sound of his own snoring. Her pretty mother is sleeping even harder, breathing face down into the pillow, not so much snoring as sort of gasping—the way, Tavy thinks, a young girl named Tavy does when she's been crying and she's ready to stop but it's not always so easy to stop crying as soon as you decide to stop crying.

In fact, it is her mother, a woman without aplomb but passionate and truthful, who sleeps so deeply that Tavy is half afraid she might not be able to wake her up even in an emergency. There could be a tornado. There could be a big flood. There could be an earthquake. Parents don't always know everything that can happen. There could be someone, or something, out there, in the dark, waiting.

About the Author

PHOTO BY MEG THENO

Kelly Cherry is the author of more than a dozen books of fiction, poetry, and creative nonfiction, including the critically acclaimed memoir *The Exiled Heart,* the recently reissued novel *Augusta Played,* and *Writing the World* (University of Missouri Press). Her work has been represented in *Best American Short Stories, Prize Stories: The O. Henry Awards,* and *The Pushcart Prize.* She is Eudora Welty Professor of English at the University of Wisconsin–Madison.